Don't Let Go

REBECCA DEEL

Copyright © 2019 Rebecca Deel

All rights reserved.

ISBN-13: 9781070855790

DEDICATION

To my amazing husband, the love of my life.

ACKNOWLEDGMENTS

Cover design by Melody Simmons.

CHAPTER ONE

Zoe Lockhart spread icing over another batch of cinnamon rolls, the delicious scent of cinnamon and sugar making her mouth water. She peeked at the clock on the wall to check the time. Perfect. She still had a few minutes before an instructor from PSI picked up the rolls for the bodyguard trainees' breakfast.

Who would stop by the bakery today? Usually the transporter was Nate Armstrong, an operative and chef who prepared meals for trainees and instructors. More often in the past few weeks, Simon Murray had volunteered for pick-up duty.

A smile curved her lips. Nate was nice, but Simon made her heart skip beats and starred in her dreams. Who was she kidding? Simon was hot. Zoe thought he was working up the courage to ask her out on a date. He didn't have to worry that she would turn him down. No one held a candle to Simon. "Thanks for coming in on your day off to help me out with the baking, Macy."

"It's not a problem. Now, what are you smiling about?" Macy Aldridge, her assistant, placed blueberry muffins on a rack to cool.

"Nothing."

"Ha. That smile says it's something. I'll bet you're thinking of a man six feet tall with dark hair, dreamy dark eyes, shoulders a mile wide, and muscles of steel."

Zoe's cheeks burned. Her friend knew her too well. "Maybe."

"I knew it." Macy pumped a fist in the air. "Has Simon asked you on a date yet?"

She shook her head.

"Of course not." She rolled her eyes. "I would have heard about it if he had. Gossip is the favorite pastime of Otter Creek's busybodies." A quick glance her direction. "Do I need to drop hints to the dense operative the next time I see him?"

"He'll ask when he's ready." If he was interested in her. Maybe Zoe had misread the signals. "Time to start the coffee."

"I have a pan of muffins ready to come out of the oven."

"I'll handle the coffee prep, then." She finished spreading icing on the last cinnamon roll and stripped off the rubber gloves covering her hands.

Zoe crossed the kitchen and into the front portion of the bakery. She prepared the coffee makers and turned on the machines. Whoever picked up the cinnamon rolls would appreciate a to-go cup of coffee.

She didn't know exactly what Simon and his friends did at the training school, but their days started early. His team also traveled frequently. Something hush-hush. Would he tell her the details one day?

Like most of her Tennessee town's inhabitants, Zoe wanted to know about Simon and his teammates. Whatever their jobs, the men were always well armed. In fact, the police department used the two teams who ran Personal Security International as Otter Creek's SWAT teams.

She backtracked to the kitchen and filled trays for the bakery's display cases. The muffins looked and smelled amazing. They wouldn't last long, she knew. Otter Creek residents loved the variety of muffins the bakery offered each day. Once the filled trays were inside the cases, she slid the rest into the cooler to refill the trays as needed.

She shifted to filling the pastry trays and the scones. Sasha Ramsey, owner of Perk, also stocked muffins, scones, and pastries from Zoe in her display cases. Her friend had decided it was better to buy her baked goods from Zoe than to make them herself or buy from an outside source. The decision had proved to be a profitable one for both women.

Zoe grinned. Besides, Sasha wanted to spend more time with her husband, Cade, a teammate of Simon's. She didn't blame Sasha. At the moment, Zoe didn't have a boyfriend or husband to complain about the extremely early and long hours she kept at the bakery despite Macy's help. Soon, she'd need to hire help in the afternoon because the hours were starting to wear on her.

After stocking the display cases with the scones and pastries, she filled a to-go cup of coffee and capped it without adding cream or sugar. None of the PSI folks added anything to their morning joe. Customers who preferred more than straight coffee usually went to Perk to fuel their caffeine addiction with Sasha's fancy additives.

Zoe returned to the kitchen and set the coffee on the counter. She frowned. Where was Macy? Another batch of cinnamon rolls was ready to come out of the oven. Grabbing oven mitts, she removed the pan and quickly shifted the rolls to a cooling rack. The last batch she'd iced was ready to be placed in the aluminum pans and covered with the plastic lid for transport to PSI.

After boxing the last of PSI's rolls, she glanced toward the darkened hall that led to her office and the employee restroom. Was Macy sick? "Macy?" she called. "You okay?"

No response.

Growing more concerned by the second, Zoe checked the cooler first, then the walk-in pantry. No Macy. Unless she had left the shop, the only places still to check were her office and the restroom.

At the entrance to the hallway, she flipped the light switch but the hall remained dark. Zoe's brows knitted. To Simon's annoyance, she had changed the light bulb last week. He caught her on the rickety ladder and made her promise to call him the next time one of the shop bulbs needed changing.

She walked toward her office. No light on in there. Bathroom, then. Zoe knocked on the door. "Macy? Are you okay?"

Silence.

She pounded on the door. "Hey, you're scaring me." When she still didn't get a response from her friend, Zoe tried the knob. It turned easily under her hand. "Macy?"

More silence.

Twisting the knob, Zoe pushed open the door. The light was off. That was weird. She reached for the switch and light flooded the small bathroom.

Zoe clamped a hand over her mouth and backed away until her back hit the wall. Someone had stabbed Macy. She needed to call for an ambulance. Racing to the kitchen for towels to staunch the blood flow, Zoe grabbed her cell phone.

Her call connected to Otter Creek's emergency dispatcher as she snatched towels and sped back down the hallway to the bathroom. "This is Zoe Lockhart. I'm at the bakery across the square. I need an ambulance and the police."

"What's the nature of your emergency?"

"My employee has been stabbed. Please send help fast. There's so much blood."

"Are you safe?"

Zoe rushed into the bathroom and knelt in an area clear of Macy's blood. "I don't know."

"Get out of the building and go to a safe place in case an intruder is still in the shop."

"I can't leave." She pressed a wad of towels on the chest wound still bleeding profusely. "Macy will bleed out if I don't put pressure on the wound."

"Stay on the phone with me. I dispatched an ambulance and the police will be on site in less than two minutes."

Not enough pressure with one hand. Zoe set the phone on the bathroom sink and used both hands to press down on the chest wound. "Come on, Macy. Hang in there."

She heard a noise in the hallway. Were the police here already? Why hadn't they called out? She hurried to the hallway and pivoted toward the kitchen, expecting to see one of Otter Creek's finest. No one stood there. Had she imagined the noise?

A brush of fabric against the wall made goosebumps surge up her spine. That hadn't been her imagination. Unfortunately, she'd made a serious mistake. The noise had come from her office, not the kitchen.

Zoe started to turn when hard hands gripped her head and slammed her against the wall. Her world went black.

CHAPTER TWO

Simon Murray parked behind Zoe's Bakery and turned off the SUV's engine, anticipation firing in his blood at seeing the baker again and having a chance to talk to her for a couple minutes while they loaded the sweets for PSI's breakfast.

He needed to grow a spine and ask Zoe if she would be interested in going out to dinner with him. Rumors were circulating around PSI that several of the single trainers and trainees had either asked her out or were thinking about it.

Simon scowled. If he didn't make a move soon, one of the other men might wheedle a date and that would make her officially off limits to Simon. He didn't poach on another man's territory. The thought of Zoe belonging to someone else made his stomach tighten into a knot.

What was the worst she could say? If she said no, he'd get over the soul-crushing disappointment of the woman of his dreams rejecting him and avoid contact with her for a while. No big deal.

Except that it was a big deal. He was crazy about Zoe Lockhart. He wanted the right to run his fingers through her chocolate-brown hair and kiss that luscious, tempting full mouth. Yeah, he'd be toast if she wasn't interested.

Maybe he should broach the subject with Piper McCoy, his best friend's wife. Piper and Zoe were close. If anyone knew the truth about Zoe's feelings regarding him, Piper would. He considered that for two heartbeats and rejected the option. A highly-trained black ops soldier could handle a woman's rejection. This was his move to make. So why did he feel like a thirteen-year-old boy experiencing his first crush?

As Simon slid to the pavement, he glanced toward the far end of the alley where a man sped around the corner on foot and disappeared. Unease filled him when an engine cranked up seconds later and someone sped away from the area with a squawk of tires.

Not sure what to make of that, he turned toward the bakery's back entrance. The door stood ajar. Concern morphed into alarm between one heartbeat and the next. Zoe never left the back door open. He'd talked to her often about shop security since he and Piper's husband, Liam, installed the bakery's alarm system. She followed all his recommendations, including keeping the door locked at all times until she checked the security screen to confirm the identity of her visitors.

Hand resting on the grip of his Sig, Simon nudged the door open wider and stepped into the well-lit kitchen filled with delectable scents. No Zoe or Macy. He resisted the urge to call out in case trouble lurked in the bakery. If he scared the women, he would apologize and send flowers or a pound of fudge to atone.

His gut said something was wrong and he'd learned to trust it. Moving further into the kitchen with soundless steps, he glanced around. The door to one cabinet filled with dish towels stood open. A towel or two had fallen to the floor as though someone yanked out a cloth. The ovens were on and from the scent emanating from the interiors, something was nearly finished baking. Zoe should be checking on her baked goods.

Simon glanced toward the dining area at the front of the shop. The door between the dining room and kitchen remained closed. He noted the to-go cup of coffee that Zoe had prepared for whoever happened to pick up the PSI order.

He glanced into the dining area. Empty. That left the cooler, Zoe's office, and the bathroom. Covering the distance to the cooler in a few swift steps, he determined the room was empty aside from muffins, scones, cookies, cakes, and cinnamon rolls waiting to be added to display cases or boxed for customers.

Simon pivoted and moved into the darkened hallway. His breath caught when he spotted the body on the floor near the bathroom. In the spill of light, he recognized Zoe's long tresses.

Heart in his throat, he sprinted the remaining feet between them and dropped to his knees. He pressed shaking fingers to her throat and breathed a sigh of relief when he felt the steady throbbing of her pulse.

Simon glanced into the bathroom and stilled. Oh, man. Macy. He took in the scene at a glance and realized Zoe had been attempting to help Macy when she'd been attacked herself.

He rose and angled himself into the small bathroom to check on Macy. The coppery scent of blood filled the small space, almost choking him with its intensity.

Simon pressed his fingers to Macy's throat. She had a pulse, barely. He noted Zoe's phone on the bathroom sink as he heard sirens approaching. At least she'd been able to call for help. If Macy survived, Zoe's quick thinking would make the difference.

At that moment, Zoe moaned. Simon returned to her side. "Zoe, can you hear me?"

"Simon?" She struggled to sit up. "Macy."

He eased her down to the floor. "Lie still. We don't know what kind of injuries you have."

"Macy."

"Help will be here in a minute. Don't move. You might have internal injuries."

"Will she be okay?" Zoe whispered.

Simon wanted to tell her that Macy would be fine. He couldn't lie to her. Zoe needed to know he would be truthful with her. If she gave him a chance, there would be times he couldn't tell her anything because of his missions.

"Police," one of Otter Creek's finest shouted from the kitchen. "Hands where I can see them."

He glanced over his shoulder, not recognizing this officer. A rookie. Terrific. "I'm Simon Murray with PSI. I'm armed. I'm a friend of both victims."

"Back toward me, fingers interlocked behind your head. Move slow."

Not only a rookie, then, but a nervous rookie. Simon preferred not to deal with a bullet wound today on top of everything else.

"No." Zoe moved closer to Simon. "You don't understand, Officer. He didn't hurt me or my friend."

"Ma'am, move away from him. Do it now."

"Simon." Her voice broke.

"Everything will be fine, baby. The important thing is for you and Macy to receive the help you need." He rose, interlocked his fingers, and backed slowly toward the nervous cop. "Call Blackhawk, Santana, Kelter, or Armstrong," he told the officer. "They'll vouch for me." A moment later, metal bracelets restrained his wrists behind his back.

The Otter Creek police chief and the three detectives on the force were friends of his. Any one of them would confirm that he wasn't a threat to Zoe or Macy.

Being cuffed in front of Zoe galled him. Sure, his unit ran afoul of the law on occasion because of misunderstandings like this one, but he didn't want Zoe to believe he and his teammates were a bunch of lawless thugs. Thugs and terrorists were the people Bravo fought against and brought to justice.

Someone was a threat to Zoe and Macy. Simon vowed to unmask that person. He wouldn't rest easy until he knew Zoe was safe.

"Cut him loose."

The lightly accented voice issuing the order brought a sense of relief to Simon. "Perfect timing, Nick."

"Are you sure, sir?" The rookie looked from Simon to Detective Nick Santana. "I found him standing over the victim."

Nick's dark gaze shifted to Simon. He frowned. "Zoe?"

"And Macy. Macy's been stabbed. She's on the bathroom floor."

"Ambulance crew is right behind me."

"Get them in here. Macy's in bad shape."

Once Nick directed the EMTs to the bathroom, he glared at the rookie. "Cut him loose, Wilson. I'll vouch for him."

"Yes, sir." With a resentful glance at Simon, the cop unlocked the handcuffs and stepped away from him.

"You the first officer on scene?" Nick asked Wilson.

"Yes, sir."

"Set up a perimeter. I'll take a look around, talk to Zoe and Simon, then get your take on things."

Wilson squared his shoulders, chest expanding with an exaggerated sense of his own importance. The officer rushed from the kitchen. Seconds later, he could be heard issuing orders for a hapless pedestrian or two to move along.

"I can't remember being that green," Nick muttered.

Simon chuckled. After a quick glance at the ovens, he grabbed the nearest oven mitts and pulled cinnamon rolls and muffins from the interiors. Not seeing other pans ready to enter the ovens, he closed the doors and turned them off. Whatever Zoe had to bake today would have to wait until another time. He already knew her bakery would be closed for the day at least. The shop was a crime scene and Zoe needed to be checked by a doctor.

"Ma'am, you should remain still until we check you," one of the EMTs said.

"I'm fine. Focus on Macy."

Simon reached the hallway in time to witness Zoe struggling to her feet. She swayed and caught herself with a hand to the wall. He hurried to her side and slipped his arm around her waist. "Come into the kitchen. The EMTs need room to work on Macy." One glance into the bathroom revealed the medical personnel scrambling to stabilize Zoe's co-worker and prepare her for transport.

Simon eased Zoe against his side and walked with her to the barstools at one of the counters. "I pulled muffins and cinnamon rolls from the ovens. Should I dump the contents on the racks?"

Her focus shifted from the hallway to the baked goods on the baking sheets. "I can do it." She hopped down from her stool before Simon could stop her. Zoe's knees buckled.

"Whoa." He caught her against his chest.

Zoe closed her eyes and swallowed hard, hand pressed to her forehead, a forehead bruised and swelling.

"You need to sit." Simon lifted her to the barstool again and kept a hand on her shoulder to insure she stayed in place. "Do you have an ice pack?"

"In the freezer. Right side, bottom shelf."

Once he found the ice pack, Simon wrapped a towel around it and pressed it gently to her forehead. "How is your vision?"

"Blurry," she admitted.

"You probably have a concussion. You should go to the hospital."

"I have a bakery to run."

Nick Santana moved to her side. "You won't be able to open today, Zoe. I'm sorry."

"I have orders to fill. I can't afford to turn away business."

Simon thought through options and came up with one that might work. Zoe would also be in a secure environment where he could keep an eye on her. "I might have a solution to your problem if the doctor clears you to work."

That earned him a frown. Too bad. Shock masked symptoms. Zoe might have more injuries than she realized.

The EMTs maneuvered their stretcher toward the kitchen and through the back door, carrying Macy to the ambulance.

"I need to ask you a few questions," Nick said to Zoe, shifting her attention back to him.

"Anything I can do to help."

"She needs to go to the hospital to be there for Macy and to be checked herself, Nick."

"I'm fine."

"So you've said. You're not. Not even close."

"After I have basic information, you can take her." Nick grabbed his notebook and a pen. "Tell me what happened here, Zoe. Try not to leave anything out."

"Macy and I arrived at 2:30 this morning to start our baking."

Simon stared. Holy cow. Did she start this early every morning? No wonder she ducked out early from any dinner Bravo's members and their wives attended.

"Did you notice anything unusual when you arrived?"

She shook her head and winced.

"Did you see or hear anyone?"

Zoe paused. "I heard a cat."

"You're sure it was a cat?" Simon asked.

"I heard a noise, like something had brushed against a metal trashcan, then a cat howled and streaked from a dark part of the alley." She swallowed hard. "I assumed the cat was responsible for the sounds I heard."

"Go on," Nick prompted.

"I arrived at the bakery first. I unlocked the door and turned off the alarm, then relocked the door. Macy arrived fifteen minutes after I did. She's usually a few minutes late." Zoe wiped away a tear that escaped. "Anyway, we dived into baking muffins and cinnamon rolls. We were pushed more than usual this morning. We have an order from PSI to fill." Zoe waved at the stack of covered aluminum pans on the other end of the counter near the door. "I prepped the coffee since Macy was pulling baked goods from the ovens. When the coffee was ready, I filled a to-go mug for Simon."

Nick's gaze shifted to Simon. "You were already here?"

He shook his head, reminding himself that Zoe always prepared to-go coffee for the operative who picked up PSI's orders. Wasn't logical, but he had the sense that she prepared the coffee for him. Yeah, he was pitiful, imagining a kindness specifically for him when Zoe was kind to all of them.

"I usually have coffee ready for whoever picks up the order." Though Zoe kept her gaze from Simon, her cheeks flared with color. Might be wishful thinking, but it sounded as though Zoe hoped he would be the one to stop by.

"Then what happened?" Nick asked.

"When I returned to the kitchen with the to-go coffee, I pulled baked goods from the oven and put in more. Macy wasn't in the kitchen. I thought she might be in the bathroom so I boxed the last of PSI's cinnamon rolls. When Macy still hadn't reappeared, I became worried. Since she wasn't in the cooler, I walked down the hall. I tried to turn on the light, but the bulb must have burned out again because it didn't work."

Simon frowned. He'd changed the bulb himself last week.

"Because my office was dark, I knocked on the bathroom door and asked Macy if she was all right." She drew in a ragged breath. "When she didn't answer, I twisted the knob and looked inside. I saw her on the floor, blood everywhere in the bathroom."

He wrapped his arm around her shoulders and eased her against his chest. Although he worried she might pull away, Zoe leaned against him.

"You were in the shop, but you didn't hear anything or see anyone?" Nick's pen hovered over the pad, his gaze locked on Zoe.

"It doesn't make sense. I was in the dining room for ten minutes. How could someone slip into the shop and hurt Macy without her making a sound? It's impossible."

Simon exchanged a grim glance with Nick, a veteran cop. Yeah, it was possible. Simon could have done the wet work in less than five minutes. So could any trained operative or professional. Would she be afraid of him if she knew the truth?

"Are you sure Macy locked the door when she arrived?" Nick asked.

Zoe nodded. "I heard the lock snick into place."

"But she would open the door for someone she knew. Is she having problems with anyone? Friends, family, or a boyfriend." A slight pause. "Her employer."

Zoe stiffened. "You think I hurt Macy?" She sounded outraged.

"I'm eliminating possibilities. You know I have to ask these questions."

"I would never hurt her. She's my friend."

"Friends fight."

"We haven't had disagreements since she started working for me. Without Macy, I would be working even longer hours."

"Is she fighting with her family or friends?"

"She didn't talk about her family, but Macy isn't from Otter Creek. Her family lives in Kansas City."

"What about a boyfriend?"

Zoe bit her bottom lip.

What was Zoe hiding? "Holding back will slow down Nick's investigation. The person who hurt Macy could go after her again if we don't stop him."

Nick's eyes narrowed. "We?"

He refused to apologize for putting himself in the middle of Nick's investigation. Whoever attacked Macy hurt Zoe, too. That made the attack personal for Simon.

"Macy's dating Isaac Lyons."

Simon frowned. "He's one of our trainees." And a troublemaker.

"Does he have the skill to pull this off?" Nick asked.

"Yeah, he does." Barely. Simon was training others who could do the job faster and with more skill. "Unless they were fighting, I don't see a motive."

Nick turned back to Zoe. "Do you know if they were having problems?"

"Isaac was controlling and Macy was growing tired of his unfounded jealousy. I don't spend time with them when they're together."

"Because you don't want to horn in on their dates or is there another reason?"

"He doesn't want me around and I'm uncomfortable with him."

Simon considered Zoe's careful word choice. Suspicion growing, he vowed to hunt down Isaac and have a talk with the recruit before the day was over.

Nick frowned. "What happened after you found Macy in the bathroom?"

"I called the emergency dispatcher while I grabbed kitchen towels to slow the blood loss. I set my phone on the bathroom counter while I put pressure on the wound. Maybe a minute later, I heard something in the hall and thought the police or EMTs had arrived. When I checked, no one was there." Zoe shivered. "I heard a noise behind me and started to turn. Someone grabbed my head and slammed me against the wall. I must have blacked out because when I opened my eyes, Simon was with me and the policeman you sent outside arrived."

Nick scribbled a few notes on his pad before flipping to a clean page and turning to Simon. "Your turn."

Simon summarized events from the time he arrived at 5:15 until now.

"Did you get a look at the runner?"

"Afraid not. I can't say for sure that the runner was a man, but that was my impression from the stride and size of the person. I saw him for a second before he rounded the corner and disappeared. Not long after, an engine turned over and the vehicle sped away. There is probably some tire tread left on the pavement. Traffic cameras might come in handy. With Zoe's permission, I'll access the video feed from the shop and give you a copy."

"I'd appreciate it." He glanced at Zoe. "Do I need a warrant?"

"Of course not. I know this is a crime scene, but can I have my phone? It was in my pocket except when I called the dispatcher."

"I'll return it later today. I need to make sure no trace evidence was transferred to your phone case." Nick glanced back at Simon. "Anything else to add?"

"Not at the moment."

"I'll prepare your statements and have them ready this afternoon. Stop by the station to sign them. If I'm not there, Stella Armstrong will be on duty and able to amend the statements or answer questions. If you think of anything else that might help, contact me. I'll be in touch soon with follow-up questions. In the meantime, don't leave town unless you inform me first." He held up a hand at Simon's raised eyebrow. "Within reason, of course. I know Fortress Security might deploy your unit at a moment's notice."

Nick laid a hand on Zoe's shoulder. "I'm sorry about Macy. Go to the hospital to be checked. I might see you there."

"What about the cinnamon rolls for PSI?" Zoe gestured to the stacks of covered aluminum containers a few inches from her hand. "Is it all right if Simon and I make the delivery? Please?"

"The stacks weren't disturbed at all?"

"No."

"All right. Don't touch anything else, though."

"Thank you, Nick."

He moved toward the hallway with his flashlight in hand.

Simon and Zoe quickly transported the cinnamon rolls to his SUV. She glanced at her kitchen, a worried expression on her face. "You'll be back tomorrow, maybe the day after at the latest."

"Thank goodness I don't have a wedding cake to prepare this week. I would have a hard time meeting a deadline after losing two days. As it is, I'll have to discount the baked goods stored in the cooler."

"No one will complain about that." Simon cupped Zoe's elbow. "Where's your purse?"

"My office."

He glanced down the hall. "Nick, Zoe's purse is in her office. Will you take it to the station or drop it off at PSI?"

"No problem," the detective called back.

Simon led her toward the alley behind the bakery. "Come on. We'll be in the way if we stay longer."

"Take me to PSI to deliver the cinnamon rolls. After that, I need to check on Macy. Should I call someone to drop me off at the hospital?"

"I'll drive you." Simon refused to let her out of his sight unless she was with someone he trusted and that list was a short one.

He opened the passenger door and tucked Zoe inside his SUV. She looked so sad and lost that Simon had difficulty keeping his hands to himself. All he wanted to do was hold her and tell her everything would be fine. He couldn't and this wasn't the time. The sooner she was checked by a doctor, the better he'd feel.

He glanced at the bakery bustling with policemen. Simon wondered when Nick would realize that from the back, Zoe and Macy were similar in build, as well as style and color of hair. The intended victim might not have been Macy.

CHAPTER THREE

Zoe turned to look at Dr. Anderson, Otter Creek's favorite physician. "What's the verdict, Dr. Anderson?"

"You have a mild concussion. You'll have dizziness and a headache for a few days along with bruising. You'll be baking decadent treats that tempt me to overindulge in a day or two."

"May I leave now?"

"I'll write a prescription for a mild pain reliever. The medicine might make you sleepy so wait two days before you drive. Once the nurse brings your discharge papers and a list of symptoms to watch for, you can leave."

Zoe breathed a sigh of relief. She could handle a headache for a few days. Perhaps Simon would drop her off at the bakery for the next two mornings. He seemed to be awake at all hours of the night based on the text messages she'd received from him over the past few months. A text from him between midnight and three in the morning wasn't unusual. "Thank you."

The gray-haired physician chuckled and patted her shoulder. "You don't enjoy our hospitality?"

"I hate hospitals."

"I understand, my dear. If your symptoms worsen or you develop new ones, come back in so we can evaluate you."

"Yes, sir." She'd promise anything as long as he let her leave after seeing Macy.

A cell phone chirped with an incoming message. Dr. Anderson sighed and pulled out his phone. After glancing at the screen, he said, "I have a patient coming in by ambulance. I'll see you later, Zoe." He left.

A light tap sounded on the door and Simon entered the room. "What did the doctor say?"

"I have a hard head." She smiled at his raised eyebrows. "You were right. I have a concussion. Dr. Anderson is giving me a prescription for pain, but I probably won't take it."

"Why not?"

"The medicine will make me sleepy and I don't have time for naps during the day. If the medicine hits me too hard, I'll be flat on the floor. I'm a lightweight when it comes to medicine."

"If you let the pain get out of control, it's harder to kill. We'll talk to Matt or Rio at PSI. They can help."

Matt Rainer, Simon's teammate, was also Bravo's medic. Although Zoe didn't know mission details, she was aware of how often the members of Bravo returned with injuries.

A knock sounded on the door and Grace St. Claire, the wife of Simon's team leader, walked in with a sheaf of papers in her hand. "How do you feel, Zoe?"

"I've been better."

"I can imagine." She went over the instructions and symptoms to watch for. "If anything changes or your headache grows worse, come back in immediately. Be good to yourself. Take the pain medicine and rest. Give your body a chance to heal before you go back to the bakery."

"I don't have much choice right now. Nick forced me to close the shop while he processes the scene."

"Don't worry. You'll make up for lost sales. People are busybodies in this town. The bakery will be packed when you open again for business."

"Have you heard anything about Macy?"

"She's still in surgery."

"Do you know how much longer they'll work on her?" Simon asked.

Grace shook her head. "If you plan to wait for news, let the desk nurse know. The doctor will update you when the surgery is complete. He's the best surgeon in the area, Zoe. Macy is in good hands."

But would that be enough? "Thanks, Grace."

The nurse glanced at Simon. "Take care of Zoe."

"I plan to."

After hugging Zoe, Grace left to continue with her tasks. Simon held out a hand to Zoe. "Let's fill your prescription while we wait for word on Macy."

The desk nurse gave them directions to the hospital pharmacy. Although unsure if she could tolerate the medicine, Zoe supposed being sleepy today wouldn't matter. If Nick allowed her to open the bakery tomorrow, Zoe would stick to over-the-counter pain relievers. A foggy brain from medicine combined with hot ovens was dangerous.

Once her prescription was ready, they walked to the cafeteria for a soft drink for Zoe and coffee for Simon. She sipped the fizzy drink, hoping the carbonation would settle her stomach. Between nausea from the concussion and worry over Macy, Zoe wouldn't be eating for a while.

Simon eyed her a moment, then said, "I'll be right back."

She watched as he crossed the cafeteria to the worker manning the cash register. After he spoke to the lady for a minute, he walked to the salad bar and grabbed a handful of crackers and returned to his seat.

He slid the packets of crackers toward Zoe. "Eating some of these might help."

"How did you know I'm feeling sick?"

A slow smile curved his mouth despite the concern in his eyes. "Everything you feel shows on your face."

She hoped that wasn't true. Otherwise, Simon Murray would know she was crazy about him, an embarrassing situation if he didn't reciprocate her feelings. "I've never been a good liar."

"It's a quality I value. I know if you tell me something, it's true." Simon's phone signaled an incoming text. He glanced at the screen. "It's Grace. We need to go back."

Zoe dumped the packages of crackers into her medicine bag. Simon tugged her to her feet and they returned to the waiting room. He informed the desk nurse that they were waiting for information on Macy and returned to sit beside Zoe.

The wait was interminable even though she suspected the actual wait time was only a few minutes.

Finally, a man wearing scrubs entered the waiting room. He zeroed in on them immediately. "Are you here for Macy Aldridge?"

Zoe nodded. She hurried toward the surgeon, Simon a step behind. "I'm Zoe, Macy's friend. How is she?"

"I'm sorry. We did everything we could, but the injuries and blood loss were too severe. Ms. Aldridge died in surgery."

CHAPTER FOUR

Simon enclosed Zoe in his arms. "I'm so sorry." And ticked off over Macy's senseless death. His heart ached for Zoe. Simon didn't envy Nick the task of informing Macy's next of kin about her death.

Zoe burrowed closer to him, body trembling as she wept for her friend.

Helpless to do more than offer solace, Simon held her until the storm of tears passed. When she quieted, he kissed her temple and turned her toward the parking lot.

As he walked her to his vehicle, Simon quartered the area. His nape prickled as though someone watched him through a scope. He doubted a sniper in Otter Creek waited to nail him in the back. Then again, he hadn't survived this long in Special Forces and black ops work by being careless and ignoring the warnings from his gut. The question plaguing Simon was whether the watcher was interested in him or Zoe.

Simon scowled. If he was the target, Zoe was in the line of fire by associating with him. Zane Murphy, Fortress Security's tech wizard, would know if Simon's name had come up in recent Internet searches. Zane could run a trace on Zoe's name to see if someone showed interest in her.

He urged Zoe to move faster across the parking lot, anxious to secure her in the safety of his reinforced vehicle. Simon tucked Zoe into the passenger seat, buckled her in, and handed her a box of tissues he kept in his console.

"Thanks," she whispered.

After a gentle squeeze of her shoulder, Simon circled the front of the vehicle and slipped behind the wheel. He cranked the engine and activated his Bluetooth. When Nick Santana answered, Simon said, "It's Simon. Macy didn't make it."

A long sigh came over the speaker. "I'm sorry to hear that. Has Zoe seen a doctor?"

"She has a mild concussion. She'll be fine in a few days."

"Good. Keep close tabs on Zoe. I have a feeling there's more to this situation than we know."

"Already planned to do that. Later, Nick."

Simon drove to the main road. He glanced at Zoe. She'd leaned her head against the seat. Tears trickled down her cheeks.

His heart squeezed. Simon wished he could alleviate her anguish. Multiple losses in his military units and a few fellow operatives over the years taught him that nothing but time would dull the ache although it never fully went away. You lived with the ghosts and memories.

One thing he could do for Zoe was keep her mind occupied. Maybe she'd like a tour of PSI. He had a class to teach in a few minutes. While one of his teammates would cover for him, seeing the facility and the training regimen might focus her attention somewhere other than Macy's loss.

"Where are we going?" Zoe looked at Simon. The sorrow in her gaze gutted him.

"PSI. I have a class to teach and I thought you might enjoy a tour of our facility."

"You can take me home, you know. I'll be fine."

Praying she wouldn't reject him, Simon wrapped his hand around hers. "Not a chance. You shouldn't be alone." If he had his way, she wouldn't be alone again until the killer was caught or dead.

"You don't have to babysit me, Simon. I'm sad about Macy and will be for a long time, but I'll be all right by myself. I'm usually alone."

"Not this time." He drew in a deep breath. He'd hung out in the shadows, watching Zoe and longing for something more with her. Time to put up or shut up. "Although the circumstances are lousy, I'm glad for any excuse to spend more time with you."

She twisted to stare at him. "You are?"

"Are you interested in having dinner with me sometime soon? You don't have to give me an answer right away. Just think about it."

"Would this be a dinner between friends or a date?"

Simon stole a glance at her before returning his attention to navigating through town. "We're already friends. I'd like this to be the beginning of something more."

Zoe was silent a moment.

Was the delayed response good or bad?

She grabbed another tissue and blotted her face. Fresh tears tracked down her cheeks.

Not good. Panic roared to life in his gut. He was out of practice, but he'd never expected to make a woman cry when he asked her for a date. "It's okay, Zoe. Forget I asked." Man, saying those words hurt. Guess he'd been gently relegated to friends-only status.

She gave a watery laugh. "No way, Simon. I'm not letting you back out."

"I made you cry."

"It's not you. Earlier this morning, Macy said she hoped you would ask me to go on a date soon. Too bad she's not here to see her wish become reality." She turned her hand over and entwined her fingers with his. "To answer your question, I would love to go to dinner with you."

Thank God. "Excellent. Maybe this weekend?"

"I'd like that. A date with you gives me something special to look forward to after a week sure to rank at the top of the worst weeks of my life. I've been hoping you would ask me out for months."

"This isn't Victorian England. You could have approached me."

"Ha. I've heard the women around town bemoaning their rejections by you when they made the first move. I almost caved last week and asked you to breakfast, but I didn't want you to see me as one of the hordes of females vying for your attention."

Interesting. She knew him better than the women who had been putting themselves out there, hoping to win a date like he was some kind of prize. If those women knew what he'd done over the years, they wouldn't be interested in a date with him.

The women also reminded him too much of military groupies. Simon had learned his lesson well. Most women who thought they could handle him and his job were wrong.

"While it's true I turned them down, the reason wasn't because they made the first move. I wasn't interested in them. I wouldn't have rejected you."

She groaned. "Wish I'd known that sooner."

Her tart tone made him chuckle. "What kind of food do you like?"

"Anything except Asian. I can't handle the MSG."

"We're a perfect match. I'm not a fan of Asian food myself. Other than that, I'll eat anything that doesn't eat me first."

"I guess you've eaten interesting things while you and your team were deployed."

"Oh, yeah." He frowned. "Durango has it much easier than we do. Nate Armstrong can cook anything and make it taste like a gourmet meal. The man is truly a food artist. Bravo, on the other hand, has to pack in food on missions. None of us cook more than the basics. Fortunately, we can grill with the best of them. We don't have Nate's skill, but we don't starve when our MREs run out, either."

"MREs?"

"Meals ready to eat." Simon lifted one shoulder. "Not half bad, especially if there's nothing else handy. We burn a lot of calories and have to eat frequently."

"Must be nice," she muttered. "If my metabolism was like yours, I wouldn't be packing around ten extra pounds."

Although he wanted to refute that statement, they were approaching the security gate at the PSI compound. Simon lowered his window and swiped his ID card through the scanner.

He drove to the back of the main building and parked. When Simon came around to open Zoe's door, he said, "My class starts in fifteen minutes. I'll give you a tour when I'm finished."

"What class are you teaching?"

"Hand-to-hand combat." He laid his hand on her lower back as they walked to the building's back entrance.

"You teach bodyguard trainees to fight?"

"They must be able to defend themselves and their principals. The bad guys don't pull punches and if they land too many, our bodyguards and their principals will die."

"Do you and your teammates take turns teaching that class or is hand-to-hand your specialty?"

"The only class we don't take turns teaching is the first-aid course. Rio or Matt handle that class."

"Having medics on your teams must come in handy."

More than she knew. Matt had saved his life more than once while Bravo was deployed and the other members of his unit would say the same.

He swiped his card through another scanner and entered a personalized code into a keypad beside the back door. When the lock disengaged, Simon opened the door and led Zoe inside the building.

Hand firmly wrapped around hers, Simon navigated the hallways, nodding to co-workers when he passed them.

At the entrance to the dining room, Matt Rainer waited. He straightened from the wall when he saw them and headed their direction. Matt folded Zoe into a tight hug, dropping an affectionate kiss to the top of her head. "I'm sorry about Macy."

"So am I," Zoe said. "How did you know we lost her?"

"Grace has been communicating with Trent who kept the rest of us in the loop." Matt released her and tipped her head up to examine her bruised forehead. "What did the doctor say about you?"

"Mild concussion. No driving for a couple of days."

The medic studied her face for a moment. "Headache? Nauseated?"

She nodded.

Matt glanced at Simon. "Soft drinks are in the refrigerator in the kitchen. If you can't find what she needs there, check the fridge in the infirmary. I'll escort Zoe into the dining room."

He squeezed Zoe's hand. "Stay with Matt or another member of Bravo until I return." After a pointed glance at Matt, Simon hustled down the corridor to the kitchen's secondary entrance.

Nate Armstrong, Durango's EOD man, turned toward him. "How is Zoe?"

"Concussion. She needs a soft drink."

The chef tipped his head toward the first refrigerator. "We're stocked up. Sorry to hear about Macy. Police have any leads yet?"

"Nick's working the case. Nothing yet, though."

"Stella is on day shift this month. She'll give Nick a hand if another case doesn't take priority. The bakery's closed for a while?"

"At least through tomorrow. Do you mind if Zoe uses our kitchen to complete bakery orders already promised to customers?"

"No problem. We'll make it work."

"Thanks, Nate."

"Let me know if she needs anything besides a soft drink."

"If you want help with something that won't tax her strength or require much concentration, she needs to keep her mind occupied. I'm in classes all day and I don't want her alone right now."

"I'm making strawberry shortcake for our lunchtime dessert. I could use a hand with that. Zoe can sit at the counter and slice strawberries while I handle the shortcakes."

Simon's mouth watered. Nate's strawberry shortcake was legendary. "I'll tell her you need help and let her decide if she's up to doing light work."

He walked into the dining area and scanned the tables until he found Zoe seated with Matt on one side and Liam on the other. Simon threaded through the tables, speaking to trainees and instructors who hailed him as he headed toward Zoe.

When he drew close, Liam met him far enough away that Zoe wouldn't overhear their conversation. "Have you spoken to Lyons yet?"

"No, but I'd planned on it. Why?"

"Do it before he finds out from someone else that his girlfriend is dead. He's a jerk, but he deserves to hear the news before it spreads."

"Where is he?"

"East corner with his buddies. He's been shooting intense looks at your girl."

"Good or bad?"

"The kind that would earn him a fist in the face if he looked at Piper that way."

Simon glanced at Lyons and saw what Liam meant. A protective streak surged to the forefront. "I'll take care of it and be the bearer of bad tidings."

"Good luck, buddy. Need backup?"

"What do you think?"

Liam grinned. "I'll go with you anyway. Lyons is a cheater."

Simon rolled his eyes. The day he couldn't handle a two-bit thug like Lyons was the day he would have to turn in his black ops card. "Suit yourself."

"I usually do."

The two men headed toward Isaac Lyons who eyed them with disdain. When Simon and Liam reached the table, Lyons leaned back in his chair, arms folded. Instead of greeting them, he stared at the two men. Fine. He wanted to do it this way, Simon would accommodate him. "We need to talk to you, Lyons."

A sneer crossed his face. "What did I do this time? Forget to fill out my time card or tie my boots the wrong way?"

Lyons's friends cracked up, laughing like loons. Their amusement subsided when they realized Simon and Liam weren't amused.

Simon doubted anything bothered this guy, but he'd give him the courtesy of telling him the bad news about Macy in private. "Come with us."

For the first time, the trainee looked uneasy. "What's going on?" he asked as he followed the operatives from the dining room to the interrogation room.

"Have a seat." Simon motioned to one of the chairs at the plain wooden table as Liam leaned against the door. After the trainee dropped into a chair, Simon said, "There's no easy way to say this. Macy was at the bakery this morning when someone broke in and attacked her with a knife."

Lyons's jaw dropped. He surged to his feet. "She's at the hospital?"

"I'm sorry, Isaac. She died on the operating table."

"We have plans for tonight. I'm taking her out of town for dinner. Why are you lying?"

"Sit down."

He stared a moment, gaze raking over Simon's and Liam's faces. "It's true, isn't it? Someone killed Macy." Lyons slowly returned to his seat. Fury and anguish burned in the depths of his eyes. "Who did it? Who murdered my girlfriend?"

"The police are looking into it."

"This is a hick town. I wouldn't trust the cops in Otter Creek to hunt for a dog much less track down a killer."

"Josh Cahill, head of PSI, is part of the Otter Creek police force," Liam reminded him. "His brother-in-law, Ethan, is the police chief and Special Forces. If the local police department needs further resources, Fortress will provide it. The killer won't get away."

"Class starts in ten minutes," Simon said. "We'll clear it with St. Claire and Cahill if you want to take the day."

"Staying busy will help you cope with the loss." Liam straightened from the door.

"Is that what you'd do if someone killed your wife? Stay busy?" Lyons stood so fast his chair tipped over backward. "I'm not a cold, heartless machine like you, McCoy. I need time to come to grips with this."

Liam's eyes glittered, but he remained silent as the trainee stalked his direction and shoulder-checked him as he pushed past. He waited until Lyons's footsteps faded before he turned to Simon, his lips curving. "That went well."

Dragging a hand down his face, he sighed. "Come on. I want to check on Zoe."

Simon and Liam entered the dining hall in time to see Lyons running full-tilt at Zoe.

CHAPTER FIVE

Zoe glanced up to see Isaac Lyons racing toward her, raw fury and hatred marring his features. Shock rolled through her when she realized Isaac wasn't going to stop.

Before she could do more than process that thought, Matt was on his feet along with Cade Ramsey, Matt's best friend and teammate. The two men intercepted Isaac.

Macy's boyfriend tried to fight them off and ended up face down on the floor. Cade and Matt worked in tandem to control a cursing and thrashing Isaac.

"Knock it off," Cade snapped. "This isn't the way to handle your grief."

"She killed my girlfriend." His eyes pinned Zoe, leaving her in no doubt as to who he meant. "She has to pay."

Why would he blame her?

"That doesn't make sense, Lyons. Zoe was also injured in the attack. You trying to say that she killed Macy and bashed her own head against a wall hard enough to give herself a concussion?"

"She could have had help. Maybe her boyfriend helped her get rid of a problem."

Boyfriend? Rage filled Zoe when she realized Isaac was accusing Simon of murdering Macy on her orders. What was his problem? Who else would he accuse next?

Simon reached her side at the same time Josh Cahill and his sidekick, Alex Morgan, strode into the dining room, grim expressions on their faces.

Being here was a bad idea. She should have insisted that Simon take her home. She was disrupting PSI's routine and causing dissension between trainers and trainees, not to mention the homicidal rage she'd inspired in Macy's boyfriend.

Simon sat in the chair next to Zoe's and wrapped his arm around her shoulders. "You okay?" he murmured.

"This isn't going to work, Simon."

He stilled. "This?"

"Me being here. I'm disrupting everything."

The operative lifted her hand to his lips and kissed her knuckles. "I need you with me."

She dragged her gaze away from the drama playing out in front of her and focused on Simon, his words making her breath catch. "Why?"

"You scared me today. I thought I'd lost you before we had a chance to begin. I need time before I'm ready to let you out of my sight."

"Can I tell you a secret?"

"Anything."

"I was afraid I would die this morning before I had a chance to kiss you."

Eyes filled with emotion, he cupped her cheek. "Zoe." His voice sounded choked.

He'd thrown her for a loop with the quick turn in his emotions. Simon would have to deal with her confession. "Too much, too soon?"

"You have no idea how happy that makes me." Simon leaned close to her ear and whispered, "I'll be happy to remedy the lack of kisses after we leave PSI."

"Promise?"

His eyes darkened as his gaze dropped to her mouth. "Oh, yeah. Kissing you will be a pleasure and an answer to a prayer."

That brought a smile to her lips. Zoe wished she could have shared the news with Macy. She would have gotten a kick out of this.

More shouting and accusations from Isaac had Zoe turning in time to see the trainee break free from Cade and Matt's hold to sprint the remaining few feet separating him from her.

Between one heartbeat and the next, Simon shoved Isaac back against the wall, his forearm pressed to the man's throat, holding him immobile. The dining hall went totally silent except for Isaac's buddies who rose and started toward their friend. Alex pointed his finger at them and shook his head. The two men froze.

Zoe's attention rocketed back to Simon when she heard Isaac dragging in a strained breath.

"If you think I'll let you touch a hair on her head, you're delusional," Simon said. "You get one free pass because of Macy. If you come after Zoe again, I will take you down hard. Are we clear?"

Isaac shifted his gaze back to Zoe.

Simon must have done something different, maybe shifted his weight, because blood drained from Isaac's face. "Last chance, Lyons."

"I got it," the trainee choked out.

After another minute, Simon released him and stepped back, keeping his body between Isaac and Zoe. "Go cool off. Either head to your room or hit the track and run out some of the aggression. I don't want to see your face the rest of the day unless it's time for a meal. You will stay away from Zoe."

"Yeah, sure."

Simon shifted toward him. His voice dropped. "Try again, trainee."

"Yes, sir," Isaac snapped out. With a last glare at Zoe, he stalked past Simon and his teammates.

Trent St. Claire used some kind of hand signal and Cade left the dining room.

Zoe was finally able to drag in a full breath after Isaac was gone. Oh, man. That had been painful to watch. Scary, too. For a second, she'd wondered if she would end up at the hospital again with another injury.

Unfortunately, Isaac blamed her for Macy's death. Considering the way he'd tried to get his hands on her more than once in the past two minutes, Zoe knew he wanted to hurt her. She didn't understand why. Zoe would never hurt Macy.

Was Isaac responsible for Macy's death? If he had been, wouldn't he have killed Zoe, too? Maybe he didn't have time. Simon might have scared off the killer before he had a chance to do more than bash Zoe's head against the wall.

If Simon had interrupted him, the killer might come back when the operative wasn't around and finish the job. Zoe shuddered. She didn't understand everything about Simon's job, but knew he deployed with his teammates every other month or so. That meant his team would be sent to handle another job soon. If Bravo deployed before Macy's killer was caught, what would happen to Zoe?

Simon laid his hand on her shoulder, staking his claim in front of the trainers and trainees. Zoe had a feeling the gesture was a warning to the other men and a reminder to her that they were a couple now and he'd do whatever it took to protect her. But he couldn't protect her from afar.

She'd protect herself. The other women married to operatives did it all the time. Zoe wasn't a shrinking violet. If she planned to do the dating dance with the dangerous operative, she couldn't be a weak woman.

The whispers and murmurs swirling around the dining room fell to total silence when Josh Cahill strode to the center of the room. "Time for the day's classes to begin," he reminded them. "Lyons won't be joining you today. His girlfriend was killed early this morning. Move out."

Trainers and trainees alike rose, deposited the dishes and cutlery in the appropriate places, and scattered for various parts of the building, leaving in small groups. Conversations were muted as the people walked to the first training session of the day. Many of them cast sly or questioning glances Zoe's direction.

"Do you teach hand-to-hand combat to all the trainees at once?" Zoe asked Simon.

He shook his head. "The classes are broken up into groups of 50. I'll teach four sessions today." Simon tugged Zoe to her feet. "Nate is serving strawberry shortcake at lunch today. He needs help slicing strawberries. Do you feel like helping him?"

"I'll still be able to watch you teach one of the sessions?"

"I have two sessions before lunch and two after."

"In that case, I'd love to help Nate for a while."

Simon guided Zoe toward the kitchen with a hand at the small of her back. Instant kitchen envy hit Zoe when they walked inside. The stainless-steel commercial-grade ovens and dishwashers gleamed in the overhead lights. The breakfast cleanup was in full swing with Nate issuing orders to another worker.

The chef turned at their entrance. Zoe had to smile at the irony of Nate Armstrong the food artist also being an operative. She didn't know his specialty but could guess. The Otter Creek police department had called on him and Cade to handle more than one bomb.

What was Simon's main job? That was a question she intended to ask later. Was he allowed to tell her? Bravo and

Durango didn't talk about their jobs aside from the PSI training. Maybe they couldn't.

Nate's gaze softened as he hugged her. "I'm sorry about Macy."

Tears stung her eyes again. "So am I."

"Otter Creek police are the best. With Fortress to back them up, it's only a matter of time before the killer is run to ground." He released her. "Please say you're here to work. My helper is going to class."

The woman stripping rubber gloves from her hands smiled. "I can't be late. Mr. Murray will make me run extra laps if I don't arrive on time."

Zoe grinned. "Voice of experience?"

"Yes, ma'am." With a glance at Nate, who nodded in dismissal, the woman hurried from the kitchen.

"What do you say, Zoe? Willing to help me slice the strawberries for shortcake?"

"Show me where to set up."

"Excellent." He looked at Simon. "Better get moving. Trainees have long memories."

Simon chuckled and turned to Zoe. "Stay with Nate. If you need me, I'll be in the large classroom to the right of dining room."

"I'll be fine."

"If your symptoms worsen or...."

Amused and exasperated by his protectiveness, Zoe laid her hand on his chest. "Simon, don't worry. I'll tell Nate if I need help. I promise."

Nate clapped Simon on the shoulder. "I'll keep an eye on her. Go."

With one last glance at her, Simon left.

The chef inclined his head toward a stool at the counter. "Sit there. I've already washed the strawberries." He slid a knife and two oversize bowls across the counter to Zoe. "One for scraps, one for the berries. We have a lot of work ahead of us. The trainees will be starving by the time lunch rolls around."

"Yes, sir." She gave him a lame salute, unable to resist when he sounded so much like a military officer.

Nate rolled his eyes before gathering supplies for the shortcakes and dumping measured ingredients into a commercial mixer.

The two of them worked in silence for a while. Once the first batches of shortcakes were in the oven, Nate started placing more shortcakes on baking sheets. "How is the nausea?"

She grimaced. "Alive and well."

"Still have a headache?"

"Oh, yeah." If she could, Zoe would crawl into bed and drag the covers over her head to block out the light.

Nate wiped his hands, dimmed the overhead lights, and grabbed his phone. He tapped in a text, then shoved it back into his pocket before washing his hands again and resuming work.

Five minutes later, Matt arrived. "I brought something for the nausea."

Zoe frowned at Nate. "You ratted on me."

He lifted one shoulder. "I'll lose my kitchen assistant if she's hugging a porcelain bowl, puking her guts out. There's no need to suffer, Zoe."

She rounded on Matt. "What more can you do? I've already taken the pain medicine. I can't take another dose for several hours."

"An anti-nausea patch will help." The medic ripped open a packet and pressed the patch behind her ear. "Lying down will help the headache."

"I can't. Nate needs me."

"If you're miserable, go to the infirmary." Nate frowned. "I can handle the work."

Zoe shook her head and almost cried at the spike of pain. "I want to finish slicing the strawberries and I don't want time to think."

"Running from reality won't stop pain, sugar. Although I appreciate the help, you aren't doing yourself any favors by wallowing in denial."

"When I'm ready, I'll deal. I can't fall apart right now." Not until she was alone. Giving in to the pain with an audience? Nope, not going to happen. "I have to function, Nate. Nick and Stella need all the information I can give them."

"All right." He glanced at Matt. "Ice packs?"

The medic nodded. "Might help long enough for Zoe to get through the day." He faced her. "Twenty minutes on, two hours off. One against your forehead, the other on your nape. If the headache worsens, have Nate or Simon notify me. You can't mess around with head injuries. Understood?"

"Thanks, Matt."

"Another soft drink might help or Nate can brew chamomile mint tea for you." He squeezed her shoulder and left.

Zoe picked up the knife and resumed slicing strawberries. "Where did you find the recipe for the shortcakes?"

"My parents own a restaurant. Strawberry shortcake is one of their specialties. I've been using this recipe since I turned ten." Nate moved to the walk-in freezer and returned with two ice packs that he wrapped in kitchen towels. "The ice would help more if you lie down."

"I'm fine."

"Of course you are." The operative pressed the smaller pack to her forehead and draped the larger one around the back of her neck. "What happened this morning at the bakery?"

Images of the bloody bathroom filled her mind. Zoe swallowed hard and shoved the mental images aside. "I don't want to talk about this now."

"You need to." Nate's voice was gentle. "You'll remember more details as you think through what happened. Retelling the incident will also help your mind begin processing it."

Slowly, her delivery halting, Zoe told Nate everything she could remember about the incident. He listened without comment until she finished, then took her back through everything step-by-step, asking her more detailed questions.

The operative leaned against the edge of the counter, arms folded across his chest. "Who wants you dead?"

CHAPTER SIX

Simon stood on the left side of the large training classroom, watching paired students run through a sequence of moves he'd taught them. He scowled when a trainee flubbed a move more than once and took his frustration out on his partner.

When the second man ended up with a fist to the jaw, flat on his back, Simon stepped onto the mat and approached the pair. "Take a breather, Dolan," he said to the trainee still on the floor. "Next time, block the punch and contain the threat. If an attacker takes you down, your principal is toast."

"He's my training partner."

"Anyone who attacks you is a threat. You contain a threat or you end up dead."

"Yes, sir." Dolan rolled to his hands and knees and got to his feet. He moved to the side to watch, rubbing his jaw.

Simon motioned for Dolan's partner to approach. "Let's go through the sequence again, Kenwood. You've almost got it."

The trainee ran through the exercise with Simon stopping him to correct stances and strikes, slowing the pace until Kenwood nailed the movements. When the motions were in muscle memory, he sped up the exercise.

Triumph filled Kenwood's eyes when they finished.

"Excellent." Simon clapped him on the shoulder.

"Thank you, sir."

"You're quick and have a solid strike. The next time you're frustrated with an exercise, ask for clarification. The point is to learn the moves, not beat your partner into the ground with a sucker punch."

"Yes, sir."

"You're lucky Dolan has a slow-burn fuse, Kenwood. Your partner is strong. He'll mop the floor with you if there's another incident, and I'll let him."

Cheeks flaming, Kenwood gave a short nod. "I'll remember."

Simon motioned for Dolan to return. As Kenwood offered an apology to his partner and the two men resumed the exercise, Simon walked around pairs of trainees, correcting moves when needed, complimenting pairs when they proved to be quick and fast.

After introducing another series of movements and counter strikes, Simon watched students running through the routines, correcting angles and stances as he walked the classroom's perimeter.

An hour later, he glanced at the clock on the wall. Simon called a halt to the session, assigning further practice before the next close-quarters-combat training in two days. "Practice with as many classmates as possible before the next class. Dismissed."

After the trainees left, Simon ran a damp mop over the floor, readying the room for the second session. Finishing his task, he checked the clock again. He had enough time to check on Zoe before the next class started.

Simon strode to the kitchen. Alarm roared through him when he found the kitchen empty. Where was Zoe?

He hurried to the door leading to the hallway and saw Nate standing guard outside the women's restroom. The EOD man glanced up as Simon approached. "How is she?"

"Matt gave her an anti-nausea patch. Her headache is worse."

"Maybe I should take her back to the hospital."

"That's something you need to ask Matt or Rio. She needs to lie down but your woman is stubborn."

His woman. Simon couldn't deny that he liked hearing the phrase. "Zoe is a strong woman."

The bathroom door opened. Zoe walked out and into Simon's arms. "Hi."

He hugged her tight, grateful for the right to hold her at last. Simon frowned when he realized she was trembling. Fatigue or something else? "How do you feel?" he murmured.

"Like I've gone a few rounds with a world-class boxer and lost."

Simon tightened his grip at the reminder that he could have missed out on this opportunity forever. "Is the patch working?"

Zoe scowled at Nate. "Seriously? You gossip more than Maeve at the hair salon."

He gave her an unrepentant shrug. "It's fact, not gossip. I told Matt because he could help. Simon cares about you. Besides, you can't deny you're better now with the patch behind your ear." Nate shifted his attention to Simon. "You have another class?"

He nodded. "Ten minutes. I've got her if you want a quick break."

As the other operative walked down the hall, Simon nudged Zoe's face up to his with the side of his hand. He looked at her forehead and winced. "You have a colorful bruise forming." Just seeing it made Simon want to pound on the face of the man who had hurt her.

She wrinkled her nose. "I saw it in the mirror."

He kissed her temple. "I'm sorry you were hurt, but I'm grateful it wasn't worse. Tell me what's wrong."

Zoe dropped her gaze to the middle of his chest. "I'm fine."

"Try again."

"I will be fine."

"I won't let anything happen to you." He'd kill anyone who tried to harm her and wouldn't lose a second of sleep over it. Simon tilted her face up to his. "What upset you?" If Lyons had taken another run at her, Nate would have told him. "Talk to me."

"Nate asked me who wanted me dead." Her gaze flew up to his face. "Before today, I'd have said no one."

"And now?"

"I don't know who to trust anymore. One of my friends may be a wolf in disguise."

"You can trust me. No one is more important to me than you. I'll keep you safe, Zoe." No matter the cost to accomplish that goal.

Time to lighten the mood. He leaned down until his mouth brushed against her ear. "You have no idea how much I want this day to be over."

She shivered. "Why?"

Her physical response made him smile and gave him hope that the chemistry he felt when they were together went both ways. "I promised you kisses and I always keep my promises. Having your mouth against mine is all I can think about. You are one serious distraction."

Zoe's breath caught. "Simon." Her voice sounded strangled. She inched closer.

He had to back off before he pushed them farther than they needed to go. But, man, was it tough. He wanted to sweep her into his arms and carry Zoe out of town. He'd love to spend several weeks with her in a place where he knew she was safe and he could concentrate only on her. "Are you still helping Nate?"

"We're making strawberry glaze in a few minutes and finishing the last preparations for lunch."

"If you feel up to it, would you like to sit in on my afternoon classes?"

"I'd love to watch you work." Her eyes sparkled, worry and sadness momentarily forgotten.

"After I finish, I'll give you a tour of PSI, then take you to dinner." He smiled. "Our first official date."

"I thought our first date was this weekend."

"I can't wait until then. As long as you feel up to it, I'd love to spend more time with you this evening." Maybe by then he'd have figured out a way to inform Zoe that she wasn't staying by herself until Macy's killer was behind bars.

While coaching the trainees, Simon had contemplated the few facts he knew about Zoe's situation. He agreed with Nate. Although Macy was dead, Simon couldn't help but worry that Zoe was the real target. If he hadn't arrived when he did, the killer might have finished the job and Simon would have lost Zoe forever.

"I may not be able to eat tonight."

"I'll make sure the restaurant menu includes lighter options in case your stomach is still upset. You need to eat, though. You have to take care of yourself."

When Nate returned, Simon dropped a quick kiss on Zoe's mouth and released her to the other operative's care. He trotted back to the classroom and started his next session.

Ninety minutes later, he dismissed his class, damp-mopped the floor, and entered the crowded dining room. His gaze zeroed in on Zoe as she walked to the serving area with a large tray of shortcakes in her hands. Nate was on her heels with a large bowl of strawberries mixed into a glaze.

Simon's stomach growled, a loud reminder that breakfast was a distant memory. Except for the coffee Zoe had prepared for him, he hadn't consumed anything since he left his house at four this morning. On a normal day, he would have grabbed a snack from Nate between classes. He didn't regret the few minutes he'd been able to hold Zoe in his arms and couldn't wait to do it again.

Zoe smiled when she saw him. "Ready for lunch?"

"More than. Have you eaten yet?"

She shook her head.

Nate laid his hand on Zoe's shoulder. "Everything is under control. Eat while you have a chance before Simon's next class."

"No offense, Nate, but I can't stomach eating spaghetti today."

"I have something else that I think will settle better. Go sit with Simon. I'll bring your lunch in a few minutes."

"Don't go to any trouble. I feel guilty enough as it is leaving you to handle the lunch crowd and clean up by yourself."

"It's not a problem. Don't worry about the cleanup. Meredith, my assistant, is free until the second afternoon session. We have it covered."

Simon grabbed a plate and filled the white surface with the noodles and meat sauce. After picking up the bundled utensils and napkin, he escorted Zoe to the table occupied by his teammates. He seated her, then poured himself a glass of iced tea and returned to the table where she waited.

Soon, Nate set a plate in front of Zoe along with utensils and a large mug of hot tea. "Chicken pot pie. Comfort food that should settle well."

"Thanks, Nate. This smells fabulous."

An hour later, Zoe walked with Simon to his classroom. Trainees streamed inside and Simon demonstrated the first sequence of moves with a volunteer from the class.

After pairing up the students, Simon walked the perimeter of the room until he was sure the trainees had a handle on the routine. He called a halt to the practice session and asked for another volunteer to demonstrate the second sequence.

A trainee stepped forward, one of Lyons' friends. Simon motioned for Moran to join him in the center of the room. Although suspicious of the trainee's motives, Simon began the demonstration, giving detailed explanations of the moves and countermoves. Nearing the end, he started to step back when Moran threw a roundhouse punch at Simon's face.

Simon heard Zoe gasp as he blocked the punch and plowed his fist into Moran's gut. The trainee dropped to his knees, wheezing as he dragged in air and absorbed the pain from Simon's blow.

Simon glanced at the other trainees watching the exchange in stunned silence. "Work with your partner on this sequence. In ten minutes, you switch partners and go through the exercise again. Hollister."

The second of Lyons' friends stepped forward, wariness in his eyes. "Sir?"

"Come here. The rest of you get busy."

The occupants of the room that had been frozen into immobility at the sudden aggression from Moran shifted into groups and started practicing on each other.

Hollister, a big bruiser with a buzz cut and a scar over his left eyebrow, lumbered forward, jaw hardened and tight. "Yes, sir?" he practically spat out when he stood in front of Simon.

"You plan to take a swing at me, too?" Simon could see the temptation in the depths of the trainee's eyes. Hollister remained silent. Maybe he had more sense than his buddy. Simon wasn't holding his breath, though. After all, Hollister was close friends with Lyons and called his judgment into question.

"You want to come after me, take your best shot. If you and your friends go after Zoe, it will be the last thing any of you do."

"We heard what Isaac said. Your girlfriend killed Macy."

"He isn't rational at present. Zoe didn't hurt Macy or ask someone to do it for her. I found Zoe unconscious. And, no, I didn't do the wet work myself. If I had, Macy would have been dead at the scene and Zoe wouldn't be injured. I'd sooner cut off my own arm than harm her. You and Moran should do yourselves a favor. Find a better friend than Lyons."

"Yes, sir," Hollister snapped.

Yeah, that was a waste of air. "One final warning. If you or Moran come after me again, you'll be out of PSI so fast, your head will spin and you won't have a second chance to enroll."

Moran staggered to his feet, arms still clutched over his gut. "Understood, sir. I apologize for my lack of control. It won't happen again."

Hollister slid a withering look at his friend but remained stubbornly silent.

"Pair up and practice the routine."

The two men moved to the other side of the room and went through the exercise. Moran threw himself into the practice session while Hollister slopped through the routine, casting sullen glances Simon's direction.

Five minutes later, Hollister spun on his heel and stalked from the room, leaving Moran standing with a scowl on his face.

Simon dragged a hand down his face, then called out, "Change partners and go through the exercise again. Moran, you're with me."

Fifteen minutes later, Moran had nailed the routine. "Good job," Simon said, clapping the other man on the shoulder.

"Thank you, sir. Again, I apologize for the cheap shot."

"What's Hollister's deal?"

"He and Isaac are from the same town. They've been best friends since kindergarten. If Isaac said he hung the moon, Chris would believe him."

"Find a new friend group, Moran. Unless I see a huge turnaround, Lyons and Hollister won't last much longer at PSI. Don't let them take you down, too."

After calling a halt to the practice session, Simon dismissed the class. He crouched beside Zoe. "The last class starts in fifteen minutes. You need a break or another soft drink?"

She gently waggled the green bottle in her hand. Clear liquid sloshed inside. "I have enough to get through the class."

"What did you think?"

"Watching you gives me a whole new appreciation for what you and your teammates do here. You're a good teacher, Simon."

His cheeks burned at her compliment. "Thanks. Do you have questions about what you observed?"

Zoe watched him a moment before cupping his cheek. "Do you often have trainees attack you?"

"Not if they plan to complete the training. Lyons and his buddies have burned their only reprieve. If it happens again, they'll be out."

"I don't want anything to happen to you."

"Trust me." He leaned over and brushed his lips over hers. "This is what I'm trained for."

She smiled against his mouth. "Kissing?"

Simon chuckled and stood before he gave in to the temptation to indulge in a longer, deeper kiss. "I need to damp mop the floor before the next class arrives."

"I can help." Zoe followed him to the supply closet.

He handed her a damp mop, then grabbed a second one for himself. Between the two of them, they cleaned the floor in five minutes.

Simon glanced at his watch. He had enough time to coax another kiss or two from the woman of his dreams before the last batch of trainees arrived. Just as he was reaching for her, his phone rang.

He checked the screen and placed the call on speaker. "You're on speaker with Zoe."

"How are you, Zoe?"

"I'm okay, thanks to Simon. Do you need something, Nick?"

"When are you and Simon free this afternoon?"

She looked at him, eyebrows raised.

"Two hours," Simon said. "Why?"

"Bring Zoe to Macy's house."

His hand tightened around the cell phone. "What's going on?"

"Someone broke into Macy's home."

CHAPTER SEVEN

Zoe's grip on Simon's hand tightened as he drove closer to Macy's two-bedroom bungalow. Who would break into her friend's house? Was it a thief who learned Macy was dead and sought to take advantage of the empty house?

What was Nick looking for at the house? Macy was killed at work, not at her home.

An invisible band tightened around her chest at the remembered horror of the small bathroom. Blood everywhere, the copper tang filling the air and choking Zoe as she stood inside the space.

She'd have to remodel the bathroom. She wouldn't be able to step foot in there after what she'd seen. Zoe needed to call Mason Kincaid with Elliott Construction. He was a master carpenter and worked on house rehabs all over Otter Creek and Dunlap County. If she bribed him with free coffee and baked goods for a year, maybe he'd move her to the top of his busy work schedule. He'd have to set aside the flea market dresser he was stripping and staining for her to revamp a bathroom filled with nightmare memories.

She shuddered. Before the remodel, the bathroom would have to be cleaned with a ton of disinfectant and an ample supply of rubber gloves. The prospect of facing that task made bile rise into her throat.

Zoe clamped a hand over her mouth. She couldn't barf in Simon's SUV.

"What's wrong? Are you sick?" he asked. When she nodded, Simon pulled off the road and parked behind a grove of trees. He turned off the engine and hurried to her door.

Zoe unlocked the seatbelt and threw it aside as he opened the door. Simon plucked her from the seat and carried her a few feet deeper into the tree cover.

As soon as her feet touched the ground, she lost her battle with the nausea. Zoe doubled over and retched repeatedly until her gut felt hollowed out.

By the time her stomach was empty, tears streamed down Zoe's face. The whole time she threw up, Simon held her hair back with one hand and supported her with an arm across her collar bone.

He nudged her back against a tree. "Stay here. I'll be right back." Simon returned a minute later with a full soft drink bottle. He broke the seal and handed her the drink. "Sip this."

She did as he suggested and sank into his embrace when Simon eased her against his chest. "Sorry. I'm so embarrassed."

"Don't apologize, Zoe. I'm surprised you held on this long."

"You expected me to barf?"

"I puke every time I have a concussion."

She frowned. "Have you had many?"

"Enough to know they aren't pleasant."

"Understatement."

"Do you feel better?"

She nodded.

"Good. We should get going. Nick must be wondering where we are."

They arrived at Macy's house fifteen minutes later. Two Otter Creek police SUVs were parked in front of the small house.

The sight sent a sharp spear of pain into Zoe's heart. This was so wrong. Macy should be inside, getting ready for another backyard barbecue instead of lying in the morgue.

Simon laced his fingers with Zoe's and led her to the front door which stood ajar. He nudged it opened with an elbow to the center panel. "Nick?" he called out.

"In the kitchen. Come on back but don't touch anything."

Zoe followed Simon into the interior of the living room, her gaze firing around the neat area. She frowned. "I don't see anything amiss."

"Nick must have a reason for believing there was a break-in." He led her toward the murmured voices coming from the back of the house.

A moment later, they walked into the kitchen to see Nick and his fellow detective, Stella Armstrong, checking surfaces for fingerprints.

Zoe felt a breeze brushing against her skin and her gaze zeroed in on the French door standing open with a broken window pane beside the knob.

"Thanks for coming." Stella looked up from her work. "Nick and I need you to look around the house and tell us if you notice anything missing." She smiled. "No touching. We've collected carpet fibers so you don't have to watch where you step."

"Stella, go with her," Nick said. "Simon, stay with me. I have questions for you."

Simon dropped a quick kiss on Zoe's mouth and turned to stare at Stella.

The detective rolled her eyes but gave a short nod before setting aside the brush she'd been using to dust with fingerprint powder. "Let's take a tour, Zoe. Tell me if you notice anything missing or out of place."

Zoe held back her curiosity until she and Stella were out of earshot, then asked, "What was that look about?"

"A not-so-subtle order to keep you safe. The members of Durango and Bravo are an overprotective bunch. If you're involved with Simon, be prepared for a man who treats you like a treasure to be protected at all costs." She slid a glance Zoe's direction. "Looks like my warning is too late, though."

"Any words of advice?"

They stopped outside the bathroom and Stella turned toward her. "They're tough, fierce men with hearts of gold. When they fall in love, they fall hard. Loving them isn't a cakewalk. You have to take the good with the bad and accept the secrecy that's inherent in their jobs. They take risks no one else would take to save innocent lives. They're worth every minute of worry and loneliness during those long night hours when the team is deployed."

"Do you regret taking a chance with Nate?"

"Never." Stella's response was immediate. "I adore that man. He's my heart."

Longing tugged Zoe, a longing for Simon. Would he one day look at her the way Nate looked at Stella? "Simon had to pull over to the side of the road on the way here so I could throw up."

The detective's eyebrows snapped up. "And he didn't run for the hills?"

Zoe shook her head. "He was surprised I hadn't been sick before then."

"That settles it. Simon Murray is a keeper. A man not totally committed to you would have bailed at that point."

Walking into the bathroom, Zoe mentally refocused. No point in obsessing over Simon when they hadn't been on a date yet. She already knew Simon was a keeper, multiple secrets or not. The question she wanted answered was whether or not he saw her as a keeper.

A glance through the bathroom cabinets and linen closet didn't reveal anything missing or out of place. She and Stella shifted their search to the guest room where they found nothing amiss aside from the dresser being in a slightly different position and the drawers not fully closed. Odd since Macy was obsessive about orderliness, but not alarming. Her friend might have been looking for something in a hurry and neglected to close the drawers.

Zoe choked back tears when they reached Macy's bedroom. The idea of her friend never coming back to the sweet room they had painted a soft gray two months ago was almost more than she could bear.

She forced herself to examine the room and compare it to the most recent visit to this part of the bungalow. Nothing new or different except the dresser drawers were slightly open in here, too. Perhaps Macy had been looking for something. Other than that, the room appeared as it had the last time she'd been here for a barbecue two weeks ago.

"I'm sorry to make you do this," Stella murmured. "I know it's painful."

"If I can help, I want to try." She wiped away a tear that had escaped. "I don't see anything wrong, Stella. This isn't a random burglar wanting to steal jewelry or electronics for a quick buck, is it?"

"Thanks for coming out."

"Can't say anything, huh?"

"That's the nature of the job." She tossed another glance at Zoe. "I'll say one more thing about our earlier discussion. Men like Nate and Simon don't think anything about providing what their partners need and don't expect to have their care reciprocated. Don't accept care from Simon without giving it back. He would take a bullet for you without a second thought. If you don't feel the same way about him, back out of the relationship soon." She grinned, mischief dancing in her eyes. "Other than that, I'll just say have fun. Simon's a great guy. Nate thinks highly of him."

High praise, indeed. "I won't forget. Thanks, Stella."

The women returned to the kitchen where Simon leaned one shoulder against the wall, watching Nick dusting for prints. The operative's gaze focused on Zoe. His eyes narrowed as he straightened. "Everything okay?"

"I didn't find anything missing or out of place except for the dressers in the bedrooms. It looks like Macy went through the drawers in search of something."

Nick glanced up. "Macy or the perp?"

Goosebumps surged up Zoe's spine. She moved closer to Simon. Even with two cops in the room, she felt safer with Simon at her side. Was it possible the person who broke in had searched the dressers in the bedrooms?

It was more than possible. A search by an invader was probable. No matter how rushed she was, Zoe didn't remember Macy ever leaving something undone, even a task as simple as closing a cabinet door.

Simon frowned. "If the perp pawed through Macy's belongings, what was he looking for?"

"Believe it or not, bedroom drawers are popular places to hide jewelry and money."

"Not Macy," Zoe insisted. "She was low maintenance. The only jewelry she owned was her grandmother's emerald ring. Macy never took it off."

"Did she hide money around the house?" Stella asked.

"I don't know."

"What about at your shop? Do you hide money there?"

"Not a chance. Either Macy or I deposited the cash earned each day into the night deposit at the bank. I've always been concerned that a thief would see my bakery as a soft target. I only leave enough cash in the floor safe every night to make change the next morning when we open the doors."

Simon scowled. "If the perp isn't looking for cash or jewelry, what is he looking for?"

"Something he's willing to kill to find." Zoe felt sick at the thought. Stella's earlier words reverberated in her mind. If this person was willing to kill to get what he was after, that meant Simon was in the line of fire.

As if he'd heard her thoughts skittering in her mind, Simon closed the gap between them and wrapped his arms around Zoe. "He won't touch you, Zoe. You have my word on that."

But at what cost? Zoe wrapped her arms around Simon's waist. She wanted this nightmare to end. What she couldn't handle was the likelihood of her friends and neighbors being at risk. To save them, she'd give a lot. Sacrificing Simon wasn't a price she was willing to pay and she wouldn't allow anyone else to sacrifice him, either.

CHAPTER EIGHT

As Simon escorted Zoe from Macy's house, he quartered the area. Although nothing stood out in this quiet neighborhood, his unease continued to grow. Someone was watching them.

Zoe's hand tightened around his. "What's wrong?"

"I'm not sure."

"Is it Macy's killer?"

Simon wished he could banish her fear. He didn't blame her for feeling vulnerable. She was. He would keep her safe. His priority was Zoe and he suspected she always would be. "Might be a nosy neighbor."

"You don't believe that."

He tucked her into the passenger seat of his SUV. "Expecting the worst is how we stay alive on missions. We never take things at face value." Things went wrong in the blink of an eye. You learned to plan for the worst, hope for the best, and adjust on the fly. If you didn't learn that lesson, you died. Simon didn't intend to die anytime soon because he had too much to live for.

After he brushed her bottom lip with his thumb, Simon rounded the front of the vehicle and climbed behind the wheel. As he drove, he kept an eye on the mirrors for signs of incoming trouble. "Are you hungry?"

"A little," she admitted.

"You up for a little drive?"

"Sure. I thought you would prefer a restaurant in town in case the police or your teammates need you."

"We'll be close enough." Simon squeezed her hand as he drove toward Highway 18. "I want to be alone with you. If we eat in town, people will stop to ask questions about what happened at the bakery."

Zoe grimaced. "Eating away from Otter Creek is sounding more attractive every minute. Where are we going?"

"One of my favorite restaurants in Cherry Hill. If we're needed, we can return to Otter Creek in under 30 minutes."

For the rest of the drive, Simon steered the conversation to light topics. If Zoe felt stressed, she wouldn't eat. Down time without bad memories bombarding her might help Zoe remember more to aid with the investigation.

He also wanted her to himself for a while. Simon needed a chance to start cementing their relationship before Zoe wised up and kicked him to the curb. What woman wanted to be saddled with a man who had his job and erratic schedule?

Simon drove to Stone Ridge, the best steakhouse in Cherry Hill. Although he didn't expect his date to eat much, the restaurant served baked potatoes and a creamy chicken soup that should entice Zoe to eat a little.

He parked near the front entrance and assisted Zoe to the asphalt. Inside the restaurant, the hostess greeted Simon by name and escorted them to a table in a dimly lit corner.

Zoe glanced around, her gaze settling on the crackling fire in the river rock hearth. "How did you learn about this place?"

"PSI offers specialized training to local police departments in the area. The Cherry Hill PD trained with us a few months ago and raved about the food here. My teammates and I tried it out and discovered the cops were right. Check their dessert menu. They have selections that my favorite baker would appreciate."

Zoe grinned. "Your favorite baker?"

"Yes, ma'am. Haven't you noticed that I only buy baked goods from you?" Otter Creek had plenty of options, but none were as good as Zoe's. "You spoiled me."

Her gaze dropped to the menu spread open on the table. "I'm afraid to try a steak or hamburger. Any suggestions?"

"The creamy chicken soup and a baked potato. Want to try it?"

"That sounds good."

The waitress took their orders. After she left, Zoe eyed Simon. "Will you tell me about your family?"

"Did you think I'd refuse?"

"You never mention them."

"I don't make it a habit to talk about my family."

"I'm sorry. I shouldn't have asked. I don't have the right to pry."

Simon covered her hand with his. "Hey, don't do that. I want you to be interested in every aspect of my life." He lifted her hand to his lips and kissed the inside of Zoe's wrist. "You have the right, Zoe."

The subtle tension in her face disappeared. "Did you have a hard childhood?"

He smiled. "Not even close. I have a large family and we're always in each other's business. The reason I don't talk about them except with my teammates is to keep my family safe."

Zoe blinked. "I don't understand."

"Have you noticed that none of the operatives or their wives are on social media?"

"I noticed."

"We make enemies all over the world. We keep a low profile and stay off social media. Our enemies could track us down and take revenge by harming those we love. I don't talk about my family and they don't talk about me on the Internet. The precaution is one you'll need to follow if you're involved with me."

She laughed, the sound doing funny things to his insides. "I'm pretty sure we're past the 'if you're involved with me' stage, Simon. Teach me the rules so I won't endanger you or your family. I'd never forgive myself if something happened to any of you because of me."

Simon squeezed her hand. "What do you want to know about my family?"

"Do you have brothers or sisters?"

"Two of each and I'm the middle kid. We're stair steps. Mom had us one year apart. Somehow, she and Dad survived five children ages five and under at home before my oldest sister started school. Mom says it's a miracle her hair didn't turn gray by the time she was thirty."

"Wow. Are your siblings married?"

"I'm the last holdout. I have fourteen nieces and nephews."

Zoe's jaw dropped. "Good grief."

"I filled out a spreadsheet for birthdays and anniversaries. With my wonky schedule, that's the only way I ensure I don't miss an important event. Needless to say, holidays are a riot around my parents' place. We get together as often as we can. Usually, I'm the one who misses celebrations because I'm deployed with my team."

"What jobs do your siblings have?"

"Tracey is the mayor of our town. James is a veterinarian. B.J. is a surgeon, and Cassie is a lawyer. Your turn. Tell me about your family."

She shrugged. "Not much to tell. I'm an only child. My parents doted on me to the point that I had to move across the state to keep from being cosseted until I was 50."

"Do you go home much?"

"Not as much as I'd like. The bakery keeps me busy. They've been in Otter Creek a few times since the shop opened." Zoe's eyes sparkled. "Mom badgered Dad until he brought her to visit me. Apparently, eight weeks without seeing me was long enough."

A policeman headed toward their table. Simon stood and held out his hand. "Good to see you again, Terry. How's your family?"

The man beamed. "Great. Thanks for asking. What are you doing in my neck of the woods?"

"A date with this gorgeous woman. Zoe, meet Sergeant Terry Hiller from the Cherry Hill police force. He survived two of my classes at PSI."

Hiller shook Zoe's hand. "Good to meet you, Zoe." He turned back to Simon. "Liam and his lady doing all right?"

"They're married now."

"Good for them. Thought they might be heading that direction." He inched closer. "We'll schedule another training session at PSI soon. The Chief agrees that Cherry Hill needs its own SWAT team."

"Excellent. My team is due for deployment soon so I'm not sure we'll be in town to train you. We have another team on site who will do a great job with you if we're gone."

"Is the other team as good as yours?"

"Oh, yeah. They're incredible. You'll be glad you trained with Durango." Durango was Fortress Security's only Delta team. While Bravo was amazing, Durango was on another level altogether.

Curiosity filled the cop's eyes. "I'll look forward to working with them."

A moment later, the waitress arrived with their food and Hiller took his leave with a promise to touch base with Simon soon.

Zoe breathed deep, eyeing the food in front of her. "This looks fabulous."

Progress. At least she was hungry. Simon kept their conversation light throughout dinner and convinced Zoe to share a dessert with him. At the first bite of carrot cake, her eyes lit up. By the time the plate was empty, Zoe had eaten more than half the slice of cake.

Back in the SUV, Simon asked, "How are you feeling?"

"Not bad, considering. Your suggestions were perfect." She laid her hand on his forearm. "The company was better than the food. Thank you for dinner."

"The pleasure was all mine." As he drove to Highway 18, Simon considered how best to broach the topic of keeping watch over Zoe. He didn't want to smother her or give the killer another chance at her. While it appeared Macy was the sole target of the attack, Simon refused to discount the possibility that Zoe might be in danger. If the killer decided that Zoe knew more than she did, he'd try to silence her.

As they reached the outskirts of Otter Creek, Simon's phone signaled an incoming text. Glancing at the screen, his blood ran cold. He called Trent. "Who and where?" he asked as soon as his team leader answered.

"Piper's on her way to the hospital in an ambulance. Liam's with her."

"Zoe and I will be there in ten minutes." He ended the call.

"What's going on?" Zoe asked. "Did something happen to Piper?"

"Trent sent an encoded message to say that one of our team had been attacked. When we receive that code, we drop whatever we're doing and respond immediately."

That code was Bravo's signal that one of their own was hurt. Now that Piper had been attacked, Simon faced the likelihood that Macy hadn't been the target this morning and he was responsible for an innocent woman's death.

CHAPTER NINE

Simon escorted Zoe into the hospital's emergency room entrance and steered her toward his teammates and their wives. The men were grim and the women looked afraid. Simon clenched his fist. No one had the right to terrorize the wives of his friends.

Unfortunately, they were right to be concerned. Did Bravo have a security breach? If so, all their loved ones were in danger. He had to call his family and warn them to take precautions. The rest of his teammates would do the same for their families as would Durango. If someone was targeting Bravo, Durango was also in the line of fire.

His grip on Zoe's hand tightened. Would this situation convince her that dating an operative was too dangerous? Man, he hoped not. She smiled at him and Simon was able to take a deep breath.

He focused on Liam who was pacing, face white and hands fisted. "Hey."

His best friend turned, eyes haunted.

Simon pulled him into a brief one-armed hug. "What happened?"

"She stopped by the grocery store to pick up something special for dinner, said she had something important to tell me. Someone jumped her in the driveway of our home. I was five minutes behind her. Five minutes. I found her unconscious on the ground." His voice cracked. "I can't lose her, Simon. I can't live without her. She's everything."

Simple, stark words from the sniper. "Piper is one tough lady. She'll fight to recover. We'll find the creep who hurt your wife. He'll wish he'd never laid a hand on one of our own."

Liam's expression hardened. "He better pray one of you finds him first. If I get my hands on him, he's dead."

Simon saw the truth in his friend's eyes. Those words weren't an idle threat.

"I don't need a vigilante cruising around town, McCoy." Ethan Blackhawk, Otter Creek's police chief, said as he entered the waiting room. He stopped in front of Liam. "I understand you want to protect your wife. You're welcome to do that on your turf. Actively looking for revenge will land you behind bars. I'd rather toss Piper's attacker in jail than her husband. Understood?"

The muscle in Liam's jaw twitched. "Yes, sir. As long as you understand that if he comes after my wife again, I will kill him, jail time or not."

"Let's hope it doesn't come to that." Ethan's gaze shifted to Zoe. "I heard about Macy. I'm sorry for your loss and your injuries."

"Thank you."

The police chief folded his arms across his chest. "You have a problem, Trent."

Bravo's leader rubbed the back of his neck. "So it seems."

"Find the leak before someone else is hurt or dies."

"Yes, sir."

Simon's lips twitched. Even though Ethan wasn't a teammate or their superior, the man demanded and received respect wherever he went. Ethan knew exactly what Bravo and Durango were up against. He'd been Special Forces and understood the risks they faced daily.

He needed to contact Zane. Now might be a good time to do that while they waited for word on Piper. "I'll have Zane start on the deep checks for all of us." Simon glanced at Ethan. "Does Josh know about Piper?"

A nod. "Called him on the way here. He's already tightening security around his team and their families."

Good. Josh and his wife, Del, had twin baby girls. That man was lethal. No one would touch his family and live to tell the tale.

He turned to Zoe. "I'll be back in a minute. Stay with my team." No offense to Blackhawk, but he trusted his teammates to protect the woman who was coming to mean so much to him.

He looked at Matt, who nodded, accepting responsibility for Zoe's safety. That done, Simon walked outside the ER doors and grabbed his phone.

When his call was answered, he said, "Zane, we might have a serious problem brewing in Otter Creek."

"Talk to me."

Simon summarized the events. "Start a deep run on Bravo and Durango and our families. We have to know if there's been a security breach. If there has, plug it fast. We can't afford to advertise our presence in Otter Creek. We'll be a danger to everyone in this town."

"I'll contact you as soon as I know something."

"I don't care what time it is, Z. Day or night."

"Copy that. Anything else?"

"I need a secure phone sent to me as soon as possible."

Silence, then, "Zoe?"

"Yes."

"You finally made your move. Congratulations, my friend. The phone should arrive at PSI by tomorrow afternoon along with her cover."

"Appreciate it, Zane."

"Yep. Later."

Simon returned to Zoe. "Anything yet?"

She shook her head. "Liam won't be able to hold himself back much longer."

"Is Grace working?"

"She's in the room with Piper and the doctor."

Maybe Matt could learn something. He worked a few shifts a month as a paramedic for Dunlap County. Simon started to approach him when Grace walked into the waiting room. She was surrounded by Simon and the others.

She held up her hand and the questions stopped. "Liam, come with me. The rest of you have to wait here." She led Liam to an examination room.

The minutes passed at an excruciating pace. Simon checked his watch again for the tenth time in the past ten minutes. What was taking so long? Was Piper that seriously injured?

Grace returned. "Piper will be fine. The doctor is going to admit her overnight for observation. If all goes well, she should be released tomorrow morning. Simon, Liam is asking for you and Zoe."

Relief swept over Simon with the force of a tidal wave. Thank God Piper would recover. He held out his hand to Zoe and together they followed Grace to the examination room.

He stepped into the room only to pull up short when he saw his best friend. Liam's arms were wrapped tight around Piper and tears were trickling down his cheeks.

Simon's brows knitted. "Is everything all right, Liam?"

He waved to the chairs at the side of the bed. "We have something to tell you." His voice came out gruff. After they sat, Liam pressed a gentle kiss to Piper's mouth before easing back and facing Simon and Zoe.

"Do you need anything before I go, Piper?" Grace asked. "A soft drink?"

"I would love a soft drink. Nothing with caffeine."

A smile from the nurse. "No problem. I'll be right back." She left.

Liam smiled at Simon and Zoe. "We wanted you to be the first to know that Piper is pregnant."

"Oh, my goodness." Zoe hopped up and hugged Piper. "Congratulations! I'm so happy for you."

When Zoe moved aside, Simon kissed Piper's cheek. "You're going to be a great mom, Piper."

She smiled. "Thanks, Simon."

"What happened at the house? Did you pass out?"

Her smile morphed into a scowl. "Some guy dressed in black with a ski mask on shoved my head against the SUV. I blacked out. The next thing I knew, I was in here with Grace telling me I was going to be fine and Liam was anxious to see me."

Anxious? Liam McCoy, a sniper reputed to have ice in his veins, had been frantic to see his wife. "You're sure the attacker was a man?"

Piper grimaced. "Positive. Hard hands, muscular build, over six feet tall. He was in good shape."

"Did he say anything?" Liam asked.

She shook her head.

"Was he waiting for you to arrive?"

"He came from the porch. I remember being surprised the porch light was out. I got out of the SUV and walked to the cargo area to carry in the groceries."

"You should have waited for me." Liam kissed Piper's temple. "From now on, you aren't to carry anything heavy and that includes groceries."

"I understand you want to protect me and the baby, but you'll be deployed soon. I have to take care of myself while you're gone."

"We'll talk about it more later."

Simon knew that stubborn look. Piper might not know it yet, but she'd just lost that argument. Knowing his friend,

Liam would arrange for a member of Durango or one of the PSI personnel to go with Piper to get groceries while they were out of town. He wasn't above bribing or blackmailing someone to help his wife.

"I called Zane. He's searching for a leak. If he finds anything, I'll let you know."

A nod. "Appreciate you taking care of that."

"I did it for myself, too. If we've had a security breach, Zoe and the rest of our teammates' wives are at risk as well as Durango and their wives."

Blood drained from Piper's face. "One of your enemies is targeting us to get to you?"

"We don't know that, baby." Liam wrapped his arm around her and tucked her against his side. "If there's any activity on the Net, Zane will find it. In the meantime, we'll take extra precautions to be sure you and all the other women are safe."

Zoe frowned. "You and your teammates better be taking extra protective measures for yourselves, too."

"We're trained to handle this, Zoe."

"You aren't invincible." She rounded on Simon. "Promise me you'll be careful."

"Always." His job was risky, but he had no intention of making Brent Maddox, his boss at Fortress Security, notify his family that Simon had been killed in action. He'd promised his mother to come back to her alive, not in a pine box. He always kept his promises.

"Call Zane," Liam said. "Tell him to access the security footage at the house and send it to your email and mine. Maybe we'll see something to indicate who we're looking for."

"I'll take care of it. Concentrate on Piper." Simon stood and helped Zoe to her feet. "Trent and the others will want to see you and Piper. We'll be in the waiting room until the visits are finished. I'll keep watch tonight. No one will get to you on my watch."

And that brought up another problem. What would he do with Zoe? Simon refused to let her go home by herself, especially now that it seemed the attacks on Zoe and Piper might be related.

On the way out, they passed Grace who was returning to the room with a soft drink for Piper. "Exciting news, isn't it?"

"The best," Zoe said. "Would it be possible for us to stay with Piper and Liam tonight?"

Simon stared at her. She planned to stay with him? Although that relieved his mind about her safety, Zoe had to be exhausted after the long and horrible day she'd had.

"I expected Liam and Simon to stay. You, on the other hand, just left this hospital earlier today. You should go home to rest, Zoe."

She shook her head. "Piper is my friend. I'm not leaving until she walks out of here tomorrow." Her lips curved. "I don't have to get up at 2:30 tomorrow morning. Nick still hasn't released the bakery so I can't open the shop for business."

Simon frowned. "Didn't you say you had orders to fill for clients tomorrow?"

"I'll have to call and cancel. I don't have an industrial-size kitchen at my disposal."

"Nate said you can use the kitchen at PSI. He'll work around you."

Zoe glanced over her shoulder at Liam and Piper, wrapped in each other's arms again. "But you're on guard duty through the night. I know you won't allow me to go to PSI on my own and I won't ask you to leave them vulnerable."

Grace slipped past them. "Work out the rotation with Trent and the others. An orderly will be taking Piper to her room in a few minutes and I know one of Bravo will want to be with them during the transport."

"I'll send one of the others down here." Simon led Zoe to the waiting room. "Matt." He motioned for the team medic to join them in the hall.

"What's up?" Matt asked, voice low.

"An orderly will be transporting Piper to her room soon. Thought you and Delilah might want to go along. I need to work out the guard rotation with Trent."

"No problem." The medic frowned. "You wanted me to go first for a reason. Is something wrong with Piper?"

"Not like you mean. She has a head injury similar to Zoe's. I'll let Liam and Piper tell you the reason she's being admitted overnight. You'll be able to offer more information and advice than the rest of us."

Matt's eyebrows soared.

Simon grinned. "You'll understand when they talk to you."

His friend pivoted and held out his hand to his wife. When she joined him, she and Matt walked down the hall to the examination room.

Trent met Simon and Zoe at the entrance of the waiting room. "Anything I should know?"

"Liam and Piper have news, but the information should come from them. We need to work out a guard rotation. I'll take the first shift. I have to leave at 2:00 tomorrow morning. Zoe has baking to do for customer orders tomorrow. I'm taking her to PSI to use the kitchen."

Trent motioned for Cade to join them. "Guard rotation. I'll take the last rotation."

Cade snorted. "You aren't fooling us. You want a date with your wife when she's off shift tomorrow morning."

"Maybe. You want the first shift or the second?"

"I'll take the second with you. Figured Liam might like to have Matt around to keep a knowledgeable eye on Piper the first part of the night."

"What about Sasha?" Zoe asked. "Simon doesn't want me to be alone and I'm sure you're just as concerned for your wife's safety. What will you do with her while you're here?"

"She has to go into the coffee shop early. Matt won't mind taking Sasha home with him and Delilah. He'll make sure Sasha is at her shop on time and stay with her until one of her employees arrives. Delilah doesn't have to open Wicks until later in the morning."

"We set, then?" Trent asked. When Simon and Cade nodded, he said, "Anything happens during your watch, I need to know about it. We can't afford to let down our guard. I'm not sure exactly what's going on, but these attacks aren't random. Someone is targeting our team through those we care about. Whoever it is isn't finished."

CHAPTER TEN

Zoe woke with a start when someone entered Piper's hospital room. She opened her eyes to see Simon and Liam standing, weapon in hand, bodies between her and Piper and a potential threat. Adrenaline poured into her bloodstream until she heard Grace's soft voice.

"Sorry. I didn't want to disturb Piper."

Simon slid his gun away as did Liam. "No problem."

"Not for you," Zoe muttered. "I almost had a heart attack."

Grace patted Zoe's shoulder. "I'll knock next time. How's Piper, Liam?"

"Sleeping, finally. She's been restless and in pain. Although the doc has offered medicine safe for the baby, Piper is worried about taking anything that isn't over-the-counter." He sounded frustrated.

"I don't blame her. She's doing all she can to protect your child, just like you're doing by staying awake all night despite having two teammates keeping watch."

"My wife, my child, my responsibility."

Grace shifted her gaze to Zoe. "Do you need anything?"

"Aside from a vacation on a deserted tropical island, no."

"Sounds good. I'll have to put in a request with Trent to take me to the beach on his next rotation at home." She squeezed Zoe's shoulder. "I have to go. I'll check in later."

When Grace left, Liam looked at Simon. "Need a break?"

"I need coffee."

"Take Zoe." He smiled. "I wouldn't say no to a cup."

"You got it." Simon tugged Zoe to her feet. "We'll be back soon."

Matt glanced up when they left the room. His wife, Delilah, remained slumped in her seat, sound asleep. "Everything okay?"

"Coffee run. Need some?"

"Oh, yeah. I worked an EMT shift before reporting to PSI yesterday. I'm on my fourth wind," he admitted.

"I'll find the strongest coffee they make here."

The medic flinched. "I would like to retain my stomach lining. Strong and black will do."

"Will Delilah want some?"

"Doubt it. I'll get her coffee on the way home if she wants it."

"Any problems?"

Matt shook his head. "Liam's awake?"

Simon nodded and wrapped his hand around Zoe's. "We'll return soon with coffee."

They rode the elevator to the bottom floor and walked to the cafeteria. "If you're hungry, choose a snack to tide you over. Cade and Trent will take over the watch in an hour, and I'll drive you to PSI to start your baking."

"Are you experienced in a kitchen?"

"I'm not in your league, but I can hold my own."

"You're hired. I need help with two large orders to complete."

"I'll be glad to help." He winked at her. "For a price."

Zoe's lips curved. "What's the price?"

"A kiss and the promise of another date."

"Deal. You already owe me a kiss."

"Hmm. You're right. I didn't fulfill my promise." He opened the door to the cafeteria. "I'll remedy that today. I don't want you thinking I don't keep my word."

"Extenuating circumstances."

They returned to the sixth floor with coffee and snacks. The fact that Simon kept his gun hand free and maintained an alert vigil didn't escape Zoe's notice.

She breathed a sigh of relief when Matt and Delilah came into view. If anything happened, Simon needed backup. Bravo was on high alert, protecting Liam and Piper, giving her time to rest and Liam the security he needed to concentrate on his wife.

Zoe's gaze shifted to Simon. He was no different than Liam or the others. He would have gone without sleep to keep her safe if she'd been admitted to the hospital.

Simon handed a to-go cup to Matt. "You're safe. The cafeteria worker assured me the coffee was fresh."

"Excellent. Thanks." He caught the apple his friend tossed him one-handed.

Simon tapped on the door and pushed it open. Zoe walked in behind him to see Liam sliding his gun back into his holster. Wow. These guys weren't messing around. Everything and everyone was considered a threat until they proved otherwise.

"Coffee." She handed a cup to Liam along with an apple and a pack of peanut butter and crackers. "If you want something else, we'll get whatever you need."

"This is fine. Thanks."

A cell phone signaled an incoming text message. Liam and Simon pulled out their phones to check the screens.

"It's mine," Simon said. He was silent a moment as he read the message. When he looked up, his expression was blank.

Zoe's stomach knotted. She'd been around Simon enough to know that when he or his friends lost all expression, something bad was happening. "Simon?"

"In the hall," Liam murmured, glancing at his sleeping wife. "I don't want to disturb Piper."

Matt rose. "What's wrong?"

"Zane sent me a message. The attacks in Otter Creek aren't random."

"We have a security breach?"

A nod. "Maddox plugged it, but the damage has been done."

"Who is Maddox?" Zoe asked.

"Our boss at Fortress Security," Liam said. "How bad is it, Simon?"

"Level six breach."

Blood drained from Liam's and Matt's faces. "What does that mean?" How bad was a level six breach?

"One of our operatives divulged classified information to the enemy," Simon said.

She remembered the confrontation with Isaac Lyons the day before. "Are you sure it was an operative?"

"Positive. Trainees wouldn't have access to the information leaked. The breach came from one of the internal servers. No question it was one of our own."

"Who?" Liam snapped.

"Z didn't tell me."

"Won't take long to find out," Matt murmured.

"No," Simon agreed. "All we have to know is who's missing."

Zoe frowned. "I don't understand. Why wouldn't Zane tell you who this person is? Wouldn't it be better to know so you can protect yourselves?"

"If we find out who leaked the intel, the traitor is dead," Liam said flatly. "The traitor is a threat to all of us and our families."

"The database breached has all the information on the operatives' real identities, locations, and their families and their locations," Simon added.

Horror filled Zoe. "He sold you out."

"Not only that, he endangered you, too." Simon cupped her cheek. "I'm sorry, Zoe. I shouldn't have gotten involved with you. My job has thrown you into the line of fire."

"Don't. I'm not made of glass."

He just shook his head.

Zoe's heart sank. If she couldn't find a way to convince him otherwise, Simon would end their relationship before it had a chance to flourish. His protective streak was a mile wide.

"We need to notify Trent," Liam said.

"I'll call him." With another lingering look at Piper, one filled with remorse and disappointment, Simon moved a short way down the hall and pressed his phone to his ear.

"How much do you care about him?" Liam asked Zoe, his voice soft.

"Why do you ask?"

"He'll distance himself from you to protect you. Don't let him. Simon might be slow to make a move, but when he does, it's because he feels deep. He won't think twice about crippling himself emotionally if the end result is you being safe."

Zoe stared. "Are you saying that Simon loves me?"

"If you want him, fight to keep him in your life. Otherwise, he'll decide he's too dangerous to be around any woman, especially you."

"Especially me?"

"Because you matter."

Stubborn man. Why wouldn't Simon accept that she'd be safer with him in her life?

Simon rejoined the group in front of Piper's door. "Team meeting at PSI as soon as Piper is released. Trent's hoping to get her released by seven. If she doesn't feel like going to work, Trent said to drive her to PSI. She can sit in on the meeting or one of the instructors can watch over her in the infirmary."

Liam frowned. "My preference is to keep her where I can see her."

"Give her the options. I need to talk to Zoe for a minute."

Liam's gaze flicked to her in silent warning before he slipped into the room where his wife was slept.

Simon eyed the medic. "Matt?"

"Yeah, I got this. Don't do anything stupid." He glared.

Zoe looked into the room across the hall. Empty. Perfect. What she wanted to say and do wasn't for an audience. Protecting her was one thing. Being a martyr for the cause was another. "In there," she said, motioning to the room.

He motioned for her to precede him.

Zoe closed the door after he was inside. "Before you say a word, I'm calling in your marker."

He blinked. "What?"

"The kiss, Simon. I'm collecting on your promise."

"Zoe, that's not a good..."

She wrapped her arms around his neck and pressed her lips to his, stopping his words in the sweetest way possible. Heat engulfed her despite Simon's arms remaining by his sides. Electricity sizzled along her nerve endings. When the man in her arms remained still, Zoe changed tactics. She caressed his mouth with butterfly kisses, one after another, gambling that the alpha male in him wouldn't be able to handle the gentle assault for long without his controlling tendencies kicking into high gear.

Following an agonizing minute when Zoe worried she'd miscalculated, that he didn't want her as much as she wanted him, Simon growled deep in his throat.

His arms wrapped around her and he spun them, pressing Zoe's back against the wall as he took control of the kiss, plundering her soft depths with the ferocity of a man starved for her taste. Simon explored her mouth with a desperation that told Zoe he thought this would be his only chance to be this close to her.

Tenderness filled her. Did this tough operative believe she'd walk away at the first sign of trouble? Not a chance. She'd waited so long, praying he would see the real Zoe Lockhart. Now that he had, she wasn't giving him up without a fight.

When he broke the kiss and tried to step back, Zoe tightened her hold and dived in for a kiss hotter than the last one.

The next time they came up for air, their breaths were coming in ragged spurts. Simon rested his forehead against hers, careful to avoid contact with her bruise. "We shouldn't have done that."

"Why not?"

"Now that I know what you taste like and how you feel in my arms, letting you go will be almost impossible."

She smiled against his mouth. "Good."

He groaned. "Have a heart, Zoe."

"Nope. Sorry. I'm just as addicted to your taste and touch. It's too late to back out now."

"Sweetheart, please. Don't make this harder than it is already."

Zoe shivered, loving the sweet endearment. Simon never called women by pet names. Even if Liam hadn't given her a hint at the depth of Simon's feelings for her, that alone would have clued her in. "You're not throwing me out of your life in some misguided plan to protect me from harm."

"It's the safest thing I can do for you. You deserve better than me anyway."

"Stop. Both of those statements are flat out lies. I will never be safer without you in my life and I deserve the best man. You, Simon."

"How can you say that? Macy is dead and you're hurt because of me. You could have died in that kitchen yesterday morning."

"We don't know the attack was because of you."

"Nothing like this happened until I showed interest in you."

"A chance with you is worth the risk. I trust you to keep me safe."

He wrapped his arms around her and held her tight. "And if it turns out I'm to blame for Macy's death?"

"Then you'll double your protective measures."

"I'm afraid it won't be enough. You don't know what it will do to me if something happens to you on my watch."

"Do you want me out of your life, Simon?"

"Are you kidding? I've wanted you for months. Giving you up hurts more than I can bear."

"Don't push me away. I need you. You're the only man I trust to keep me safe from the danger stalking us all."

His hold tightened. "Dirty pool, Zoe."

The other Fortress operatives assigned to PSI were well trained and could protect her. They weren't Simon Murray, the man she'd dreamed about every night since he arrived in Otter Creek. She fought to preserve their budding romance. She loved his protective streak. His tendency to put himself last? She didn't love that.

"Stop fighting with me and start fighting for me, Simon," she whispered.

He remained quiet for a while, silently fighting an internal battle, his body tense and still. Finally, his muscles softened and he sighed, his warm breath against her ear sending another cascade of shivers through her body. "Are you sure?"

"Yes." No hesitation.

"You'll do everything I tell you, when I tell you?"

"When it concerns my safety or yours. Anything else depends on the importance of the topic and how strongly I feel about an issue."

Simon's rough laughter rumbled in his chest. "Fair enough. I hope you don't regret your decision." He ushered Zoe into the hall.

Matt straightened. "Well?"

"She won't do the smart thing and kick me to the curb." Simon's voice held a mixture of concern and relief.

A smile curved the medic's lips. "Good for you, Zoe. Bravo women don't run when trouble hits. They dig deep and stand strong."

A Bravo woman. Zoe liked the sound of that and felt honored to be included in those ranks. Only time would prove whether she and Simon were perfectly suited for each other, but she couldn't imagine her life without him.

She and Simon returned to Piper's room for the remainder of their shift.

At the top of the hour, Trent and Cade arrived to spell Matt and Simon. Simon handed off the watch and escorted Zoe to his SUV.

He drove from the parking lot. "We have enough time to stop by your house for you to change clothes and head to PSI. Do you want me to stop at the diner for hot drinks?"

Zoe shook her head. "I'll make coffee while we bake."

Minutes later, Simon followed her to the front door of her home.

Zoe shoved her key in the deadbolt and frowned. The door wasn't locked. Chills bumps surged up her back. She never left her door unlocked, no matter how tired she was. She removed the key and moved away from the door until her back pressed against Simon's chest.

His hands cupped her upper arms. "What's wrong?"

"The door is unlocked. I know I locked it."

Simon eased her to the side and pulled his gun. "I'll go in first. When I signal you, come inside and stay by the door."

"Be careful."

He squeezed her hand, then twisted the knob with his shirt-covered hand. Simon turned on the light and uttered a soft whistle.

Zoe frowned. "What is it?"

The operative moved aside. "Take a look."

She walked into the living room and gasped. Someone had broken into her house. Unlike Macy's place, the person who broke in here wasn't concerned about hiding his presence. Books littered the floor along with couch cushions. Pictures had been swept off her bookcase and lay among broken shards of glass around the floor. Decorations that had been on the wall now lay scattered around the room.

"We should check the rest of your place," Simon murmured. "Stay behind me."

Zoe believed that precaution wasn't necessary. Why would the person who broke in be waiting for her return? She followed Simon throughout the rest of the house.

When they reached her bedroom, Simon growled.

"Is it safe to look?" she whispered.

"Yeah." He wrapped his arm around her shoulder as she took in the new paint on her walls.

Written in red were the words, "Next time, I won't miss."

CHAPTER ELEVEN

Simon snapped pictures of the interior of Zoe's house while Nick interviewed her and took notes. The detective had scowled at him when Simon walked toward the house. Tough. He wanted visual proof of the destruction. Partly for the insurance company. Partly to see if there was a pattern to the destruction. Right now, he was too angry to see past the red haze in his mind.

Someone was out to terrorize Zoe and doing a great job. What was the point? The creep had to know Simon would protect her from threats. Was he hoping to make her run, separate her from Simon? If that was the goal, the plan was doomed to fail. Zoe Lockhart wouldn't cut and run. She was made of sterner stuff than that.

On one hand, he was thrilled to find a woman strong enough to stand in the face of adversity. At the same time, fear for Zoe's safety settled deep into his bones. He wanted to whisk the sexy baker far away from Otter Creek and place a battalion of guards around her.

The last shot he took was the wall vandalized with red paint. At least the words had been scrawled with paint instead of blood. Although he hadn't touched the mark with his finger, Simon had scraped a small sample into a bag to send to the lab Fortress used. The scent had been of fresh paint, not blood as he'd feared. Whoever this guy was, Simon wouldn't have been surprised if the thug had used animal blood or Macy's blood to scrawl ugly words on Zoe's wall in an effort to heighten the terror quotient. As it stood now, he doubted the lab would discover anything distinctive in the paint to nail the creep targeting Zoe.

He made his way through the house to the front yard where Nick and Zoe stood by Simon's SUV.

"Are you sure nothing is missing?" Nick asked her.

"Positive. This is like Macy's house."

Not quite. Macy's break-in artist looked around and moved the dressers. Zoe's place looked as though someone threw a temper tantrum and destroyed as much as possible.

The detective frowned. "You haven't received threats?"

She shook her head.

"No former boyfriends with an ax to grind or a man you turned down for a date?"

"I haven't dated anyone seriously in three years. The last relationship ended by mutual consent. Grant Caldwell is now happily married to one of my friends from high school. He's not attacking my friends to win me back."

"But men have asked you out on dates in recent months."

Simon slid his arm around Zoe's shoulders and drew her against his side in silent support.

"I've had some offers."

Some? From the talk around town and PSI, a long string of civilians, operatives, and trainees had been turned down by Zoe.

"Did you go out with any of them?" Nick asked.

She shook her head. "The only man who has interested me for months is Simon. Before that, setting up the bakery and getting the business off the ground took up all my time."

"Did anyone seem insulted that you turned them down?" Nick held up his hand before she could respond. "Think about it and get back to me. I know several men asked. Madison and Del's store is a central gossip point for the town busybodies. My wife mentioned the string of men hitting on you because the old biddies were wagering on who would win the first date."

Simon chuckled. "Who won the bet?"

A quick grin from the detective. "Ethan's aunt. Ruth is sharp as a tack and she noticed how you and Zoe acted when you were in the same room together…" His smile faded. "Could these incidents be connected to you, Simon?"

Simon hesitated. In a matter of hours, Josh Cahill, Nick's brother-in-law, would inform his entire family about the security leak. Nick should keep a close eye on his wife. "It's possible."

Nick's scowl deepened. "Explain."

Simon summarized what he knew about the security leak, precious little at this point. If Zane didn't come up with information soon, Simon would go over his head to Maddox. Zoe was his to protect. He would keep her safe. If he failed, Simon would spiral into the darkness. He'd lost many friends to the war on terror. He refused to lose Zoe, too.

"Does Josh know?"

He nodded. "Durango and Bravo are meeting at PSI to discuss the situation and devise a plan to handle the fallout and security measures."

"If Maddox handled the security leak already, the only loose end is the party the traitor sold the information to."

They didn't know who was gunning for them. If the traitor sold the information to more than one interested party, Otter Creek would become a blood bath.

Simon's hands fisted. They would uncover every bit of information the traitor leaked and stop the attacks. He couldn't help but wonder if more than one person was breaking into houses. "Don't let down your guard, Nick. Something isn't adding up."

"Meaning?"

"We might be dealing with more than one group."

Nick dragged a hand down his face. "Great. Just what we need. Look, I know your missions are classified and I respect the reason for the secrecy. But my wife's safety is at stake as well as the safety of Otter Creek citizens. I need more information."

"I'll pass along as much as I can. So will Josh. We know what's at stake." He wouldn't be able to forget. The responsibility for Zoe's safety weighed heavy on Simon's mind. There was no limit to what he would do to protect her. "Do you need anything else? I'm taking Zoe to PSI. She has bakery orders to complete."

The detective closed his notebook. "I have what I need for now. If you leave town, I need to know."

"Yes, sir." Simon helped Zoe into his SUV and drove them toward PSI. When Zoe remained silent, staring out the passenger window, he said, "Are you all right?"

"Not really." She twisted to face him. "Why did he destroy my belongings? Breaking in and scrawling those words on the wall would have done the job."

"Fortress will replace everything." Especially since it appeared that Zoe's connection to Simon might be the cause of her current troubles.

"Why did he escalate to that level of destruction when a threat would have been sufficient to get his point across? What caused him to destroy instead of threaten?"

Zoe frowned. "Some creep killed Macy with a knife and bashed my head against a wall. Someone broke into Macy's house but didn't take anything. He looked around and moved the dresser a little. Piper is injured in an attack. My house is trashed and a verbal threat is painted on my wall. Do we have two different groups preying on Bravo's women?"

That was the question. "Noticed that, did you?"

"You already knew."

"I suspected. I don't know if the two groups are related to the Fortress leak or not."

"Find out. I don't want more of my friends at risk."

His lips curved. "Yes, ma'am." If he'd had any doubts about Zoe's ability to handle the potential danger of being involved with a black ops soldier, those doubts were a long distance behind him. Zoe Lockhart had the courage of a lion and a steel spine. A blessing and a curse.

He held her hand until they reached PSI's security gate. After carding them into the compound, Simon parked in the employee lot and ushered Zoe inside the main building.

The hallways were shrouded in shadows, the place quiet in the early morning hour. He walked with Zoe to the kitchen and turned on the lights. "What are we making this morning?"

"Blueberry muffins and cranberry-orange scones. I'll replace Nate's supplies when Nick releases my bakery."

After washing their hands, they started to work. Simon measured and dumped ingredients into the industrial mixer while Zoe prepared the pans needed for baking muffins and scones.

Once the first batches of muffins were in the ovens, Zoe made coffee. Two hours into their work, Nate arrived.

"Good morning. How's it going in here?"

Zoe smiled. "We're right on schedule. Turns out Simon is a great kitchen assistant."

The EOD man's eyebrows rose. "Is that right? Guess I know who to call if I need a hand in here."

"Don't get your hopes up, buddy." Simon wiped his hands on a nearby towel. "I'm a world-class follower of directions. Zoe is a champion director."

"I can work with that."

Simon sent his friend a narrow-eyed look to Nate's amusement.

The other operative sobered. "How's Piper?"

"Resting comfortably when we left the hospital. She refused pain meds for the headache."

Nate frowned. "Liam should have insisted."

Simon hesitated but Nate and the rest of Durango would learn about the baby in a few hours. "Piper is pregnant."

"That's great! Stella will be thrilled for them." Nate washed his hands and went to the refrigerator to grab ingredients for breakfast. "How's the nausea this morning, Zoe?"

"Better."

"Good enough that you can tolerate the scent of meat cooking?"

She held up the mug of tea she'd brewed a short time earlier. "I remembered your breakfast plan. I have chamomile mint tea. If I need something stronger, I'll grab another soft drink."

"Need help, Nate?" Simon asked.

"You have a decent hand with bacon?"

"It's a staple of my breakfast menu." Not that he'd be opening his own restaurant anytime soon, but he had a fair hand with breakfast items.

"You're hired." Nate tossed him a large package of bacon.

"I'm baking enough muffins and scones to include with your breakfast burritos," Zoe said.

"You're going to be the VIP at breakfast this morning, sugar. Thanks for thinking about us."

"It's the least I can do for allowing me to use your kitchen."

They made breakfast burritos and finished baking muffins and scones several minutes before trainees and instructors arrived for the meal. They boxed up muffins and scones to be delivered to Sasha's coffee shop, Perk.

Zoe secured the lid on the last container. "I need to deliver the order before six. I promised Sasha I would deliver at the normal time."

"I'll help you load up." Nate tossed aside his towel and went to a supply closet where he pulled out a cart. "This should work to transport the containers to the SUV."

They loaded the cart with baked goods and stored them in the cargo area of Simon's vehicle. "Thanks, Nate."

"See you when you return. I'll save breakfast for you."

As he and Zoe drove from the PSI grounds, Zoe said, "I didn't want to hurt Nate's feelings, but I'm not sure I can eat what he's serving today."

"Good thing you made muffins and scones." He winked at her. "They smell amazing. Thanks for thinking of trainees and instructors. We always appreciate having your baked goods. Eating your baking two days in a row will put everyone in a good mood." Well, maybe not everyone. He couldn't imagine Lyons and his buddy, Hollister, being happy about anything right now, especially knowing the treats were made by Zoe's hands.

They arrived at Perk with ten minutes to spare. Cade's wife hugged Zoe when she and Simon stepped inside the shop. "Are you okay?"

"Just a little bump on the head."

Sasha brushed Zoe's hair off her forehead to examine the bruise and winced. "Ouch. I'm glad you're all right, Zoe." She stepped back. "Come on. We need to unload the muffins and scones so I can fill display cases. People will be banging on the door in ten minutes. I'm amazed how desperate people are for their coffee fix."

Simon chuckled. That necessary coffee fix was the reason Cade met the woman he married. The three of them quickly unloaded the baked goods, and the women filled the display cases while Simon checked the security in Perk. Couldn't be too careful and Cade was on watch at the hospital until Piper was released.

Once he was satisfied that Perk's security hadn't been tampered with, he returned to the dining room. "Will you be alone for long?"

Sasha shook her head. "My assistant will be here by 6:15. Don't worry, Simon. Perk is jammed with customers until ten o'clock. I won't be alone. In fact, my helpers will be overlapping by thirty minutes the rest of the day. Cade and I talked about the security arrangements as he brought me to the shop this morning. I'll be fine."

"If anything bothers you, whether you can figure out what it is or not, contact Cade. We'll have someone here in minutes."

"I will. I know you have things to do. You don't have to babysit."

Determined not to leave her until the shop was open and filled with customers, he said, "How about a to-go cup of coffee for me and hot tea for Zoe? We've been slaving away since 2:30 on your order."

The expression on Sasha's face told Simon she wasn't fooled at his delayed departure, but she turned away to fill their orders without comment. Once the orders were finished, she unlocked the door and admitted Ethan Blackhawk, the first person in line.

Simon wondered if he had an ulterior motive for appearing on Perk's doorstep this early when his own wife, Serena, made the best coffee in the county. "Good morning, Ethan."

The police chief's dark eyes locked on his. "Simon, I need you to come with me to the station."

CHAPTER TWELVE

Simon's eyebrows winged upward as he studied Ethan's grim expression. "What's going on?" He felt Zoe's hand slip into his. Her cold hand trembled.

The police chief glanced at the customers streaming into Perk. "Not here, Simon. I need you to come with me now."

Ethan's insistence on talking to him at the station wasn't good. Concern for his family sent ice water racing through his veins. No way. If his family was hurt, Maddox or Trent would contact him, not Otter Creek's chief of police. "I'm parked in the alley. I don't want Zoe walking through the square." He refused to leave her in Perk and give the person after Zoe an easy target. Two Bravo women in the same place without an operative to safeguard them? Too much temptation for an enemy combatant to pass up.

A reluctant nod from Ethan. "No detours," he murmured.

He was a suspect? "Two minutes," he promised.

"Want coffee, Ethan?" Sasha asked as she handed Simon and Zoe their drinks, her eyes filled with concern.

"I wouldn't turn down a cup." Ethan pulled out his wallet and dropped a few bills on the counter to pay for his drink. When the coffee maven handed him a to-go cup, he nodded his thanks, turned a pointed glance Simon's direction, and walked from the shop, stopping to speak to a few customers who greeted him by name.

After he paid Sasha for their drinks, Simon cupped Zoe's elbow and escorted her out the back door. "I don't know what's going on, but I don't want you to leave the police station without me or one of Bravo at your side."

"Something's wrong."

"Oh, yeah. We'll find out what I'm suspected of doing soon. If you're a suspect, too, don't make a statement without an attorney present."

Her eyes widened in alarm as he helped her into the SUV. "I don't know any attorneys, Simon."

"Call Trent. One of the Fortress lawyers will represent you."

"But I'm not guilty of anything illegal."

He couldn't say the same for himself. He tried to abide by the law. In some cases, skirting the law was the only way to complete his mission. Had one of those instances come back to haunt him? "I'm not saying you've broken a law, especially since I'm the one Ethan came after. Considering what's been happening the past 24 hours, keeping the attorney option open might be wise."

Simon parked in the visitor section of the station's lot and escorted Zoe inside the building.

The desk sergeant looked up. "Help you?"

"I'm Simon Murray. Chief Blackhawk is expecting me." More like commanded him to show up at the station or else Ethan would come after Simon himself. He didn't want Ethan Blackhawk on his six. The six-foot-four cop was one of the most dangerous men Simon had ever met and that was saying something considering the terrorists he'd fought over the years. Ethan could have easily been a member of Delta Force, but was rumored to have chosen to stay in the Rangers to be more accessible to his beloved aunt.

The cop inclined his head toward the plastic chairs against the wall. "Have a seat. I'll let him know you're here."

A minute later, Ethan opened the double doors into the inner part of the station and motioned for Simon and Zoe to follow him. Once they crossed the threshold, the chief led them down a hallway to a smaller room.

One glance inside had Simon casting a questioning glance at Ethan. "You're taking us to an interrogation room?"

"Two rooms. You're in this one. Zoe will be in the second one."

Simon slid his arm around Zoe's waist. "I'm checking the second interrogation room. It's not negotiable, Ethan."

After a slight nod, the police chief led them to a second interrogation room. No windows and a two-way mirror on a wall butting up against an observation room. "Satisfied?"

"She can't be alone. Someone tried to hurt her yesterday morning. I'm not taking chances with her life."

"I'll have an officer stay with Zoe until one of the detectives arrives to question her."

"Only if it's a cop I know and trust."

That brought a scowl to the chief's face. "You don't have the control here, Murray."

"You wouldn't trust some random cop with Serena's life. Why would you expect me to hand over Zoe's safety to a stranger? Come on, Ethan. You know what's at stake here and the kind of people Bravo fights against. A run-of-the-mill beat cop can't handle our enemies. I'm not risking her life with unproven assurances and loyalties."

"Wait here." Ethan strode from the room, phone in his hand. Two minutes later, he returned. "Finish your drinks. Zoe's bodyguard will arrive in five minutes."

Trusting Ethan to choose someone with the right skill set to protect his girl, Simon seated Zoe at the wooden table and dropped onto the seat beside hers. Ethan returned after a minute and sat across from them with his own coffee cup in hand.

The three of them navigated a stilted conversation about town happenings while they sipped their beverages. By the time they finished their drinks, a brush of fabric against the wall heralded the approach of someone new. Simon's hand automatically went to his Sig. At least his weapons hadn't been confiscated the moment he entered the station. He'd expected to have to relinquish them. Perhaps that meant the coming interrogation was a formality.

"Stand down," Ethan murmured. "It's the bodyguard."

When Josh Cahill entered the room, Simon's worry for Zoe's safety faded. He trusted Josh at his back and knew Zoe would be safe with the Delta Force soldier turned cop and black ops operative.

Josh nodded at him and greeted Zoe before turning to his brother-in-law. "How long will I be tied up? We're spread thin at PSI with Bravo having four members in limbo."

"You'll be free to leave when Stella arrives. She was with Nick at the crime scene fifteen minutes ago."

Crime scene? Simon stared at Ethan. Something else must have happened in the hours since he'd left Nick standing in front of Zoe's house this morning.

At that moment, someone else approach, the steps light and quick. Stella walked in. She glanced at Ethan. "Sorry for the delay. Are we questioning them together or separately?"

Them? Simon frowned. He didn't like the sound of that. Suspecting him of something nefarious was one thing. Zoe shouldn't be under suspicion.

"Separately." Ethan glanced at Josh. "Keep her safe and secluded until we're ready to talk to her."

"Copy that."

"Let's go, Simon. The sooner we do this, the better this will go for you."

The hairs rose on the back of his neck. Not good. If Ethan arrested him, who would protect Zoe?

The woman in question drew in a ragged breath. "Simon, what's going on?" she whispered.

"Everything will be fine." Please, God, let that be the case. Simon didn't want to hand responsibility for her safety to anyone else, even his teammates. She was his. He brushed her lips with his. "I'll be next door." If she needed him, he'd get to her no matter who he had to go through to reach her side. Rising, he sent a pointed glance at Josh.

Understanding dawned in Josh's eyes. "I've got her, Simon. No one will touch her. You have my word."

Unable to resist, Simon kissed Zoe again before making himself leave the room. The sooner he cleared up whatever they thought he'd done, the faster he would return to Zoe's side to act as a shield against the danger stalking her.

Ethan and Stella followed Simon into the first interrogation room and the chief closed the door. Stella sat at the table and waved Simon to the seat across from her. Ethan took up a position against the wall near the door, arms folded across his chest. Seriously? Did Ethan believe Simon would bolt from the room and leave Zoe vulnerable?

Another thought occurred to him, this one sending a spike of disappointment through him. Perhaps Ethan was here as protection for Stella. He'd never hurt Nate's wife. Stella was a friend.

He shifted his gaze to the detective. "Enough secrecy, Stella. Why did you send Ethan to find me when a simple phone call would have brought me here voluntarily?"

"Do you know Isaac Lyons?"

He glanced at Ethan and, no surprise, got nothing in the way of a clue from the police chief. Simon refocused on

Stella. Had Lyons filed charges against him for slamming his back against the wall and choking him? If so, the trainee was going to be out of PSI on his ear before the day was finished. Not only that, any charges he might have filed against Simon wouldn't stick. He had a room full of witnesses who would state the trainee had been going after Zoe. "He's one of PSI's trainees."

"How well do you know him?"

"He's been training as a bodyguard for three months. In that time, he's rotated through my classes twice a week, sometimes more depending on whether or not I covered another instructor's class. But I'm guessing that you know this. What's this about, Stella?"

"When did you see him last?"

Frustration bubbled inside him at the deflection. "Yesterday morning at breakfast. Cade and I broke the news about Macy's death to him. We didn't want him to hear about it through the town grapevine. Lyons and Macy were dating. No one deserves to hear news like that through gossip."

"I understand you had an altercation with him in the dining room."

Now they were getting somewhere. "He was upset over Macy's death and, for some reason, blamed Zoe. Matt and Liam stopped him when he went after Zoe. They took him to the floor and got him under control, then let him up when he calmed down. By that time, I was beside Zoe. However, once Lyons was free, he came at Zoe again. I stopped him."

"How?"

"Shoved him against the wall and pressed my forearm against his throat."

"What did you do then?"

"Warned him off. Told him if he tried to hurt Zoe again, I would take him down hard."

"Anything else?"

What was she looking for? "I told him to take the day off from training and go to his room or run until he had himself under control, but he was to leave Zoe alone."

"Did you see him again after that time?"

Simon frowned. "No. I already told you I didn't. Talk to me, Stella. Is Lyons filing assault charges? If he is, I have about 200 witnesses to verify my story. He didn't have a mark on him when he left the dining room."

"Where were you this morning between two and five?"

He laid his hand on her forearm. "Stella, talk to me."

Ethan stirred, his gaze hard. "Simon."

When he looked at the chief, the man shook his head slightly.

Okay, then. This was definitely official and Ethan was here as Stella's backup. Having Ethan with her was a wise move on Stella's part. If Simon had intended to harm her, Stella wouldn't have been able to stop him by herself.

He released her and sat back. "At two o'clock, I was standing in front of Zoe's house with Nick Santana. Zoe's home was broken into and trashed sometime yesterday. We discovered the mess after we left Piper's hospital room. Once Zoe packed an overnight bag under Nick's supervision, we drove to PSI for her to use the kitchen to bake muffins and scones for Perk. We stayed in that kitchen until 5:30 when we loaded my SUV with baked goods with Nate's help and drove to Perk where Ethan found me at 6:00."

"When did Nate arrive?"

"A few minutes before five o'clock."

"Did you leave Zoe's side at any time during those hours when the two of you were baking in the kitchen?"

"No."

"Even to go down the hall to the bathroom?"

"Again, no."

"Will you provide access to the security footage at PSI to verify your story?"

"Of course." But they all knew he could have tampered with the footage to make it appear he'd never left the kitchen. Even if he didn't have the skill to pull off the deception, he knew enough people at Fortress with the ability who also owed him a favor and would keep their mouths shut if requested to do so. The footage wasn't definitive proof.

"I'll expect that footage from Zane by the end of the day, Simon."

He looked at Ethan. "I'm getting my cell phone." He didn't particularly want to end up with another bullet hole in his body.

A nod from the chief.

Simon pulled his cell phone from his pocket and sent a text to Zane, requesting the security footage at PSI for the times in question. That done, he laid his phone on the table. "Zane will send the information by the end of the day. What's going on, Stella? I answered your questions. It's time for you to answer mine."

"Isaac Lyons is dead. He was found in his car with his throat slit."

Stunned, Simon sat in silence for a moment. Lyons was dead? "Where was he found?"

"Half a block from Zoe's house."

Could Lyons have broken in and trashed Zoe's place in a fit of anger over Macy's death? That would explain the stark difference between the search through Macy's house and the utter destruction in Zoe's. "You think I killed him."

"You're capable of subduing Lyons and slitting his throat. He was found down the street from her house, a place you admit to being this morning. You had motive to kill the man. He threatened your girlfriend. I know exactly how protective Fortress operatives are when their women are in danger. Lyons was a threat to Zoe. Seeing him that close to Zoe's house could have sent you over the edge. He was a danger to your woman. You dispatched the danger to keep her safe. No muss. No fuss. No regret for protecting what's yours."

Despite the maelstrom of emotion, Simon forced himself to think. On the outside looking in, he appeared to be the perfect suspect. But he hadn't seen or touched Lyons since breakfast yesterday morning. "If I thought Zoe's life was in imminent danger, I wouldn't hesitate to do what was necessary to protect her. In this case, I didn't have to. I didn't know Lyons was parked near her house and I was more interested in driving her to PSI to complete her baking than killing a pathetic excuse for a man who was mouthing off."

He probably should shut his mouth and call the Fortress lawyer, but he wanted to say a few more things on the record. "Three things to remember. If I had killed Lyons in self-defense while protecting Zoe, I would have owned up to the deed like a man and turned myself in, even if the result was jail time. But the fact is I didn't kill him. Second, if I determined Lyons' death was necessary, I'd kill him somewhere other than close to my girlfriend's house and take the time to hide the body where you'd never find it. Third, you both know what I'm trained to do. I'm capable of pulling off the crime without throwing suspicion on myself or Zoe. This is clumsy work. I'm not clumsy or careless."

"Let's go through everything again." Stella flipped her notebook to a fresh page. "Back up to when you arrived at the bakery yesterday morning and go from there."

Simon went through everything again. When he finished, he looked from Stella to Ethan. "Do I need to call a lawyer?"

"That's your right." Ethan's tone reflected nothing but professionalism. Frustration bit at Simon. Ethan would have made a great operative. He was impossible to read. "At the moment, you are a person of interest in the murder of Isaac Lyons. If we file charges, you'll have the opportunity to call the Fortress lawyer."

"What about Zoe? Is she a person of interest, too?"

A slight nod.

Simon scowled. "That's crazy, Ethan. She would never be able to sneak up on Lyons, hold him steady, and slice his throat. He might not have been fully trained, but he could have overpowered her in seconds. Zoe doesn't have the strength to pull this off."

"The element of surprise and a sharp knife would take care of the job."

"Not a chance. She doesn't have it in her to kill someone."

"Everyone has that capacity if the stakes are high enough."

"To protect herself?" Simon shook his head. "No way."

"What about to protect you?" Ethan asked, voice soft.

"I can take care of myself. Zoe knows that."

"Does she? You haven't been together long. I'm betting she doesn't know who and what you really are."

Simon bit back a further protest. Ethan had a point. He hadn't had a chance to talk to her about his job.

The muscle in his jaw twitched. Zoe's character precluded her from harming anyone even if she had underestimated Simon and his abilities. Besides, Zoe didn't have the opportunity to sneak off and kill Lyons. She'd been by his side since she'd joined him in the PSI classroom yesterday. "You're wrong, Ethan. Zoe hasn't been alone since I found her unconscious on her bakery floor yesterday morning. Don't waste your time looking at her. Zoe didn't kill Lyons."

Stella stood. "We had to ask you these questions whether we wanted to or not. It's our job. We can't show favoritism to friends. We have to consider every angle, every alternative. It's how we eliminate suspects and move on to new ones. The questions weren't meant to be personal."

Ha. They were plenty personal to him. "Do you believe I killed him?"

She stared at him. "I know you're capable of killing without an ounce of remorse if doing so saved your girlfriend's life. I don't believe you would have slit his throat from the back seat of his car. That smacks of cowardice. You're an in-your-face man. If you believed Lyons needed to die to save an innocent, you would have taken him on face to face, not attacked him from behind." She smiled. "And no, I don't think you'd have been stupid enough to kill him close to Zoe's house and point the finger at yourself or her. I believe Lyons would have disappeared, never to be seen again. You are far from careless. If you were, you wouldn't be a member of one of Fortress's top operative teams."

Relief loosened the knots in his stomach. Stella hadn't given him the all-clear, but neither did she believe he was guilty of murder. "I think I'm insulted. One of Fortress's top teams? Bravo is the best team I've ever worked with."

"You and your teammates are exceptionally good," she admitted. "I've seen your training maneuvers and watched when Bravo acted as a county SWAT team in that hostage situation last month when Nate and the others were out of the country. But however good you are, you aren't Durango."

Those words would have rankled more if she hadn't been right. Durango was special, and Simon had the greatest respect for them and their skill. Fortress was lucky to have that team.

Stella rounded the table and headed for the door. "You're free to leave the room. There's a vending machine in the lobby and you're welcome to the coffee in the squad room. It's Serena's Home Runs blend so you won't have to worry about losing your stomach lining." Stella glanced over her shoulder at Simon. "I don't know exactly what's going on yet, but be on your guard, Simon. Someone wants to hurt you and those you love."

CHAPTER THIRTEEN

Zoe glanced at her watch again and grimaced. What was taking Stella and Ethan so long with Simon? What did they want with her? She hadn't forgotten Ethan's order to Josh to keep her safe and isolated until they were ready to talk to her. What did they want to talk to her about?

She longed to pace, but she didn't want to appear afraid in front of Josh Cahill. The man might be one of the leaders of PSI, but he was first a cop for the Otter Creek police. He'd tell Ethan and Stella what she said and did while in his care.

Zoe frowned. Unless he didn't have to report anything. Her gaze scanned the room and settled on a camera in the upper left corner. Was it recording? She didn't want to make herself or Simon look guilty of anything. They weren't guilty unless sharing kisses that singed Zoe to her toes counted. Man, that operative had serious skills in the kissing department.

"Relax, Zoe," Josh said. "Being tense and worried use up more energy than you can spare."

"This waiting is driving me crazy. Is that camera recording everything I say and do in this room?"

His eyebrow rose. "Got something to be worried about?"

She glared at him. Was he deliberately baiting her?

The cop's lips curved. He glanced at the camera. "It's not on. You're safe."

Nothing about this situation was funny. Something was wrong and Josh was joking with her. She inclined her head toward the mirror. "What about in there? That's an observation room, right? Is someone watching us?" Zoe must sound paranoid to Josh. She couldn't help it. Her skin felt as though ants were crawling all over her body from the tension and anxiety racing through her system.

With a sigh, Josh rose, stepped out into the hall, and opened the observation room door. He was back in seconds. "Empty."

He resumed his seat. "You and Simon are an item now?"

Zoe's cheeks heated. "It's new."

Josh grinned. "About time. You've been dancing around each other for months. What made him man up and say something?"

"Macy's death. He believes his arrival prevented the killer from doing more than knocking me out."

"What do you think?"

She sighed. "I don't know. I thought Macy was the target. Now, I'm not convinced she wasn't an accident while I was the main target."

That brought a frown. "Why do you say that?"

"Someone broke into my house yesterday, trashed the place, and left a painted threat painted on my wall."

He stilled. "What did it say?"

"Next time, I won't miss."

He gave a soft whistle. "Any idea why you're a target?"

"Simon is afraid this is connected to his job and the security leak from one of the Fortress operatives turned rogue."

Josh's face hardened. "What do you know about the security leak?"

Was she breaking a rule? Zoe didn't want to cause Simon trouble. "Simon said it's a level six breach."

"Did he mention the operative's name who turned?"

A cold chill skittered up Zoe's spine at the look in Josh Cahill's eyes. She never wanted to be the cause of this look. At this moment, he was every inch an operative determined to protect his family, not a cop.

Good grief. How did he maintain the balance between his two vocations? He upheld the law on one job and worked outside it with the other. That particular look in Josh's eyes reminded Zoe of Simon's eyes when he'd acted as her bodyguard. She gathered they weren't trained in the same way, but this interaction convinced her that Josh Cahill and Simon were cut from the same cloth.

Zoe shook her head. "No name."

A door opened close by. A moment later, Stella walked into the room followed by Ethan and Simon.

Josh rose. "Need me for anything else?" he asked Ethan.

The police chief shook his head. "Thanks for coming in on short notice."

"No problem." He slid a look to Zoe. "We'll figure out what's going on, Zoe. In the meantime, be straight with Stella and Ethan. They're the best there is and only want to uncover the truth and nab the killer."

Yes, but at what price? At least Simon didn't look as though he was going to jail for the moment. "Thanks for keeping me safe, Josh."

With a nod, he left.

Ethan turned a pointed stare at Simon. "Out."

"In a minute." Simon crouched by her side. "You okay?"

"I'm fine."

"Need a soft drink or water?"

She shook her head. She wanted this interrogation session with Stella and Ethan over as soon as possible.

Simon lifted her hand to his lips and kissed her knuckles. "I'll be outside the door if you need me." He stood and stared at Ethan.

The police chief's lips curved, but he gave a slight nod.

Seemingly satisfied with the exchange with Ethan, Simon left the room pulling the door shut behind him.

Zoe had never been uneasy in Ethan's presence or Stella's. Now, however, she drew great comfort knowing Simon was close.

"We have questions for you, Zoe," Stella said. "You have the right to an attorney if you want one."

Her heart rate zoomed into the stratosphere. She was a suspect in a crime? "Do I need one?"

"You're a person of interest. If you're charged with a crime, you'll want an attorney. Do you have one?"

"Simon said he would arrange for me to consult with the Fortress lawyer if I needed his services." The possibility of having to consult an attorney made her stomach churn. Fortress must have high priced attorneys. The bakery was making a profit, but not enough to afford the fees of a legal shark. She'd be in hock up to her eyebrows for the rest of her life if she had to pay for those services.

Ethan snorted. "One of the cadre of attorneys, you mean. Maddox keeps an army of them on retainer."

Zoe's mouth gaped. A cadre? "Wow."

Stella shrugged. "Sometimes law enforcement takes exception to the methods of the teams. Fortress lawyers stay busy." She flipped open her notebook. "Do you know Isaac Lyons?"

She stiffened. This interrogation was about Isaac? Her cheeks burned. Had Macy's boyfriend filed charges against Simon? She should have known this was connected to him. He wasn't man enough to confront Simon face-to-face, so he took the easy way out and complained to the police. "Yes."

"How well?"

"I don't like the guy. He's a creep. He abused Macy, but she never filed a complaint." Zoe had seen the violence and been on the receiving end of it once, but it was her word against his. "I'm afraid to be in the same vicinity with him," she admitted.

Ethan's eyes narrowed. "Did he hurt you?"

Zoe didn't want to lie to them, but she didn't want to set off more suspicions about Simon's innocence, either.

He leaned forward, arms folded on the table. "Zoe, did Lyons hurt you?"

She gave a short nod.

A muscle in his jaw flexed. "Did you report it?"

"No," she murmured.

"Why not?" Stella's voice was gentle.

"Macy begged me not to. She said he'd be kicked out of PSI if Josh or Trent found out."

"She was right. PSI has strict conduct standards. If a trainee violates those standards, they're out. If Lyons' behavior violated the rules, he'd have been dismissed. How bad were your injuries?"

"Sprained ankle."

"Is that what happened when you were in the walking boot?" Ethan asked.

She nodded.

"That was six weeks ago. What happened to cause the injury?"

"Isaac and Macy were fighting at her house. She and I had plans to meet Sasha and Piper for dinner, and since her car wasn't working at the time, I stopped by to pick her up.

Isaac was angry about her choosing to have dinner with us instead of spending time with him."

"What happened?"

"He slapped her so hard she fell to the ground. I got out of the car and ran toward her to help her up and get her away from him. I feared he would hurt her more. I know he's still early in his training, but he's big and strong. Macy didn't have a chance of standing up to him and winning the confrontation. Anyway, Isaac cursed at me for interfering in their lives and shoved me. I tried to keep my balance, but stumbled and rolled my ankle."

"Did Simon know about the injury and who caused it?"

"He was gone with his team for almost a month. I was out of the boot and walking normally by the time he returned. I never told him."

"Why not? You weren't dating at the time."

"We might not have been involved then, but he's protective and honorable to the core. He would have confronted Isaac about the incident." Even without having a formal dating relationship, Simon would have torn into Isaac for hurting her or any woman. "He's also one of the trainers at PSI. He would have passed the information to Trent, and I promised Macy not to say anything. I have never been close enough for Isaac to touch me again. I told Macy if anything like that happened again, I would go straight to the police and Trent St. Claire."

"You were in a walking boot which means you had medical treatment."

"Macy drove me to the emergency room at Memorial Hospital. She felt guilty that I'd been hurt coming to her aid and that was the only thing she could do to help. Once I was released, she drove me home and made me promise not to come in the next day." Zoe sat back, hands rubbing her arms as chill bumps pebbled her skin at the remembered incident. Isaac Lyons was one scary man. What had Macy seen in him?

"Will you give us permission to access your treatment record?"

She nodded. What good would it do to refuse? They already knew about the walking boot and now they knew why she'd worn it. Macy was dead. The promise she'd made to her friend was no longer valid. After the behavior she'd seen yesterday from Isaac, Zoe wondered if he was stable.

"Are you sure Simon didn't know that Lyons hurt you?"

"Positive. The only ones who knew were Macy, Isaac, and me. None of us told him. I told everyone who asked about the injury that I fell and sprained my ankle." It was the truth, though not all of it.

Stella flipped to a clean page in her notebook. "When was the last time you saw Isaac Lyons?"

"Yesterday at breakfast at PSI. Simon and Cade had just told him about Macy's death and for some reason, he blamed me for it."

"I understand there was an altercation in the dining room. Tell me about that."

Zoe related the incident and said, "Is this about Simon pushing Isaac away from me? He didn't hurt Isaac. A lot of people were there and will verify that Isaac walked away unharmed."

"What did you do after Isaac left?" Ethan asked.

"I went to the PSI kitchen to help Nate with lunch prep, then spent the afternoon with Simon while he worked with two classes of trainees. After that, we went to dinner, then the hospital to be with Piper and Liam. Early this morning, Simon drove me home where we discovered my house had been trashed. After we talked to Nick, we returned to PSI so I could bake muffins and scones for Sasha's coffee shop. I also made a supply for PSI in appreciation for them allowing me to use the kitchen. You saw us at Perk."

"Did either of you see Lyons again after the incident in the dining room at PSI?"

"No."

"Was Simon out of your sight for any length of time during the past 24 hours?"

She started to say no. Her brow furrowed. "Only when he left the ER waiting room to talk to his friend, Zane."

"What time was that?"

"Maybe 9:00 p.m."

"How long was he out of your sight?"

"Five minutes."

"You're sure it wasn't any longer than that?"

"Positive."

"Where did he go to make his phone call?"

"Outside the ER on the sidewalk. I could see him as he paced in front of the doors while he talked." Even handling business with his co-worker, Simon was still protecting her. From his position at the entrance to the hospital, he could still see her and was aware of every person who passed through the doors near Zoe.

"Was he out of your sight during the time you were with Piper?"

"A few minutes to consult with his teammates. I heard their voices in the hall."

"What about when you were in the PSI kitchen this morning? Were you separated from him?"

She frowned at him. "What's going on? Why all the questions about our movements after the dust up with Isaac?"

"Answer the question, Zoe," Stella said. "Were you and Simon alone together the whole time in the kitchen at PSI?"

"Simon never left my side while we were in the kitchen. Nate joined us a few minutes before five. After my baking was finished, Simon and I pitched in to help Nate with breakfast. Stella, please tell me what's going on. You're scaring me."

"We need to establish timelines and your locations from breakfast yesterday morning to the time Ethan saw you at Perk because someone murdered Isaac Lyons."

Blood drained from Zoe's face so fast she felt lightheaded. The next words Stella said sounded like they were coming from a great distance and the room spun.

The next thing she knew, Ethan was by her side, urging her to fold forward with her head on her knees. "Get a soft drink with sugar, Stella," he ordered.

"Sweetheart?"

Simon. His arm wrapped around her shoulders and he held her secure against his chest. "I'm okay," she whispered.

"No, you're not. You're in shock." His tone was accusatory. Was he angry at her?

"Isaac's dead."

"They told me." Then, to Ethan, "I trusted you to protect her."

Fast footsteps. Stella said, "Here."

A moment later, Simon helped Zoe sit up slowly and, keeping his arm wrapped around her to hold her steady, pressed the cold soft drink bottle into her hands. "Sip this."

"We'll give you a few minutes," Ethan murmured and left the room with Stella in his wake.

When the room quit spinning and the buzz in her ears had faded, Zoe set the drink on the table and turned into Simon's arms, drawing on his strength to ground her further in the moment.

Someone had murdered Isaac. She had thought he was to blame for Macy's death and the destruction at her house, and maybe Piper's injury as well. But someone had killed him and thrown her world into a tailspin. Was all this related to the operative turned rogue? Or did Zoe have an enemy she knew nothing about?

Zoe tightened her grip around Simon. Would the killer come after Simon next? She'd just been given the right to be with this man. She didn't want to lose him.

CHAPTER FOURTEEN

Simon kissed Zoe's temple and settled her more fully against his chest. "Better now?"

She gave a slight nod, not loosening her hold. Fine with him. He loved holding her, had dreamed of having this privilege from the first time that he'd seen her. Being with her in the company of his friends and their wives had stoked a longing to have her in his life in a more personal way.

His job and his caution had slowed the process of including himself in her day-to-day life. Now that he was involved with her, he'd never take the privilege for granted. She was his, and Simon wouldn't let her go without a fight.

"Who is doing this, Simon?"

"I don't know, but I'll find out and stop him."

"You're sure a man is responsible?"

He considered her question. "Why do you ask that?"

She gave a short laugh. "Ethan and Stella wouldn't exclude a woman from suspicion. If a woman caught Isaac by surprise, she might be able to kill him."

"In this case, I don't think so."

"Why not?"

Lyons' death had upset her. He didn't want to compound it by conveying details that shouldn't be in her head.

Zoe eased back to see his face although her arms remained locked around his neck. She frowned. "You know something more. I can handle the truth despite what happened a few minutes ago. News of his death was a shock on the heels of losing Macy."

"Did Ethan tell you where Lyons was found or how he died?"

She shook her head. "Tell me."

"He was found in his car with his throat slit. Lyons was parked down the street from your house."

Zoe's eyes widened.

"Time of death was sometime between two and five this morning."

She groaned. "That's why they want to establish a timeline and if we were apart during the past 24 hours. Why do you think the killer was a man? Fortress has female operatives. I heard you and the others mention a few."

"They're operatives, trained to kill when necessary. You're not an operative and lack the training or character to kill." No matter what the cops had implied about Zoe killing to protect him. He didn't need protection. "The killer was in the backseat and had enough strength to control Lyons to make the fatal cut. You protect those you care about, but not like this. You wouldn't kill in this manner. Lyons wasn't fully trained, but he'd have overpowered you in seconds. Besides, he wouldn't allow you to sit behind him. He'd be vulnerable to attack from behind."

Zoe sighed.

Simon believed she was innocent. The police would have questions after her encounter with Isaac in PSI's dining room. The trainee didn't touch her, but Simon had indicated that he'd do anything necessary to protect her. That made him the prime suspect in Lyons' murder.

"I have something to tell you." Her voice was soft, guilt evident on her face.

He frowned. Simon would never believe her guilty of murder, no matter what she said. Zoe didn't have the mindset or skill to be a cold-blooded murderer. "Talk to me."

"I had a problem with Isaac six weeks ago."

"Bravo was out of the country." They'd been tromping through a forest in Bolivia, tracking a terrorist group who kidnapped an American oil executive's wife, demanding an exorbitant ransom for her release. The oil executive was more interested in paying Fortress to free his wife than fund the terrorists and their activities. But while Bravo had been successful in freeing the woman and eradicating the terrorist group, apparently Zoe had been fighting against Lyons. He should have been here. "What happened?"

"Macy and I planned to meet Piper and Sasha for dinner one night. I stopped by her house to pick up Macy because her car was on the fritz. Isaac was there. He and Macy were in the middle of a blazing fight in the front yard. He was furious because she planned to go to dinner with us rather than spend more time with him. I parked in the driveway so I couldn't help but overhear their words. Isaac slapped Macy hard, knocking her to the ground. I got out of the car to help her, but he was angry and out of control. He shoved me away from her, then got into his car and left Macy and me on the ground."

Fury boiled in Simon's gut. "Go on."

"I had a bad ankle sprain and used a walking boot for two weeks after that incident. The doctor cleared me to ditch the boot before you returned home."

If Lyons was still alive, Simon would hunt him down and teach him to treat women with more respect. He longed to pound someone's face, but since the object of his fury was dead, he wrestled down the hurricane of emotion. "Why didn't you tell me?"

Zoe cupped his cheek. "I promised Macy I wouldn't. I warned her if I felt threatened by him or if he ever touched me again, I would go straight to the police, Trent, and you. She begged me to remain quiet, Simon. She said Isaac would have been kicked out of PSI and he would have left town. Macy loved him."

"She was right. He'd have been kicked out of PSI. Lyons deserved any punishment he received. You should have told me."

"We weren't dating then, Simon."

"That's not the reason you kept this a secret from me."

A gentle kiss on his mouth before she murmured, "I knew you would take him to task for hurting me when that wasn't Isaac's intention. He was out of control at that moment."

"Operatives can't be out of control any time. If he is, he can't think or react properly. On a mission, he risks his own life as well as that of his teammates or client if he loses control."

"I didn't think about that."

"If anyone threatens you again, promise that you'll tell me immediately. For me to focus on a mission, I have to know you'll tell me if anything or anyone scares you."

Another kiss from the woman in his arms, this one more of a claiming. He reveled in her claim. When she drew back, Zoe said, "I promise, Simon."

The door to the interrogation room opened. "Ready to resume, Zoe?" Ethan asked.

She nodded, her gaze still locked with Simon's.

"Wait in the hall, Simon."

After what happened during the previous interrogation session, he was reluctant to leave Zoe alone with Ethan and Stella. Simon captured Zoe's mouth in a quick, hard kiss before standing. He slid a warning glance toward Ethan before returning to stand watch in the hallway outside the room.

He called Zane.

"Yeah, Murphy."

"It's Simon. What do you have for me?"

"I pulled the camera footage from Liam's security system."

"What did you find?"

"Not much. The perp was wearing all black, including a ski mask. I'm cleaning up the images, hoping for more."

"That's not what I wanted to hear, Z. Did he get inside the house?"

"No. He couldn't get past the alarm system and locks. Liam received an alert, but in light of Piper's hospitalization, he's forgotten."

"Do you have a general description?"

"He's about six feet, muscular, moves like he's a professional. If he'd had a few more minutes, he might have bypassed the security system."

Simon frowned. "He's one of us?" Could the rogue operative be in Otter Creek?

"I don't think he's black ops. I sent the footage to your email and Liam's. Tell me what you think when you see it. How's Piper?"

"She should be released soon. Other than a lingering headache, she should be fine."

Zane remained silent a moment. "What aren't you telling me? You know something else. Spill."

The tech wizard was sharp. "She's pregnant."

A laugh sounded over the phone's speaker. "That's great! I'm happy for them. The boss will be, too. What about Zoe?"

"Blackhawk and Stella are interrogating her about Lyons' death."

"Once they eliminate you and Zoe as suspects, they'll focus their attention on finding the real killer."

"Have you sent Ethan the footage from PSI?"

"Already done. Zoe's phone should be at PSI by ten this morning."

"Excellent. Thanks, Z."

"Yep. Anything else?"

He thought about what Zoe had told him. "Tear Isaac Lyons' life apart."

"What am I looking for?"

Simon told Zane about Zoe's injury. "A man that out of control didn't wake up one day and decide to be abusive toward his girlfriend." The idea that any man would treat a woman in that manner turned his stomach.

"We didn't find anything in his background check. You know the boss wouldn't take a chance on someone like that."

"If Lyons had one hidden weakness, he might have others." One that someone could have capitalized on.

"I'll see what I can find." He ended the call.

Simon placed another call, unsure this one would be successful. Brent Maddox was not a pushover. However, he had a soft spot for women in danger.

"Maddox. What do you need, Simon?"

"To report the latest from Otter Creek and ask a favor."

"Go."

Simon summarized the events of the past 24 hours, ending with him and Zoe being summoned to the police station for questioning in the death of Isaac Lyons.

"How did Lyons die?" After Simon relayed the details, Maddox growled. "That isn't the work of an amateur."

"No, sir," he agreed. "That's why I was treated to a full interrogation by our police chief."

"Why did Blackhawk focus on you?"

"Zoe's mine."

"Ah. So, you finally made a move, huh?"

Simon scowled. "What? Did everybody in Fortress make bets on when I would claim her?"

"It's good, clean entertainment in a world filled with darkness and evil, my friend. So, yes, everyone wagered a buck or two on the date you grew a spine and asked her on a date."

"Yeah, yeah. Thanks for the vote of confidence."

"For what it's worth, I'm glad you stepped up."

He snorted. "You like your operatives happy and settled."

"Keeps them stable. What's the favor?"

"Information. I want to know the name of the rogue operative."

"Why?"

"Someone is stalking Bravo and our women, sir. Knowing the name of the rogue will help us be prepared."

"No, it won't."

He blinked. "I don't understand."

"The rogue is no longer a threat to you or anyone else. He's dead."

"What happened?"

"He went after a member of the Shadow unit."

Simon's eyebrows rose. "Which one?"

"Ben Martin."

He whistled softly. "Stupid move on the rogue's part to go up against a Navy SEAL. Ben's all right?"

"Banged up a little. He'll recover."

"Do we know who the rogue sold the information to?"

"We should have that nailed down in the next two hours. Zane assigned Bridget, Trace Young's wife, to the search. She's almost finished."

"Good. Would you have given me the rogue's name?"

"What do you think?"

Simon rolled his eyes. Should have known better than to try and weasel information from Brent Maddox.

"Keep me apprised. If you need anything, contact me. We'll take care of it."

After he ended the call, Trent sent a reminder text about the meeting at PSI scheduled for ten. Hopefully, Ethan and Stella would have the information they needed by then.

An hour later, the door to the interrogation room opened again. Ethan inclined his head toward his office in a silent order for Simon to follow him. After a quick glance inside the room where Stella and Zoe were still talking, he trailed the police chief. Once he crossed the threshold, Ethan closed the door and pointed at one of the visitor chairs in front of his desk.

"Time to tell me what's going on, Simon. I'm responsible for the safety of Otter Creek's citizens, including your girlfriend when you aren't by her side. I'll do my job more effectively if I have more information."

Simon didn't have much choice if he wanted to protect the town and woman he'd claimed as his own. "What do you want to know?"

"Was Lyons a one-man crime spree or should I be prepared for more trouble?"

"I don't know."

When Ethan glared at him, Simon held up a hand to placate the cop. "Bravo and Durango have a meeting at ten o'clock this morning. We're still gathering information from our sources. We should have more soon."

Ethan leaned against his desk, arms folded. "No more secrets. I've been Special Forces. I know the missions you take on and the enemies you make when you do your job right. How much of a threat am I looking at?"

"We had an operative go rogue. He sold information on Bravo and possibly Durango and their families. We don't know who has the information yet. We will. One of the tech geeks is tracking that down."

Ethan scowled. "And the rogue agent?"

"Dead. He made the fatal mistake of going after a Navy SEAL."

"We're looking at terrorists out for revenge against Bravo and maybe Durango." He dragged a hand down his face. "Tell Zane and Maddox that I want to be copied in on every piece of information they learn. No exceptions."

The police chief studied Simon for a moment, then said, "While it's possible terrorists are responsible for what's been happening with Zoe, that's not their typical MO. They don't harass. They kill. Who else is after your girlfriend, Simon?"

His hands clenched. "If I knew that, half this battle would be over. Bravo would go after them before they had a chance to do any more damage."

"We'll help where we can. You and Zoe are free to go. Stay available. I'm sure Stella and Nick will have more questions. In the meantime, if you leave town, we need to know." His gaze was intense and direct. "For Zoe's sake, getting her out of town might be the best way to keep her safe."

"I don't know if I can convince her to keep the bakery closed for a few more days." While she was making a living, she wasn't flush with cash.

"Figure out a way. Short on funds is better than dead."

With that grim pronouncement echoing in his mind, Simon walked to the interrogation room. "We need to leave, Zoe. I have a meeting at PSI."

Stella rose with Zoe. "Be careful, Zoe. If you feel like anything is wrong, even if you can't figure out what it is, call for help. We'd rather be on the spot for a false alarm than for you to assume your imagination was overactive when trouble is stalking you."

Zoe flinched. "I wish you had chosen a different word."

"Being blunt might save your life."

Zoe joined Simon in the hallway and they walked through the bullpen and lobby to the stairs in front of the police station. He slid his arm around her shoulders and tucked her close to his side as he led her to his SUV. While they'd been inside the interrogation rooms, Otter Creek had come alive, and now citizens streamed down the streets and sidewalks, heading toward jobs, school, or one of the restaurants in town.

"Are you hungry?" he asked as he unlocked his SUV and helped her inside.

Zoe shook her head. "Are you still angry with me?"

"I'm angry at myself."

"Why?"

"For being such a coward. If I had stepped up sooner, you'd have told me about Lyons. He would have been kicked out of PSI and maybe Macy would be alive. If Lyons killed Macy, her death is partly my fault."

"Don't, Simon. You couldn't have known."

He trailed his knuckles lightly down her cheek and shut the door. Time to go to PSI.

Simon shut the passenger door and circled to the driver's side. When he grasped the handle, he heard an engine rev nearby. Simon glanced up to see the barrel of a handgun pointed his direction.

He dropped to the ground and rolled under his SUV as bullets sprayed his vehicle.

CHAPTER FIFTEEN

Simon scooted to the other side of his SUV. "Stay inside," he ordered Zoe, and crouched by the rear wheel, weapon drawn as police officers poured from the station behind him. A blue four-door sedan sped away. A moment later, two prowl cars raced from the station in pursuit, sirens blaring and lights flashing.

As Blackhawk headed his direction, Simon stood and opened the passenger door.

"Simon!" Zoe dove into his open arms. "Are you okay?"

"I'm fine. Are you hurt?"

She shook her head. "I don't understand why none of the bullets hit the SUV. Was the shooter a bad shot?"

His arms tightened around her. "He was accurate enough."

"But the glass didn't break."

"My ride is reinforced and the glass is bullet-resistant."

"Simon." Ethan's gaze scanned over Simon and Zoe. "You two okay?"

"No injuries."

"Lucky."

He scanned the area and noticed three town citizens sitting or sprawled on the sidewalk. Officers raced to their sides to render aide. Others formed a barrier between the injured and the street in case of more trouble. A few blocks over, sirens from fire engines and ambulances could be heard coming closer, responding to the scene. "How bad are the injuries?"

"Through-and-through on one, bullets kissed the other two. Could have been worse." His dark eyes pinned Simon. "Think about what I told you."

"Yes, sir."

"Take Zoe inside the station. Call Trent and tell him you'll be late for your meeting. We need statements before you leave." Ethan turned away and organized the scene, deploying resources to the best advantage.

Simon urged Zoe toward the station, gaze constantly scanning the area in case the shooter decided to try again. Although unlikely, he wasn't taking chances with Zoe's life.

He propelled her up the stairs and into the safety of the station. The desk sergeant waved them into the bullpen. Simon didn't argue with him. The waiting area by the front desk was surrounded by glass and made Zoe more vulnerable to attack.

They hurried into the bullpen and Simon steered Zoe into the interrogation room. He didn't like having only one entrance and exit, but anyone who wanted to harm Zoe would have to go through him to get to her.

He seated Zoe at the table and dropped into the chair next to hers. Simon grabbed his phone and called Trent.

"St. Claire."

"It's Simon. Zoe and I will be late."

"What's wrong?"

"Drive-by shooting at the police station. Zoe and I have to give statements to the police." Again.

"You two injured?"

"No, but three civilians were shot. Minor injuries."

"Target?"

He glanced at Zoe whose gaze was locked on his face. "Me."

"I'll call Ethan to offer our assistance. We may have to delay our meeting. You and Zoe stay off the street. As soon as you're free to leave the station, head to PSI. We'll come up with a plan."

"Yes, sir." Simon slid the phone into his pocket. "After we finish here, we're to head to PSI."

She looked surprised. "Shouldn't we lend Ethan a hand?"

"Trent is going to offer assistance. We can't be among the volunteers, Zoe. Bravo shouldn't be volunteering, either."

"Why not?"

"That wasn't a random drive-by shooting. The shooter was aiming for me. The people injured were hit by bullets meant for me. I'm not sure whether I was meant to die to make you more vulnerable to attack or if I was the target all along."

"You think this could be related to the terrorist?"

"We don't believe in coincidence in our line of work. There's a reason for everything that happens."

"But this man could have killed people." Outrage filled her voice.

Simon was glad to hear the fury in her voice instead of the stark fear of moments earlier. "Terrorists don't care about the fallout as long as they meet their objective."

"If you were the target, they failed. We're putting our friends in danger."

"That's what we'll discuss with Bravo and Durango. We have to devise a plan to handle this situation."

"We don't know who to look for."

He cupped her cheek. "We'll find them. Trust me. Trust my team." Simon drew Zoe into his arms and held her close, thankful she was alive and unharmed.

Minutes later, Stella hurried into the interrogation room. She dropped onto the chair across the table from them. "Simon, you first. Tell me what happened in as much detail as you can remember."

After he complied, the detective turned to Zoe. "Your turn. From your perspective, what happened? What did you see?"

Zoe's story matched his with fewer details.

Stella frowned. "Not much to go on. Would Zane be willing to hack into traffic cams for us and send us the footage of the incident?"

Simon's eyebrows rose. "Don't you need a paper trail for the lawyers to hide behind?"

"We'll establish one. No judge is going to deny our request, but that process takes time that we don't have. Although you two were likely the targets, we can't be positive that's the case. By now, the shooter could be anywhere. I'd at least like a starting point. We need to find the shooter and determine if he had a grudge against one of my co-workers, or just you and Zoe."

"Zane will be glad to help. You have his number. Call him yourself."

"I can't ask him to break the law. This isn't an official request."

Understanding flooded Simon. Stella needed deniability. "If you're finished with us, I'll call Zane on the way to PSI and request the footage."

"Thanks." Her phone rang. Stella glanced at the screen and rose. "It's Nate. I have to go. I'll see you later." She left the room, phone pressed to her ear.

Simon extended his hand to Zoe. "Let's get out of here. I'll treat you to a muffin at PSI with a soft drink chaser." He could use food and coffee himself.

She grinned. "Big spender."

"Hey, I know how to take care of my girl."

DON'T LET GO

Simon held Zoe back when they reached the double doors leading to the waiting area. "Let me make sure it's safe first." He opened the door and checked the waiting room which was clear of visitors, then walked to the front entrance of the station. The sidewalk and street directly in front of the station were in a state of controlled chaos.

As he scanned the activity, one of the black PSI SUVs was waved through the police barricade and allowed to park at the far end of the side lot. Matt exited the vehicle and started toward the station.

A moment later, he opened the door and strode inside. "Ethan said you needed a ride because your SUV is evidence. I looked at the damage as I came in. You won't want to drive it in its current condition."

Simon growled. Bear, the mechanical magician of Fortress, would have a fit when he saw the damage to Simon's SUV. "I'm going to owe Bear a steak dinner at the most expensive restaurant near his house."

Matt grinned. "A dinner for him and his family."

That made him flinch. "Doesn't he have a big family?"

"He sure does." His friend's eyes glinted with amusement.

"You're enjoying this, aren't you?"

"As long as it's not me in hot water with the mechanic with magic fingers, you bet."

He glared at his friend. "You're all heart."

The medic chuckled. "How's Zoe?"

"Scared and worried for our friends and neighbors in Otter Creek."

Matt sobered and inclined his head toward the action on the street. "Looks like she has cause to worry. Let's get you guys out of here. Our meeting at PSI has been postponed until noon. Durango will be here in two minutes to assist with crowd control and anything else Ethan needs. Ethan's orders are for Bravo to keep a low profile around town. If we determine Durango is a target, they'll be off limits to the OCPD for the duration until we resolve the problem."

Simon didn't blame the police chief. If he needed more assistance than Durango could offer, PSI had bodyguards that were near the end of their training. They weren't on anyone's radar and would be able to fill the gaps while Ethan's men were busy with other tasks.

"Utilize your time to hunt for the best steak dinner near Bear's compound." Another sly grin Simon's direction.

He scowled at his friend and returned to the bullpen for Zoe. "Matt's here to drive us to PSI."

She blinked. "Why aren't we taking your vehicle?"

"The SUV's exterior is compromised and the vehicle is evidence. Eventually, I'll get it back and take it to the Fortress mechanic to repair."

"You can't just take it to a regular body shop?"

"We have specialty upgrades on our fleet. Only our people handle the vehicles."

When Zoe walked with Simon into the lobby, Matt scrutinized her. "How is the headache and nausea?"

"A little better."

His eyes narrowed. "Have you eaten?"

She frowned. "No, Mom."

The medic waggled an index finger at her. "You know better. Let's get you back to PSI where I'll ply you with food and drink suitable for someone suffering from adrenaline dump and a concussion."

"Lovely."

"Yep. Let's move unless you want to be subjected to Megan Kelter's famous interrogation techniques."

Gaze firing all around in case the reporter lurked in the shadows to ambush them, Simon gripped Zoe's upper arm and urged her forward. Meg Kelter was the editor of the town newspaper and well known for her ruthless questions. When Meg learned Simon and Zoe were the targets, she would pursue them relentlessly for an interview.

Ethan was right. Bravo needed to keep a low profile. Otherwise, the notoriety would entice their enemies to descend on this idyllic town near the Smokey Mountains.

Simon and Matt kept Zoe sandwiched between them as they walked at a fast clip to the SUV. Once inside the vehicle, Matt cranked the engine and drove quickly from the lot. He took a circuitous route to PSI, both he and Simon watching the mirrors in case the shooter had plans for a repeat performance.

They arrived at the gated entrance to PSI fifteen minutes later without further incident and Matt carded them into the compound. Once they parked and walked inside the main building, the medic headed toward the infirmary.

Instead of going to the kitchen, Simon detoured to the front office to take care of an errand that was even more important after the events of the morning. "Do you have a package for me, Kathy?" he asked the grandmother of six that Josh had hired to manage the office and keep the support staff on task.

Bright green eyes met his. "Perfect timing, Simon. A package just arrived for you." Kathy grabbed the white mailer and handed it to him. "The courier said I was to get this to you as soon as possible."

After a nod of thanks, Simon carried the envelope into the kitchen where he slit the edge and removed the black satellite phone already nestled in its protective cover along with a smaller package.

Zoe glanced at the phone and frowned. "Why do you need a second phone?"

"This is yours."

"But I already have one."

"This is a secured satellite phone. It's heavily encrypted so we can talk or text when I'm on missions." It also had a sophisticated tracker embedded into the system although he didn't plan to tell Zoe that information yet. No need to worry her more than she already was. "This is the only safe way for us to communicate. With this phone, I don't have to worry about someone intercepting our communication or pinpointing your location." Only Zane would have that ability.

"Is the satellite phone really necessary?"

He nodded. "I want to talk to you while I'm deployed, Zoe. I miss you like crazy when I'm gone. This phone will be my lifeline. Will you accept it?"

"All right." She brushed his lips with hers. "I miss you, too, when you're gone. I'll be happy to have a way to communicate with you, a way that keeps you safe."

Simon scooped up the second, smaller envelope, slit the edge, and poured the contents into his palm. A watch and a pair of earrings with a matching necklace and bracelet sparkled in the kitchen's overhead light.

He strapped the watch on one wrist, then fastened the bracelet on the other wrist and helped her with the necklace. Simon stepped back, satisfaction filling him at the sight of the potentially life-saving jewelry on Zoe.

He turned over her hand and dropped the earrings onto her palm. "These are beyond my ability to fasten. Will you put them on?"

Zoe slipped the earrings she'd been wearing into her purse and slid in the ones from Fortress. "Why did you buy me jewelry?"

"I didn't buy it, but I chose the design I thought fit your personality." Bright sunshine. That's what he thought of every time he saw Zoe. "This is another form of protection." He stroked a thumb over the cheerful sunflowers circling her wrist. "The jewelry has trackers embedded into the design. You wearing the jewelry will help me find you in an emergency."

She cupped his jaw, her touch gentle. "I'll wear them all the time. They're beautiful." Zoe glanced at the bracelet. "I'll have to put the bracelet in my pocket when I'm working so I don't decorate it with dough or icing."

Matt walked into the kitchen. He glanced at the sat phone. "What did Z choose for her cover?"

Zoe turned over the phone and grinned. "Cupcakes."

Simon smiled. Z was a smart man. "Zane also added the contact information for each member of Bravo, Durango, Brent Maddox, the Fortress CEO, and his own number. If you need help, contact me first. If I don't answer, go down the line, starting with members of Bravo."

"What if you're deployed? I don't want to call you at the wrong time and put your life in jeopardy."

"Text me. If I don't respond, shift to Durango or Zane. Day or night, Zoe. Someone will be available to help you with anything you need."

She studied him a moment. "Is dating or marrying an operative that dangerous?"

"It can be. We keep a low profile, but unexpected things happen."

"Like the rogue operative."

Thankfully, that problem didn't happen often. Otherwise, Simon would seriously question the wisdom of getting involved with Zoe.

Matt ripped open a packet. "Simon, find food for Zoe while I replace her patch."

"The nausea isn't bad," she protested.

"You'll be much more comfortable." He motioned for her to sit on a stool at the counter and replaced her patch with a fresh one. "As soon as you eat, take pain meds for the headache."

Thirty minutes later, Simon led Zoe into the classroom beside the dining hall and seated her at the back. The trainees were silent as Simon walked to the front of the room.

He faced the students who were clustered together, watching him warily. "Liam's wife is in the hospital so he won't be here for this session. We're going to the gun range today to practice your marksmanship."

"Lyons is dead." Hollister stepped forward, hands fisted at his side. "Shouldn't you be in jail?"

Gasps greeted the bold question. Others glared at the belligerent trainee. All of them waited for Simon's reaction.

"I'd have to be an idiot to kill Lyons and leave his body down the street from my girlfriend's house. I'm a lot of things, Hollister, but stupid isn't one of them. The police don't have evidence that I killed your friend."

"Doesn't mean it's not there."

"There's no evidence because I didn't kill Lyons. The subject is closed. If you can't accept that, there's the door. Don't let it hit you on the way out. If you leave, you're finished at PSI."

Hollister's jaw tightened, but he remained in place.

That was something, at least. Simon didn't like having the furious trainee at his back. He'd have to keep tabs on him since he seemed to be cut from the same cloth as Lyons.

He glanced at the other trainees. "Same offer is true for the rest of you. You can leave, but you're walking away from PSI if you do. Otherwise, it's time to work. Head to the gun range with your weapon, ammunition, and protective gear."

Simon dismissed them and held out his hand to Zoe. "Come on. I'll find protective gear for you."

"Why?"

"You're getting your first lesson in handling a weapon today." He prayed she never had to use the information he gave her.

CHAPTER SIXTEEN

Zoe let her breath out halfway and gently squeezed the trigger as Simon taught her. The gun bucked in her hand, the sound of the shot muffled because of the ear protectors she wore. When Simon motioned for her to continue, she repeated the procedure over and over until the magazine was empty.

She lowered the gun and shifted her index finger to rest outside the trigger guard as Simon checked her accuracy. Zoe looked at the scattered holes in the target and was amazed her bullets hit the paper at all.

Simon smiled, satisfaction in his eyes. "Not bad for your first time at the range."

She looked at the paper again. "Are you kidding? I emptied three magazines. If I was a decent marksman, the target would be obliterated. Shouldn't the holes be clustered together instead of spread out like a shotgun blast?"

He chuckled. "You did better your first time shooting a weapon than I did. Trust me, you'll improve. You're a natural."

She didn't know about that. "More like you're a good teacher."

Simon brushed a kiss over her mouth before he turned his attention to the other lanes where the trainees were wrapping up their practice session. He went to a panel on the wall and pressed a button. A red light came on in the corners of the ceiling. The shots slowed and finally stopped. The trainees removed their protective gear. "Collect your targets and leave them on the table at the back for Liam to evaluate. You'll be in Crime Town tomorrow." He chuckled at the groans. "Dismissed."

After collecting their gear and targets, the trainees filed out of the range building, stacking their paper targets on the designated table.

Simon turned back to Zoe. "You want yours?"

She shook her head. "I need a lot more practice to be halfway decent."

"We'll practice and you will improve."

Zoe was afraid she'd never live up to Simon's faith in her shooting ability. However, if he wanted to invest that much time in training her to be a better shot, she wouldn't complain. She'd enjoy every minute with him between deployments. "What's the plan now?"

"Meet with Bravo and Durango during lunch. We'll eat in the conference room. The other instructors will let us know if trainees become rowdy."

Simon took the gun he'd given Zoe to use and cleaned it, then returned it to the weapons vault at the back of the range building. That done, he escorted her to the dining room to grab lunch. He led her to a hallway that curved toward the parking lot. A rumble of male voices halted in mid-conversation when she walked into the conference room.

As one, the members of Durango and Bravo stood at her entrance. Liam waved Zoe and Simon to the two empty chairs to his right. Once she sat, the men dropped into their seats. Some resumed eating. Others watched her and Simon with amusement or satisfaction in their eyes.

She blew out a breath, her cheeks burning. Terrific. The members of both teams knew that she and Simon were dating.

Trent pushed his empty plate aside and nodded at Cade who typed something into a computer keyboard. A moment later, a large screen mounted on the wall came to life and a buzz-cut blond man appeared.

"Sit rep," he ordered.

Trent glanced at Simon and used a hand signal.

"The police hauled me and Zoe in for questioning early this morning in the death of Isaac Lyons."

"Why?"

"The trainee was found in his car a few houses down from Zoe's place, throat slit."

"TOD?"

"Between two and five this morning. I was with Zoe the whole time. Unfortunately, part of that time, we were at her house. According to Blackhawk and Nate's wife, Stella, I have the means, motive, and opportunity to have pulled off the murder."

Ice blue eyes shifted to look at Zoe. "I'm Brent Maddox, Ms. Lockhart."

"Call me Zoe."

He inclined his head, then returned his attention to Simon. "Continue."

Simon summarized their interrogations. When he mentioned the incident in Macy's yard involving Zoe, all the men frowned.

"Need one of the lawyers?" Brent asked.

"Not yet. So far, we're clear."

"If that changes, I want to know."

"Yes, sir."

"Tell me the rest."

Simon told his boss about the drive-by shooting, ending with, "Three civilians were injured. Status unknown."

"They're being treated at Memorial Hospital," Josh said. "Two will be released later this afternoon. The third should go home tomorrow. All will recover without long-term repercussions."

A nod. "What do you need from me, Simon?"

"I asked Zane to dig into Lyons' life. Has he come up with anything yet?"

"Yeah. You aren't going to like it. He's been receiving payments of $5,000 a month since he arrived at PSI."

Trent frowned. "Fortress flags unusual monetary activity. How did we miss that?"

"The money was deposited into a second checking account under his girlfriend's name."

Shock rolled through Zoe.

"Did Z track the money's origination?" Trent asked.

A snort. "Offshore bank account."

Simon groaned. "Let me guess. The Cayman Islands?"

"That's right."

"Any chance of tracking it beyond the Caymans?"

"Maybe. Trace's wife, Bridget, is a computer whiz and doesn't give up once she sinks her teeth into something. She's chasing the money trail. Z is handling another crisis at the moment. Between them, they'll figure out where the money came from. As soon as we know something, we'll contact you."

"Yes, sir."

"If you're the primary target of the attacks, you may have to relocate. Otherwise, we risk more innocent civilians in your town."

Trent scowled. "We aren't sending him out alone, boss."

Alarm exploded inside Zoe. Brent couldn't send Simon away from his teammates. Against a determined opponent unafraid of collateral damage, Simon would be at a disadvantage. He needed his teammates to guard his back.

The Fortress CEO's eyes narrowed. "Did I suggest we toss him to the wolves?"

"No, sir."

"We'll consider options once we have more information. In the meantime, think about your missions and scour the Internet for mention of your opponents. If someone wants revenge, he made inquiries about Bravo."

"We don't know who the rogue sold information to or what he provided to the enemy." Josh looked thoughtful. "We do know that Zoe and Piper were targeted. What if the rogue's work isn't responsible for what's happening in Otter Creek? Is it possible the attacks are connected to one of the ops Liam and Simon went on together without their teammates?"

Simon and Liam exchanged glances.

Brent frowned. "How many missions are we talking about, Liam?"

The operative rubbed the back of his neck. "At least ten. We've been partners for five years. Not all our missions required the full team."

"Four involved only the two of us, though," Simon added. "For the rest of the missions, Bravo provided backup but we didn't need assistance."

"Focus on those four," Brent said. "Let's narrow down our suspect pool." He turned his attention to Zoe. "What do you think?"

"I'm not sure the trouble we're experiencing is from one person or group."

Simon's boss straightened. "Explain."

Zoe told him why she suspected two different groups or people were responsible for the problems. "The crimes are on two opposite ends of the scale. On one end, two houses are broken into. Macy's place was searched, especially the dressers. In my house, everything was trashed, almost like someone threw a tantrum. My dresser had also been moved. I don't know for certain, but I have to wonder if my house was invaded by two people." Knowing that made her skin crawl. "On the other end of the crime scale is the murder of Macy and Isaac. Would a thief kill?"

"If he panics and is stupid enough to carry a weapon, then yeah, it's possible," Nate said.

"Most thieves don't carry weapons," Josh murmured. "They don't want to have a longer prison sentence if they're caught by the police."

"Piper was attacked in her own driveway," Zoe pointed out. "She said the man came from the front porch."

Brent looked at Liam, eyebrow raised.

He nodded. "Zane checked the video feed. The clown tried to break into the house. He had enough difficulty that Piper arrived home before he succeeded. He shoved her into the side of the SUV and ran."

"Was she home at the normal time?" Josh asked.

"Piper left work early to prepare a special meal." A slow smile curved his mouth. "She had news to tell me."

Rio, Durango's medic, tilted his head. "Don't keep us in suspense, buddy. Looks like the news was good."

"It's the best. Piper is pregnant."

That brought a round of congratulations from the members of both teams and Brent.

Josh finally held up his hand in a bid for silence. "Circling back to the topic at hand. So, Piper came home early. The perp didn't plan to confront anyone. He thought he'd have the house to himself to do his search. Piper's change in plans interfered with his agenda."

"Zane thinks the guy is a professional," Simon said.

"But it's not the same guy who killed Macy and Isaac," Cade said. "He wouldn't hesitate to use a knife on Piper like he did with Macy and Isaac."

Liam's hands clenched. "When I get my hands on the dude who hurt Piper, he'll wish he'd chosen a different profession."

"I didn't hear that," Josh said, his tone mild.

"You can also turn a blind eye when he's dropped off at the station with a few bruises."

Durango's leader scowled at him.

Nate looked at Zoe, speculation in his gaze. "Maybe we should consider another alternative."

Simon wrapped his arm around her. "What's that?"

"All the incidents are connected to Zoe, not Simon and Liam."

CHAPTER SEVENTEEN

Simon's heart skipped a beat before lurching into a rapid rhythm. "Why do you think Zoe could be the target instead of me?"

"I don't know that she is, but it's something to keep in mind. Macy was her employee and friend. Zoe and Piper are friends. Maybe the shooter at the police station wasn't aiming at you. Zoe could have been the intended victim. The shooter wouldn't know the SUV is reinforced and decked out with bullet-resistant glass. In a normal vehicle, she would have been hit with one of those bullets."

"What about Isaac's death?" Zoe asked. "Why would someone use him to get back at me? I didn't like the man and tried to convince Macy to break up with him. Killing Isaac isn't about punishing me."

"Lyons' death wouldn't punish you," Matt agreed. "But if Simon was blamed for his death, his arrest would separate you from your best protection. That could have been the point to killing Lyons near your house. It was pure luck that Simon happened to be in your home near the time of the murder. He should have been at home asleep with no witnesses to prove he was there."

"But I haven't made anyone angry enough to want to kill me. For crying out loud, I haven't even been on a date since Simon moved to Otter Creek." She stopped and covered her face with her hands. "I can't believe I admitted that to a room full of men."

Several chuckles sounded in the room. Simon couldn't help but kiss her temple, loving that she hadn't been interested in anyone else in months. He'd felt the same about Zoe.

"Perhaps you didn't make someone angry, Zoe," Josh said. "You could have seen something you weren't supposed to, something that threatens a dangerous person."

"But how does that explain Macy's death and the attack on Piper? We do things together all the time. Most of the time we included Delilah, Sasha, and Grace in our plans. How can I pinpoint something I saw that threatened someone else?"

"Get all the women together and brainstorm," Brent said. "See if you can figure out what might have been the trigger. It's possible one of them noticed something at the time or in recent days that set off warning signals."

"I'll talk to Grace about her work schedule," Trent said. "We'll arrange a meeting with the women as soon as we can."

"Good. In the meantime, we need to make contingency plans, Simon."

His gaze shifted from Zoe to his boss. "What kind of plans?"

"A place to go to ground if it does turn out that you and Liam are targets for revenge."

"Suggestions?"

"Micah Winter, our logistics coordinator, is out of town with his wife and kids. His cabin outside of Murfreesboro is empty. He's agreed to let you and Zoe use it as a temporary haven. It's not listed under his name and it's off the grid."

Simon considered that option, then shook his head. "I don't want to bring this trouble anywhere near his family or their house."

"I can appreciate that, but he's a paranoid man. Trust me, he's well prepared for trouble. There's even a secure room in his cabin."

"I still don't want to risk it."

"Rod's cabin," Josh said. "It's also outside Murfreesboro but nowhere near Micah's place. The cabin is large enough for a team of operatives to provide protection for Zoe and Simon."

That brought a scowl to Simon's face. "I can protect myself."

Durango's leader ignored his outburst. "After Rod's cabin was rebuilt, we helped him set up a shell corporation. The origination is buried deep because Z is a master geek. That should give you enough separation to keep the location off the radar and give you a safe and secure place to hide."

Maybe. At least the cabin wouldn't be associated with Micah or anyone else from Fortress. Contemplating retreating from the field of battle rankled, though. Although he'd leave Otter Creek to protect friends and neighbors, he hated to cede even an inch to the enemy. "I'll consider it."

"What about the bakery?" Zoe's voice was soft. "Nick should release my bakery soon."

"You need to have the bathroom cleaned by people who specialize in cleaning crime scenes," Josh said. "I can give you a recommendation. These guys are fast and good."

"Will I be able to work while they clean?"

"You won't want to be there. Want me to call them and set it up once Nick finishes his work?"

She sighed and gave a short nod. "Thanks, Josh."

Simon's phone rang at that moment. He checked the screen and rose, heart rate skyrocketing. To receive a call from her during the day was unusual. She always waited until after the workday to contact him. Even then, it was a text for him to call her. Like Zoe, his mother worried about calling him at the wrong time. "Excuse me. I have to take this."

In the hall, he swiped the screen with his thumb. "What's wrong, Mom?"

"Your father's been shot."

His grip around the cell phone tightened. Fury that someone would shoot his father and bone deep fear that he would lose him filled Simon. "How is he?"

A soft sob came through the speaker. "I don't know. He's in surgery right now."

"Do the police know who's responsible?"

"I have no idea."

"It's all right, Mom. I'll find out. Are you at Hanover Medical?"

"Yes."

"Do you have someone with you?"

"B.J. is here."

"Let me talk to him."

A moment later, his brother said, "Are you stateside?"

"I'm in Otter Creek." Even if he wasn't, Maddox would fly him home as soon as possible. "What do you know?"

"One shot, center mass. He has tension pneumothorax."

He scowled. "English, please."

"His lung collapsed, there's air in his chest, and it's pressing on his heart. In addition, the bullet is close to the spinal column."

"Bottom line, bro. Is he going to make it?"

"I don't know. The surgeon is working on him now. I'll know more when Dad is out of surgery. When will you be here?"

"As soon as I can. I have some things to arrange first."

"Hurry, Simon."

He ended the call and took a moment to get himself under control. His mind filled with the myriad tasks he needed to accomplish before he'd be able to leave town. He wasn't leaving Zoe in Otter Creek when danger surrounded her. He'd never forgive himself if anything happened to her while he was gone.

Simon slid his phone away and opened the door to the conference room.

Zoe took one look at him and said, "What happened?"

"My father's been shot."

Matt straightened. "Injuries?"

Simon repeated what his brother said. "B.J. won't know more until Dad's out of surgery."

Quinn Gallagher, Durango's spotter, said, "I'll cover your responsibilities here. If Durango is deployed, I'll arrange for another instructor to step in."

Maddox spoke up. "One of the jet's will be in Knoxville in two hours. You're officially off duty as of now. We'll have a vehicle waiting for you and Zoe when you land in Hanover."

"Thanks, boss."

"Let me know what you and your family need. We'll take care of it. Matt?"

"Yes, sir?"

"Pack your bags. Simon needs backup. Might as well be someone who speaks medical jargon."

Instead of agreeing instantly, the medic glanced at Simon, his gaze troubled. "Sir, in light of what's happening in Otter Creek, I don't want to leave Delilah."

"Take her with you. Simon, give me the name of a good hotel close to the hospital. I'll have Zane reserve a suite for the four of you."

"The Westgate Hotel."

"Boss, if Bravo is the target, what are the chances this shooting is a coincidence?" Liam asked.

"Zero."

"We should all go," Cade said.

"And leave our wives vulnerable to attack?" Trent scowled. "Not a chance. Grace is a nurse. She can't request time off without warning."

Maddox looked thoughtful. "The Shadow unit is down one man. Ben was injured when the rogue tried to take him out, but he's functional. The team is available for a soft assignment. They've been skating on a razor-thin edge for a while. I don't think they'll protest babysitting duty."

"If Shadow provides protection, I'll feel better about leaving Delilah here," Matt said.

"We'll trade off shifts with them," Josh added.

Trent nodded. "That will work. Have Nico contact Grace with a protection plan for the women. She'll touch base with the others to let them know what's going on. We'll meet Shadow at the airport and let them drive our SUVs to Otter Creek. That way they'll have wheels."

A nod from Maddox. "We'll reserve rooms for the rest of Bravo along with the suite at The Westgate. Zane will notify you when the jet's in the air." He ended the transmission.

Josh stood. "We'll take care of things here, Trent. Focus on Mr. Murray."

"Watch your backs. We still don't know if the rogue spilled enough information to be a danger to your team and your families."

"So far, Bravo's been on the front lines. If you remain the main target, you'll take the trouble with you."

Trent's expression turned grim. "Still, don't let down your guard and give the tangos an opening."

A slow nod from the Delta soldier and cop. "We never do."

Simon's gaze swept over each of Durango's faces. No, he supposed they didn't. "We owe you a favor."

Josh waved that aside. "No favors owed between friends. Just take care of business and get back here." He walked to the white board at the end of the room, picked up a marker, and looked at his team. "We have a schedule to rework and security plans to firm up. We need to work fast. I have a class in thirty minutes."

Trent motioned for his team to vacate the conference room. When they reassembled in the hallway, he looked at his team and Zoe. "Pack your gear. We leave Otter Creek in one hour. We'll meet back here and travel together." His gaze focused on Simon and Zoe. "I don't want you traveling alone in case someone decides Highway 18 is the perfect place for an ambush."

CHAPTER EIGHTEEN

As Simon drove a loaner SUV from the PSI parking lot, he glanced at Zoe. "Do you mind going home with me?"

"Of course not." She twisted in her seat to face him. "I want to meet your family although I'd hoped to do it under better circumstances. Besides, you should concentrate on your father, not worry about whether or not I'm safe. I don't want to be a distraction and right now I would be if I insisted on staying in Otter Creek."

She ran her fingers through her hair, giving him a peek at the bruise spreading across the right side of her forehead, a stark reminder of the danger she was in. "I also need to have the bathroom at the bakery professionally cleaned and prefer the work be done when the bakery is closed. I don't think people want the reminder of what happened while they're eating or ordering food. Hopefully, the cleaners won't take long."

The knot in his stomach eased, grateful that she understood his concern over her safety and how torn he was between wanting to protect her and be with his family. He didn't want to chase her off with his overprotective streak.

She'd have to get used to that aspect of his personality. However, he wanted to ease her into it, not hit her with the reality before their relationship had a chance to solidify from this fledging beginning. Simon didn't want to lose this woman. "Thanks, Zoe."

"You would do it for me if my father had been shot."

"I'm not sure how long we'll be gone. A few days, at least." Maybe longer, depending on how his father responded to treatment.

"I'll have to make arrangements for a few orders already placed for cakes and remind Sasha I won't be able to bake for Perk for a few days."

"Make whatever arrangements you need to." He squeezed her hand. "I want you with me."

"To protect me?"

"Yes, and because I need you." He'd never admitted that to another woman. What was it about Zoe that allowed him to let down his guard and make himself vulnerable?

"Really?"

"I've been careful about my family's safety since I entered the military, then transitioned to black ops. This is the first time my job has caused harm to someone I love. The thought of you being here while I'm out of state doesn't sit well with me." He sighed. "I'm afraid to let you out of my sight, not because you're in danger although that's true. I'm more worried that you'll realize I'm not worth the risk and move on to someone else, someone with a job less dangerous than mine."

Zoe gave a soft laugh. "No other man fascinates me like you do. You also don't know if your father's shooting is connected to your job. Isn't it possible your father was an innocent bystander and someone else was the target?"

"Maybe." He didn't think that would turn out to be the case. Coincidences didn't happen often in his line of work. "I have to call Ethan. He needs to know we're leaving town and why."

Simon called the police chief and put the call on speaker.

"Blackhawk."

"It's Simon. Zoe and I are leaving town in an hour. Bravo is going with us."

"What happened?"

"My father's been shot. The bullet is lodged near his spine."

"Prognosis?"

"Unknown."

"Do I need to provide protection for the other Bravo women?"

"We have it covered although having more eyes on them wouldn't hurt. Shadow is arriving in two hours to provide protection. Between them and Durango, the women will be well protected."

"I'll talk to Josh and offer assistance if his team is deployed. Otherwise, we'll keep our eyes open around the homes and businesses. Where is your home, Simon?"

"Hanover, Texas. I don't know how long we'll be gone." His hands clenched around the steering wheel in a white-knuckled grip. "I'm going to find out who did this."

"You won't be in Otter Creek," the police chief warned. "The cops in Hanover don't know Bravo is a team of good men."

"I'm aware."

"Forget about being a vigilante, Simon. Concentrate on your father and family. If you and Bravo learn the identity of the perp, give the information to the police. You hear me?"

"Yes, sir."

"Good. We'll be vigilant while you're gone and watch the Bravo women as well as your home and Zoe's."

"Appreciate it." He ended the call and glanced at Zoe. "Make your calls. If you'll give him permission, Zane will arrange for your cell number to be transferred to the sat phone and the Fortress carrier." He didn't tell her the bill would go to him. If Zoe insisted on paying, Simon would make sure the monthly bill was equivalent to her usual one. He'd have Zane bill the rest to him.

She called Sasha first and apologized for not being able to fill her orders for a few days and learned the Perk owner had already made arrangements with her former supplier to cover her baking needs for the next two weeks. That done, she called another baker in Cherry Hill and explained that her shop would be closed for a few days to make unexpected repairs. The other baker agreed to take care of the cakes for a baby shower, a wedding, and a retirement party. "Thank you, Misty. I owe you a huge favor." A moment later, she ended the call.

After that, she called the three customers with the cake orders and explained that she'd arranged for the Cherry Hill Bakery to provide the cakes for their events. The customers offered sympathy over Macy's death and were grateful that Zoe had worked out other arrangements despite the circumstances.

As she ended the last call, Simon parked in her driveway and turned off the engine. He circled the SUV to meet her at the sidewalk.

"You can go on home while I pack. It's daylight outside. I'll be fine."

Simon shook his head. "Most of your neighbors are at work and the person who killed Macy and Lyons won't hesitate to take advantage of you being alone. I'll wait. Is there anything you want me to do while you're packing?"

"Check the windows and doors. I don't know if the police checked them before they finished processing the house."

He kissed her. "I'll make sure everything is secure." Simon took the keys from her hand and unlocked her front door. A quick scan showed that nothing had changed since the last time they'd been in the house save for fingerprint powder coating every surface.

Zoe groaned. "It's looks even worse now than it did earlier."

"I'll help you clean when we return." One of the first things he planned to do was paint her bedroom wall. Zoe didn't need to see that every time she walked into her bedroom. He nudged her toward the hall. "Go pack while I check the locks."

She hurried to her bedroom and Simon headed for the kitchen and Zoe's French doors. He glanced at the window pane that had been broken and breathed easier. Good. Mason Kincaid, cousin to Durango's medic, had replaced the glass. A call to the contractor early that morning had netted the fast response. One less worry over the security of Zoe's house.

He still wasn't happy that she didn't have a security system here. He understood that money had been tight and she'd chosen to protect the shop first. Didn't mean he would turn a blind eye to the safety needs in her home now that he knew she'd neglected to set up the safety precautions here. Especially not since she was his.

As he checked that doors and windows were secured, Simon called Zane. "It's Simon. Need a favor."

"Name it."

"Zoe needs a security system installed at her home."

"Top of the line?"

"Yes. As soon as possible, Z. Someone broke into her home and trashed the place. I don't want her sleeping in a house that isn't secure."

"You want the bill?"

"Copy that. If she protests, we'll work something out."

"Understood. How did she like the phone?"

"She loved the cover. Pull the expenses from my account."

"Copy that. I'm sorry about your father. How are you holding up?"

Hearing those words was a painful reminder of what he'd managed to block from his mind for the past two minutes. "It's tough to know you could be responsible for your father's death."

"Let's hope that isn't the outcome of the shooting. We'll have an installation team in Otter Creek first thing tomorrow morning."

"Thanks. Zoe said it's fine for you to transfer her number and carrier." He gave his friend the information he needed as he walked to the guest room to check the windows for signs of tampering. "Any new information?"

"Should have something for you in another hour or so. We're working as fast as we can, Simon. We know what's at stake."

"Sorry. I want to help and I need information to do that." He glanced over his shoulder to be sure Zoe wasn't within earshot. "I'm worried about Zoe."

"You have reason to be." A pause, then, "I have to go. Got a call coming in from the Texas team. They're in a hot zone."

That explained why Maddox agreed with Bravo going to Hanover. The Texas team wasn't available to provide backup.

Satisfied the window in the guest room was secure, Simon crossed the hall to check the bathroom window. The window raised easily. On closer inspection, he realized the lock had been tampered with.

Frowning, he worked the lock and concluded it wasn't functional. Simon needed a way to secure the window until Mason could replace the mechanism. "Zoe, do you have a screwdriver and screws?"

She appeared in the doorway seconds later with the requested items. "Is something wrong?"

"The window lock is broken." He took the box of screws and the screwdriver from her hands. "How long has it been broken?"

"I unlocked it last weekend to open the window and let in fresh air while I cleaned. The lock worked fine."

"Huh. Makes me wonder which one of the break-in artists sabotaged your window and why." Any reason wouldn't be a good one. He looked back in time to see blood drain from her face and wanted to give himself a swift kick for scaring her more.

"Why did they mess with my window?"

Simon forced himself back to his task. If he gave in to the urge to take her into his arms, they wouldn't be at PSI on time to meet his teammates. He knew himself, and Zoe was fast becoming his addiction. The more he touched her, the greater the craving to have her in his arms grew. The need to get to his father's side pushed as hard at Simon as the need to comfort and protect Zoe. "I'll find out when we catch and question them."

A soft sigh. "Catching them doesn't seem likely at this point."

"Count on it. Have you finished packing?"

She nodded.

"Once I check your bedroom windows, we'll leave. Might be a good idea to check your refrigerator for food that will spoil soon. I'll take out the trash before we leave." She was anxious. The necessary task would occupy her and prevent unpleasant surprises when she returned.

After she left, Simon inserted screws so the window couldn't be raised without breaking glass. He'd let Mason know about the temporary fix.

When he entered the kitchen, Zoe was cinching a trash bag. Simon handed her the tool and screws, then carried the trash to the garbage can at the back of the house.

They drove to Simon's place where he added changes of clothes and extra ammunition to his bag. "We need to stop by the police station to grab my Go bag from the back of the SUV."

While he drove, he called to inform Ethan that he needed access to his vehicle.

"I'll meet you at the curb with the bag. Your vehicle is still being processed."

"If you release it while I'm gone, give Josh the keys. He can take my ride to Bear."

Ethan chuckled. "How ticked off will Bear be?"

"Enough that I'll be in deep debt for life. He takes damage to the vehicles personally."

"Good luck, my friend."

He'd have to throw himself on Bear's mercy. The problem was the mechanic didn't have much when his beloved machinery was involved.

As Simon headed toward PSI to meet his teammates, he called Mason about the broken lock. "The Fortress installation team will be at the house at 8:00 tomorrow morning. Zoe needs the repair completed before the windows are wired."

"I'll take care of it. What else can I do to help?"

Simon glanced at her, eyebrow raised.

She said, "Josh is arranging for a cleaning company to clean the employee bathroom at the bakery. When they finish, would you have time to paint the room? I need the room to look different. Any color other than what's on the walls now is fine."

"I'll make time for it." His voice was gentle. "Who has a key?"

"Sasha and Delilah."

"I'll take care of everything, Zoe."

Simon glanced at Zoe after he ended the call. "I know I should have consulted you before setting up the alarm installation, but I need you to be safe."

"Fortress systems are pricey."

"They're worth every penny. You'll receive a nice discount on the system and installation." He chanced another look and grinned. "A perk of dating an operative." She laughed, as he'd meant for her to do.

They met his team and were soon on their way to the airport in Knoxville. While the caravan of PSI vehicles parked an hour later, a Fortress jet taxied to a stop on the tarmac. As Bravo unloaded gear, the jet's hatch opened and the stairs were lowered. One by one, the Shadow team exited the jet with Ben, their wounded comrade, bringing up the rear.

Simon shook hands with Nico Rivera, Shadow team's leader. "Thanks for lending a hand in Otter Creek."

"No problem. If we play our cards right, either Serena Blackhawk or Nate will cook for us. Can't lose with either one of those chefs providing food."

"Still, I appreciate you coming on short notice."

Nico sobered. "What's the latest on your father's condition?"

"My brother sent a text a few minutes ago. Dad's still in surgery. The surgeon estimates another hour. So far, Dad's doing well, and the doctor is optimistic."

"Sounds positive. Keep us informed." Nico faced Trent. "Orders?"

"The women know you're providing security. Blackhawk and his officers will watch from a distance. If you notice suspicious activity, notify the police chief. If someone goes after our wives, do whatever is necessary to protect them."

A nod. "Anything else we should know?"

"Assign Joe and Sam to Piper. She's pregnant."

A round of congratulations to Liam followed Trent's announcement. "I'll take good care of your wife," Sam, Shadow's medic, told Liam.

"We don't have a timeline on our return," Trent continued. "If Maddox needs your team, make sure another unit replaces you. Durango will trade out shifts with Shadow. Coordinate coverage with Josh."

"Copy that." Nico's gaze shifted to Zoe. "You must be Zoe Lockhart." He held out his hand. "I'm Nico Rivera. This my team, Joe and Samantha Gray, Ben Martin, and Trace Young."

She shook his hand. "I'm glad to meet all of you. Simon speaks highly of your unit."

"That's because we're the best Fortress team," Joe said with a grin.

Liam snorted. "You wish."

Trent shifted his Go bag to his shoulder. "We need to go. Nico, the keys are with our vehicles."

"The bird's refueling and should be ready to lift off in a few minutes. Watch your backs. We'll take care of your wives."

As the Shadow team crossed the tarmac toward the SUVs, Simon noted Ben's slight limp. Looked like Maddox was right. Ben was mobile enough for bodyguard duty but not for the type of missions they usually tackled.

Simon shifted his Go bag to his other shoulder, took Zoe's luggage, and wrapped his free hand around hers. He led her toward the jet.

"I've never flown on a plane this small."

"No need to be nervous. Fortress jets are always in top mechanical condition. We never know when we'll have to leave in a hurry."

After storing their gear in the overhead compartments, he sat beside her at the back of the cabin as the others joined them in the jet. When the jet powered up, Zoe's face paled. Simon raised the arm of the seat separating them and wrapped his arm around her shoulders.

When the jet leveled out, she glanced at him. "Thanks."

Before he could reply, Trent's cell phone signaled an incoming call. Conversation inside the cabin tapered off.

Although the conversation was short and mostly one-sided, Trent's expression darkened the longer he listened.

When he ended the call, Bravo's leader looked straight at Simon. "We have a problem."

CHAPTER NINETEEN

Zoe stared at Trent. "How can that happen? He was at PSI and now he's vanished into thin air." Unbelievable. How could Isaac's friend, Chris Hollister, have slipped away? Where had he gone and what was he doing?

The questions left her feeling uneasy. From the interaction she'd witnessed between Chris and Simon, the trainee hated Simon. Did he hate the operative enough to do something drastic, like shoot Simon's father? She hadn't believed anyone in her life was that evil until a killer murdered Macy. After seeing Chris's reaction to Isaac's death, Zoe wouldn't be surprised by anything he did.

"When was he last seen?" Simon asked.

"He attended the afternoon training session and left campus. No one's seen him since."

A scowl. "PSI's dorms are gossip central, worse than the Otter Creek biddies at sharing information. I can't believe somebody didn't pry the information out of him before he took off."

"Josh and Alex questioned his friends. Hollister was upset about Lyons' death and blamed you. He thinks you killed Lyons to protect Zoe."

Didn't take a genius to figure out the only reason Simon would kill Lyons was to protect someone who couldn't protect herself. Zoe.

She shifted her gaze from Trent to Simon. "Is it possible that Hollister went to Hanover?"

Simon's body went motionless. "He had enough time to fly there."

"Then you'll be able to discover if he bought a ticket."

"If he flew commercial. He could have taken a private flight. If you pay the pilot enough money, he might leave a name off the manifest."

"Is that illegal?"

Simon's lips curved. "Money talks."

"If he has that kind of money, why is he training as a bodyguard?"

"Good question, one we'll ask Hollister when we find him." Liam folded his arms across his chest. "Lyons and Hollister were childhood friends."

"We need to learn everything we can about them." Trent pointed at Matt. "Dig into Hollister's financial background. Simon and Zoe, take his history. Cade, find out where Hollister went. It's rare for people to successfully go off the grid. Most of them make mistakes. See if he made any in the past few hours. I'll take Lyons' background. Liam, look at his money trail. We already know he was getting money through Macy's second account. See if Zane and Bridget have tracked the money back to the source and if other red flags appear. We can't do anything to help Simon's family for the next few hours. We'll push the investigation forward as far as we can while we're in the air."

"And once we're on the ground in Hanover?" Simon asked.

"Your family will be our focus. We'll unearth what we can on Lyons and Hollister in our off time. Anything you find, pass to Zane as well. Dig hard for the next two hours."

The operatives grabbed laptops from duffel bags and settled in to work. Simon reached into the overhead compartment and grabbed his computer. "Need a snack or drink?"

She shook her head. "Where do we start?"

"We'll log into Fortress Security's system and tear apart Hollister's background."

"Did Fortress run a background search on him?"

"Several. Nothing out of the ordinary showed up or Maddox wouldn't have sent him to PSI."

"That means the Fortress process is flawed or something changed since he arrived at PSI."

"No background check is infallible, but ours is thorough."

"Have you been in his face often since he arrived at PSI?"

"We don't hold their hands. These are strong and opinionated men and women. We can't coddle them. Our training is tough because we're trying to keep them and their principals alive. We don't apologize for that. The trainees know what to expect from the first day of orientation. There are no surprises."

"You have been in his face."

"Along with every other trainee at PSI." He frowned. "But you have a valid point. I have been hard on him because of his belligerent attitude. Maybe he resented it."

"He has a big ego."

"You know him?"

"Not really. Because he hung around with Isaac, running into Chris was inevitable."

Simon's eyes narrowed. "Did he touch you or hurt you?"

"Only Isaac did that one time."

Apparently satisfied, Simon booted up his computer and entered his passwords to his company's website. He clicked on a program and typed in Chris Hollister's name. "Let's see what Zane learned on the background checks." He angled the computer screen for Zoe to see the information.

She scanned paragraph after paragraph of data, impressed by the amount of information amassed. Hollister grew up in Tuscaloosa, Alabama along with Isaac. He was one of seven children in the Hollister family, all boys. His father had been a Marine. His mother had stayed at home full time until her sons were grown and had left home. She'd passed away from cancer while Chris was at college. He was the youngest child. "It's sad that he lost his mother," she murmured.

"Yeah. I can't imagine that and don't want to." He pointed at another section of the screen. "Look at this. Tell me what you think."

Her attention shifted to the new section of the document. "Chris and Isaac were competitive shooters." She looked at Simon. "Does that mean they competed in target shooting?"

"That's right."

"How are Chris's marksmanship scores at the gun range?"

"Top of his class."

"What about Isaac? Was he as skilled with a gun?"

"He scored high in our evaluations at PSI. Usually, he and Hollister vied for the top spot."

"In other words, Chris has the skill and training to shoot your father."

"Hollister is skilled with a handgun and a rifle. He could have used either one."

"Chris and Isaac attended the University of Alabama and were roommates. They were in the Army for four years before applying at PSI." Zoe frowned. "Why didn't they apply to Fortress to be operatives?"

"You have to be invited to apply. PSI is the bodyguard training school. We train operatives as well, but anyone can apply to attend the school for the bodyguard education. If Maddox likes what he sees and receives trainer recommendation, the trainees might be invited to apply to Fortress. Most of them go on to work for other companies as bodyguards and private security."

"Would Brent consider hiring them as operatives later if they didn't distinguish themselves in training?"

He shook his head.

They continued scanning Chris's background information. Zane had ferreted out an incredible amount of information.

She frowned and glanced at him. "Does Fortress have a file on me?"

"Depends."

"On what?"

"How much trouble I'll be in if I tell you the truth."

Guess that answered her question. "Do they investigate the women the operatives date?"

"Not all of them." His cheeks turned an interesting shade of red.

"Should I ask more questions or let it drop?"

"I'll owe you a huge steak dinner and the most expensive floral arrangement ever created if you'll let this go. I don't want to dig myself a deeper hole, please."

Zoe grinned. "You get a pass. For now. I'll assume I'm one of the privileged few since I have a file. Based on the questions you've asked me over the past few days, you haven't read the file."

He slid her a glance. "I preferred to learn about you the old-fashioned way."

"Definite brownie points for you on that score, Simon." Did the existence of the file mean Simon was as crazy about her as she was about him? Being this invested in a relationship alone would be heartbreaking.

"Let's get back to Hollister."

"We finished reading the background information Fortress provided. What's next?"

"Scan the Net for new information." He typed Chris's name into a browser.

Several hits filled the screen. Except for the most recent activity connected to his name, the information was the same as what they'd already seen.

Zoe leaned closer to the screen. "Is that what I think it is?"

"It's a hotel reservation for a room in Black Canyon, Texas."

"How close is that to Hanover?"

His hand clenched. "Twenty miles from town."

A ball of ice formed in her stomach. The date on the hotel reservation was for last night. Based on the information on the screen, Chris had checked in. He'd been in the area when Simon's father had been gunned down. Was he the shooter?

Trent stood. "Conference table," he ordered.

As Bravo arranged themselves around the table, Simon seated Zoe in the chair beside his.

Trent motioned to Matt. "What did you learn about Hollister and his financial situation?"

"Same situation as Lyons. He has an unknown source of income. The windfall is the same amount."

Cade frowned. "He doesn't have a girlfriend. How is he getting the money?"

"Actually, he does have a girlfriend."

The men turned to stare at Zoe.

"Who?" Simon asked.

"Wendy Oberman."

Matt's eyebrows rose. "Doesn't she work at the beauty salon with Maeve?"

She nodded. "She and Chris started dating soon after he arrived at PSI."

"How do you know about them?" Simon asked.

"Wendy has a fondness for my cinnamon rolls. She likes to stroll in each morning and brag about Chris and how well he is doing. I never knew if she was telling the truth or not about that." She had bragged about bagging Chris in record time while Zoe hadn't dated anyone in months. There had been a good reason for that, one Zoe didn't share with her customer. No other man in Otter Creek held a candle to Simon Murray.

"Have Zane look into Wendy Oberman's accounts," Trent said. "Find out if she opened a second account in the past three months. Anything else?"

"Just a gut feeling someone flipped him after the background checks were completed prior to his arrival in Otter Creek."

"Check his social media accounts," Liam said. "He probably bragged about his admittance to PSI and made himself a target."

"Maybe Wendy would talk to one of us since Hollister is MIA." Matt looked at Simon. "Anyone except you. If Hollister groused about your treatment of him, she'd have heard the complaints. I doubt Wendy would talk to you."

"One of us calling her out of the blue would raise her suspicions." Cade turned to Zoe. "Think she'd talk to you?"

Zoe nodded. "She and Macy were friends. I'll offer my condolences."

"Excellent. See if anything about Hollister or his behavior worried her." Trent nodded at Simon. "Anything new on your end?"

"He registered at a hotel in Black Canyon, Texas, twenty miles outside of Hanover."

Bravo's leader blew out a breath. "When did he arrive?"

"Last night. He was in the area when Dad was shot, Trent."

"Circumstantial," Cade murmured.

"Suspicious," Simon countered. "He's from Tuscaloosa, not Texas, and he's in the middle of training at PSI. What reason could he have for being in that neck of the woods at the time that my father was shot? And by the way, he and Lyons were competitive shooters and served in the Army. Hollister has the means, motive, and opportunity."

"Still no proof of his guilt."

"We'll find him and get the truth from him," Liam said.

Trent pointed at Cade.

"My findings confirmed Simon's info. Hollister checked into the hotel last night. A scan of security feeds confirms his identity. He arrived with two bags. One looks like a rifle case, the other a duffel bag. Hollister left early this morning, rifle case over his shoulder. He hasn't returned to the hotel from what I've seen. He hasn't checked out."

"Doesn't mean he's still in the area. Nothing new on Lyons' background," Trent said. "He grew up down the street from Hollister. They've been close friends since they were kids. Liam?"

"Zip on the money trail. Hopefully, Trace's wife, Bridget will find out where the money originated from, but that's a task beyond my computer abilities to track."

"All right. We have a few threads to tug and see what unravels. Right now, it's time to change gears. Simon, we'll work in shifts to guard your father while he's in the hospital. When he's released, where is the best place for him to recuperate?"

"Home. My folks own a cattle ranch. They have 500 acres and 20 ranch hands. The area immediately surrounding the ranch is flat, making it easy to see anyone who approaches during daylight hours."

"Lighting around the house?"

"Excellent. The security system is top of the line from Fortress. Motion sensors, cameras, the works."

"Five hundred acres is impossible to secure," Liam said.

"I can't ship him to Ft. Knox and he'll refuse to go anywhere but the ranch. Dad won't be able to work for a while, but he can oversee activities and give directions from inside the house." A smile curved his mouth. "Dad rocks at directing operations from behind the scenes."

"We'll have to be vigilant at night. Will the hands patrol the grounds once the sun sets?"

"They love Dad and will do everything possible to help."

"When you have the chance, talk to the foreman. Do your siblings or their families live at the ranch?"

Simon shook his head.

"What do you want to do about their security? Maddox will approve bodyguards for them."

"Tracy is the mayor of Hanover. She has her own security detail assigned to her. They're all experienced cops. Cassie is a district attorney. She's been assigned security until Dad's shooter is behind bars. That leaves James and B.J. I doubt either will accept protection."

"We need satellite images of the house and surrounding acreage." Trent turned to Zoe. "While we study the maps and images, talk to Wendy. Let's find out what she knows about Hollister."

Zoe walked to the back of the jet. She didn't want Wendy to know she was with Simon and the others. If the hairdresser suspected, she wouldn't feel free to talk.

She glanced through the doorway near the rear of the jet, expecting a restroom. Her eyebrows rose. A bedroom. Zoe turned on the light and closed the door.

Sliding her phone from her pocket, Zoe called Wendy, hoping the other woman would have time to talk to her.

The shop wouldn't close for another hour and the last hour of the day was the busiest.

A moment later, a female voice answered, "This is Wendy."

Thank goodness. Maybe she could help Simon and the others. "Wendy, this is Zoe."

A gasp. "How are you?"

"I've been better."

"Me, too."

"Are you okay?"

"How can I be? Someone murdered Macy." Her voice thickened. "Why would anyone do that? Macy was a good person. She didn't deserve what happened to her."

"You're right. She didn't. I've been thinking about that and Isaac's death."

"Hard not to. You should be careful."

"Why?"

"You were a few feet away when Macy was attacked. It could have been you."

A truth she wasn't likely to forget. "I know."

"People around town are saying that Simon showing up so fast when Macy was attacked was really convenient."

Zoe frowned. "What are you saying, Wendy?"

"Be careful. What if they're right? What if Simon killed Macy?"

Fury bubbled in her blood. "No way."

"You're kind of biased, you know."

Definitely. "How is Chris handling Isaac's death?"

A soft snort. "I wouldn't know."

"You haven't seen him?"

"Not for two days."

"Did you talk to him?"

"All my calls go to voice mail. He ain't answering texts, either."

"Did you go to PSI?"

"Sure. Got tired of him ducking my calls. I went yesterday afternoon after he stood me up for our date. He was gone, Zoe. Poof! Like he'd never been there at all. It's not like him to disappear like that. I talked to his friends and they don't know where he is, either."

"Maybe he needs time alone to process the loss of his best friend and Macy."

"Or maybe he got into it with Simon and paid the price for it."

"Simon was with me during the time the police estimate Isaac was killed."

"I just know what I know." Wendy's tone came across as defensive.

"Is it possible Chris ran?"

"Why would he do that? He ain't afraid of nobody, including your boyfriend."

"Simon isn't on a crime spree although someone is. Maybe Chris knew something and that's why he ran."

"Are you accusing him of killing Isaac and Macy?"

"Of course not. But it's possible he was afraid for his life." Zoe doubted that was the truth, but the scenario was a possibility, no matter how slim the chance.

"Maybe. I don't know if it means anything, but Chris and Isaac had dinner with a friend a couple weeks ago. Both of them were upset after that dinner and started talking a lot of trash."

Zoe frowned. "About what?"

"Your man and Liam and their friends."

"What did they say?"

"Stuff about how they were responsible for the incarceration of a good man. They were careful, you know? They didn't say much. I just overheard a few remarks."

Right. In other words, Wendy eavesdropped on their conversation. "Did they mention the name of the friend they met for dinner?"

"Why should I tell you? You'll just blab it to your boyfriend."

"Wendy, this man upset Chris and Isaac. Isaac's dead and Chris is missing. This man might be dangerous. You said Chris doesn't ignore you or your calls. Something is wrong. Don't you want to help him?"

A soft sigh. "I might be making a huge mistake here, but I guess I can apologize to Chris and get him to forgive me if I'm wrong."

"You aren't wrong to help him, Wendy. What was the name Chris and Isaac mentioned?"

"Well, I didn't get a first name, but the last name is Barone."

CHAPTER TWENTY

Simon glanced over his shoulder again for the tenth time in the past five minutes to see if Zoe had finished the phone call with Wendy. Still nothing. He waited a few more minutes. When she didn't return to the main cabin, he pushed back from the table and, ignoring smirks and knowing glances from his teammates, walked toward the bedroom to find out what was keeping her.

While his teammates studied the satellite images of his family's ranch and debated the best positioning of the hands, he walked into the room in time to hear Zoe tell Wendy to be careful.

Her voice and body language put him on alert. "Shift the call to speaker," he murmured.

A second later, Wendy's voice came through the speaker. "I don't understand. Why should I be worried?"

Simon walked into the room and laid his hand on Zoe's shoulder as she answered Wendy's question.

"Taking precautions seems like a smart move. Have you noticed anyone hanging around the shop or your house the past few days?"

A soft gasp. "How did you know a man's been watching me?"

Not good. "Wendy, it's Simon. How long ago did you notice someone watching you?"

"The day before Macy was killed. I didn't know I was on speaker, Zoe." Her tone made clear her displeasure.

"You weren't until a few seconds ago." Simon sat beside Zoe. "What does this man look like?"

"Brown hair, maybe six feet. He looks strong."

"Did you see distinguishing characteristics or the color of his eyes?"

"Are you crazy? I avoided him as much as I could."

"Did you call the police and report him?"

"Chris told me to call him if anybody bothered or scared me. I've been trying to reach him for two days. Now, he's missing."

"Do you have vacation days available?"

"I'm scheduled to take a week off at the end of the month."

"Ask Maeve if you can take them starting tomorrow. Do you have a place you can go that's populated but not a location someone would automatically look for you?"

"You're scaring me, Simon."

"I'm trying to keep you alive. You could be a target, Wendy."

"What should I do?"

"As soon as you finish work today, get in your car and drive to your destination. Don't go home to pack. Do you have cash on you?"

"A little. I have debit and credit cards with me."

"Don't use them. As soon as you leave work, drive to PSI. I'll have one of the instructors meet you with cash to tide you over. You can settle up with him when you return to town."

"I'm going into hiding?" Wendy's voice rose to a squeak. "But I didn't do anything wrong."

"If the man concludes that you know too much, you become a liability."

"I'm afraid to go off by myself. What if the man who killed Macy and Isaac comes after me, too? I don't have a gun or anything. How can I defend myself against a killer?"

"Go to PSI. I'll make a few calls. When you leave Maeve's salon, act as though you're driving to PSI to find Chris. Lock your doors as soon as you get in the car. Don't stop for anything or anyone until you reach PSI's front gates."

"All right. But what do I tell Maeve? I can't afford to lose my job."

"Let me talk to her. I'll explain everything."

After a few thumps and muffled conversations, Maeve's voice came through the speaker. "Simon, Wendy said you needed to talk to me. What's going on?"

Well aware Maeve was an incorrigible gossip, he told the salon owner as little as possible while still conveying the urgency of his request. He'd heard enough of Wendy's conversation with Zoe to know the hairdresser was in danger from the person who killed Macy and Isaac. Whether the killer was Hollister was another question. For her sake, Simon hoped not. The woman would be devastated to learn the man she'd been dating was responsible for two deaths and wanted to make her the third. "It's safer for Wendy, you, and your customers if you send her on vacation early. I know this puts you in a lurch, but I believe this is best for her."

"I trust your judgment. I'll figure out the scheduling. One of the other girls is begging for extra hours to pay for a home remodeling project with that cute Mason Kincaid. I'll ask her to fill in."

"Thanks, Maeve. You're the best."

Laughter spilled from the speaker. "You're a sweet talker, Simon. I'd better get back to work."

Simon handed the phone to Zoe and pulled out his own. He called Josh. "I need a favor."

"Name it."

"Wendy Oberman will arrive at PSI in an hour. Someone's been following her for the past few days. She's afraid."

"She has good reason to be."

"I convinced her to go on vacation and skip the trip home to pack. She needs cash. Wendy's afraid to leave town by herself. What do you think about sending Rayne Weatherly with her?" Rayne was a refugee of the Chicago PD and was on the fast track to becoming an operative. She'd distinguished herself in every class and worked harder than most of their trainees. Maddox was keeping tabs on her progress.

"She's a perfect choice of bodyguard for Wendy. Does Wendy have a place to go?"

"She says she does, but I don't know if the place she chose is appropriate to go to ground."

"Do you know how long Wendy and Rayne will be gone?"

"Not yet." He glanced at Zoe. "My gut says it won't be long. Hollister checked into a hotel close to my hometown with a rifle case last night."

"Confirmed sighting?"

"Security camera."

"We'll work things out with Wendy and Rayne. Keep me informed, Simon." Josh ended the call.

Simon slid his phone away and wrapped his arm around Zoe's shoulders. "Did Wendy have information we can use?"

"She and other Otter Creek residents think you killed Macy and Isaac."

He stilled. Ironic that the people he'd die to protect believed he was a cold-blooded killer. "Do you?" The possibility that she did made Simon's gut twist into a knot.

"No." No hesitation or doubt in her voice.

His muscles relaxed. "What else did she say?" Knowing Wendy, she'd said quite a few things, most of them off topic.

"She mentioned that Chris and Isaac had a meal with a friend from college. Whatever this friend said upset them."

"Did they mention the friend's name?"

"Wendy was eavesdropping and didn't catch the whole name, just the last. Does the name Barone mean anything to you?"

Ice water flooded Simon's veins. He let out a careful breath. Oh, man. Not what he wanted to hear. "Yeah, unfortunately it does. Is she sure about the name?"

She nodded, concern filling her gaze. "Simon, what is it?"

"Trouble." He stood and held out his hand. "Come on. We need to tell the others what you learned and start doing some research. We have to find out the name of the friend and where he is now." And if he was the one pulling the strings. Was Matteo Barone behind everything happening in Otter Creek?

Simon led her to the conference table where his teammates waited. They glanced up as he and Zoe approached.

"Did Wendy give us anything to work with?" Trent asked.

Simon seated Zoe before dropping into the chair beside her. "Two things. One, the town thinks I'm a stone-cold killer."

Matt rolled his eyes. "Nice."

"Unsurprising given what little they know about what we do for a living. What else?" Trent prompted.

"Wendy overheard a conversation between Hollister and Lyons. The two men ate dinner with a friend from college two weeks ago. Whatever they discussed upset the trainees. That conversation prompted them to trash me and

Liam from that point on. That's also about the time their arrogance and belligerence skyrocketed."

Liam's eyebrows rose. "Why did they zero in on us?"

"The friend's last name is Barone."

The sniper straightened in his chair, his expression grim. "She didn't hear a first name?"

"I asked her that question," Zoe said. "She's positive about the last name. Nothing on the first."

"If this friend went to college with Lyons and Hollister, he's about 28 years old." His gaze locked with Simon's. "Too old to be Matteo if he escaped prison."

"We would have been notified. Zane's keeping track of him."

Cade snorted. "Stranger things have happened."

"Must be a family member," Trent said.

"The name's not totally uncommon," Matt reminded them. "We shouldn't assume it's the same Barone family."

"Why else would this Barone be after me and Liam?" Simon shook his head. "No, it's Matteo's family."

"We need to know if Matteo is directing events from prison," Trent said.

Liam shoved back from the table. "I have to call Piper."

"Joe and Sam should know what's going on so they'll be prepared. I'll call Josh to alert Durango. Piper will be guarded at all times, Liam. That's why we requested another team. Shadow is one of the best teams at Fortress."

He grimaced. "I know. I trust Shadow and Durango to protect her. I only wish I was there to protect my wife and child. They're my responsibility." Liam stalked toward the back bedroom and shut the door.

Simon dragged a hand down his face, guilt eating at him. "I should have insisted that Liam stay home."

"Piper will be pregnant for another seven months," Matt pointed out. "This won't be the last time we're deployed while she's carrying their child."

"That doesn't make me feel better about being the reason he's away from Piper this time. This should be a time of celebration, not worry."

"That's not on you, Simon. If this is related to Matteo's family, they're to blame. Besides, if we weren't going to Texas, we would have been deployed soon. Liam still would have been away from Piper."

Yeah, he got the logic. Irrational or not, he still felt guilty.

"Are you allowed to tell me what this is about?" Zoe asked. "I don't want to be left in the dark, not with so much at stake."

"Did Piper tell you about what happened when she and Liam went to her home in Alabama?" Simon asked.

"I know her uncle was sick and he requested that she come home to take over the gaming company. She mentioned there was some trouble while they were there."

"There was trouble, all right. Matteo Barone, the father of Piper's ex-boyfriend, tried to have her killed."

She nodded. "She said Liam was injured protecting her."

"That's right. He was."

"Barone. You think this friend from college is from that family?"

"Makes the most sense. It's a stretch to think another clown named Barone would be after me and Liam."

"Liam, I can understand. But why is this guy after you?"

"I was Liam's backup."

"All of us were involved," Trent reminded him. "That makes Bravo a target."

"This is about revenge?"

"That's my best guess."

"But why kill Macy and Isaac?" The color drained from Zoe's face. "You think Chris is to blame? Why would he kill his best friend?"

"We don't know that he did, but Hollister being in Black Canyon at the same time my father is shot isn't a coincidence."

"I'll give you that one, but to kill Isaac?" Zoe shook her head. "I don't believe he'd do that."

"Maybe Lyons wouldn't cooperate in the plan." Yeah, it was a weak link. Simon had a difficult time believing that Hollister would turn on his friend, but even the best of friends could be at each other's throats if they disagreed about something strongly enough.

Zoe looked skeptical.

Trent slid his phone from his pocket and made a call.

A moment later, Zane said, "Murphy."

"It's Trent. You're on speaker with Bravo and Zoe. Do a status check on Matteo Barone."

"Hold." Two minutes passed before he returned. "He's still a guest of the government. What's going on?"

"Hollister and Lyons had a meeting with a friend from college. Last name's Barone. I wanted to confirm Matteo was still behind bars before we move on to other options."

The sound of clicking keys of a keyboard drifted through the speaker. "They attended University of Alabama. Checking alumni with the last name of Barone now." A pause, then, "Five Barones are listed. Two of them are deceased. One had cancer. The other died in a car wreck. That leaves three who are the right age. One of them is a woman."

"You can eliminate her," Zoe said. "Isaac and Chris met with a man."

"That leaves Blake and Garrett Barone. Both of them are around the same age as Hollister and Lyons. Want me to dig into their backgrounds?"

"Not right now," Simon said. "We'll handle the background research and have you assist if we run into a roadblock."

"Good enough."

"Did Bridget trace the money Hollister received?" Trent asked.

"The same Cayman Islands account that dispersed money to Lyons also transferred money to Wendy Oberman's account. She drew out the money in cash every month, but her spending habits never changed."

"And from there?"

"Bridget finally traced the money to the Barone family trust. I confirmed her findings five minutes ago."

"Do you know who has access to the fund?" Simon asked.

"I'll get started on it soon. I have tasks with a higher priority in front of your request."

"As soon as you can, then. Thanks, Zane."

"No problem. Report to the boss. He'll want to know the latest."

"Copy that." He ended the call and looked at Trent in silent inquiry.

Trent motioned for Simon to handle the call.

Seconds later, Brent Maddox's deep voice came through the speaker. "Yeah, Maddox."

"It's Simon. You're on speaker with Bravo and Zoe."

"Sit rep."

Simon summarized the new information they had gathered, including the financial link to the Barone trust. "Zane's looking into who has access to the trust funds."

Maddox growled. "I thought we were finished with Barone and his crazy family. Even though Barone is behind bars and his organization disbanded, that doesn't preclude his family members from plotting revenge against the men responsible for the patriarch's incarceration. Let me know if Bravo needs backup. The Texas unit's mission is wrapping up and they should be available soon. Zoe?"

She jerked. "Yes, sir?"

"How do you feel?"

"Better than yesterday."

"Good. I handpicked your installation guys. They're the best technicians we have. Your alarm system won't be online for a couple of days. The technicians will watch over your property until your home is secured."

"Thanks for taking care of the details. When should I expect a bill?"

"Focus on healing and being there for Simon and his family. We'll settle up later. Simon, what's the latest on your father?"

"At last check, he was still in surgery. I'll text B.J. in a few minutes."

"Keep me updated."

"Yes, sir."

"Trent, Nico reported that Bravo's wives are fine. He's guarding Grace."

Trent's face showed his relief. "Excellent. Thanks." After the call ended, he said, "We have two hours before we land. Back to work."

"Simon, can I help with anything?" Zoe asked.

He turned to Trent. "With your permission, I'll turn her loose on the background information for Blake and Garrett Barone while we work on the security arrangements for my parents."

At Trent's slight nod, Simon retrieved his computer and logged Zoe in. "Find out what you can about the Barones." He tapped the secured Internet browser Fortress employees used to do research on the Net.

"I'll save what I discover in two files."

"Perfect." He brushed his mouth over hers. "Thanks for the assist."

She smiled and turned her attention to the computer.

Simon returned to the conference table and used Liam's computer to project Hanover Medical Center's schematics on the television mounted to the wall. Time to study the layout of the hospital. If they were lucky, Bravo would bag a killer before he struck again.

CHAPTER TWENTY-ONE

Two hours later, the Fortress jet touched down at Hanover International Airport. When the jet taxied to a stop, the Bravo team surged to their feet and retrieved duffel and equipment bags.

Zoe unlatched her safety belt and stood by the time Simon had their bags in hand. Although she offered to carry her own, Simon wouldn't relinquish his hold. She followed him to the door.

Simon paused when he stepped on the first stair and scanned the area, his body blocking hers. She didn't know what he'd expected to see since it was dark outside. Apparently satisfied that all was well, he assisted her down the stairs.

Once they reached the tarmac, Trent, Cade, and Matt formed a wall of protection in front of her, Simon and Liam. She wanted to shake the men. They were more concerned for her safety than their own.

Simon ushered Zoe into the terminal behind Trent. The other four operatives stayed behind with the bags.

In short order, the rental papers were signed and the keys for the SUVs Zane had reserved were handed over.

Liam and Simon loaded their bags and Zoe's into the back of one SUV while the other operatives went to the second vehicle.

After placing Zoe in the shotgun seat, Simon slid behind the steering wheel and cranked the engine. He drove quickly from the lot, leading Trent's SUV onto the interstate.

"How far to Hanover Medical?" Zoe asked.

"Fifteen minutes."

Fifteen minutes too long from the sound of Simon's voice. She didn't blame him. If her father had been shot, she would have been anxious to be at his side, too.

Although the drive was uneventful, Zoe couldn't help but breathe a sigh of relief when they walked into the hospital unscathed. Having a target on her back gave her the creeps. She didn't know how Simon dealt with that all the time.

He bypassed the information desk and headed straight for the elevator. After a short ride to the sixth floor, he strode to the ICU nurse's station and gave them his name.

Two minutes later, a man who was obviously one of his brothers entered the hall and gripped him in a one-armed hug. After a soft conversation, Simon gave a short nod and held out his hand to Zoe.

She slid her hand into his. The brother's eyes lit with speculation.

Simon said, "B.J., this is Zoe Lockhart."

The man who resembled Simon smiled at her. "Zoe, I didn't think I'd ever have a chance to meet you."

Simon scowled. "Knock it off, bro."

B.J. clapped him on the shoulder. "I'm glad you finally grew a spine. She's everything you said and more."

Zoe blinked. Interesting comment. Amusement zinged through her when she noticed Simon's flushed face.

Simon's brother inclined his head to the room behind him. "Dad's still out of it, but Mom's with him. She'll be thrilled to see you and meet your friends." A quick grin curved his mouth. "Especially Zoe."

Simon pointed at him. "Zip it."

B.J. chuckled and waved them into the room while he stepped to the nurse's desk and struck up a conversation with the nurse.

With Zoe's hand clasped in his, Simon led her into the room. An older woman with beautiful salt-and-pepper hair sat at the bedside of a man who looked like an older version of Simon.

Wow. Simon Murray would grow more handsome as he matured. And his mother? Zoe could only hope to look as good when she was Mrs. Murray's age.

His mother glanced up at their entrance and stood, tears forming in her eyes. "Simon. I'm so glad you were able to come."

He released Zoe's hand and wrapped his arms around his mother. "I wouldn't be anywhere else." Simon eased away from his mother after a moment and drew Zoe to his side. "Mom, this is Zoe Lockhart. Zoe, my mother, Lisa."

Lisa's eyes widened in surprise. "I'm glad to meet you at last. Simon has talked about you since he moved to Otter Creek."

The corners of Zoe's mouth edged up. Simon had been her primary topic of conversation with her parents from the moment he'd blown into town. "I'm glad to meet you, too. I wish it was under better circumstances."

"Please, sit for a few minutes." Lisa gestured to the two chairs at her husband's bedside. "I don't know how long the nurse will allow you to stay. I have a feeling they're making exceptions because B.J. is one of the doctors on staff."

Simon motioned for Zoe to take one of the seats although he remained standing, his gaze locked on his father. "How is Dad?"

"Sleeping off the anesthetic. B.J. said Don could be out of it for a while."

"What does his doctor say his chances are?"

"As long as there aren't any post-surgery complications, he's optimistic."

"Any chance of paralysis?"

"We won't know until your father is awake." A tear streaked down Lisa's pale face. "I don't know how he'll react if he's paralyzed. Your father has always been in robust health. He'll be devastated if he's confined to a wheelchair."

"Dad taught me the meaning of strength. He'll deal with whatever comes."

She drew in a deep breath. "We both will. You and Zoe must be tired. You should go to the hotel and rest. I'll call if there's a change."

Simon shook his head. "I'm not going anywhere. In fact, the rest of Bravo came with me."

Lisa blinked. "Why did they come? I know it can't be only for moral support."

"Sit, Mom." When she complied, Simon crouched and clasped her hand. "There's a good possibility that Dad's shooting is related to my job. This is my fault."

Her brows knitted. "Why do you think you're to blame?"

"It's a long story. Do the police have leads?"

"I don't know. Tracey might."

"I'll call her in a few minutes. Don't worry about anything. Focus your attention on Dad. My team and I will provide protection for you and Dad."

Zoe's gaze rested on Simon's face. His determination to find the man who shot his father glinted in his eyes. If there was a way to track down the shooter, Simon and the rest of Bravo would find it.

"Protection?" Lisa's voice rose. "Is Don still in danger?"

"It's a precaution," Simon soothed. "No one will hurt him again. You can trust Bravo with his safety."

"But he could still be a target?"

"Yes, ma'am."

"What about your brother and sisters? My grandchildren." Her hand clamped on his. "Simon, the kids."

"Cassie and Tracey are covered as are their families. I'll talk to James and B.J, but I'm not holding my breath that they'll cooperate."

"I want them and their families protected. That's the only way I'll have peace of mind."

"I'll tell them. Until Dad is released from the hospital, one of my team will be inside this room and a second will be outside the door."

She stared. "Will they let you do that? They have a strict policy about the number of people visiting patients."

"They'll accommodate us. We have favors we can cash in to get it approved if necessary. I don't think it will be. The hospital won't want to be responsible for the Murray family safety with rent-a-cops. Besides, Tracey is the mayor. What sane administrator wants to land on her bad list?"

"Hanover has a good police force."

"They're good. They aren't Bravo." He stood. "I'll be back. I'm going to talk with B.J. about the security arrangements."

Simon kissed Zoe before leaving the room.

Nothing like staking a claim in front of his mother. Feeling her cheeks heat, she glanced at Lisa Murray and saw her smiling.

"I'm just relishing the fact that my son is wise enough to recognize and treasure a gift when he sees one."

A gift? "That's kind of you to say."

"It's the truth. You're here with Simon to support him instead of working in your bakery. Your sacrifice isn't lost on me, Zoe, and I know he appreciates your presence."

"I wanted to be with him." She didn't know how much information Simon had told his mother about the deaths in Otter Creek. No need to terrify her further. The woman would soon discover Simon and his friend, Liam, were in danger. "He's an amazing man. I admire him and what he does to protect others."

His mother shifted her gaze to the still form of her sleeping husband. "Simon reminds me of his father."

"Then you're truly blessed."

Simon returned. "All set. The administrators agreed to cooperate with our security arrangements. My team leader is briefing hospital security now."

A low moan drew their attention to the bed. Lisa gripped her husband's hand. "Can you hear me, Don?"

The older man breathed deeper and grimaced. His eyelids fluttered and lifted.

Lisa smiled despite tears trickling down her cheeks. "It's about time you woke up."

Although Don Murray didn't respond verbally, his confusion showed.

"You're in the medical center. You were shot this morning."

The beep from the heart monitor sped up as his eyes widened.

Simon moved into his father's line of vision. "Dad, calm down."

Don's gaze darted to Simon, back to his wife, then returned to Simon.

Zoe frowned. He was trying to tell Simon something but what?

Simon gripped his father's other hand. "I have you and Mom covered. My team is here with me. No one will hurt Mom. You have my word. We're working on security for the rest of the clan. Focus on recovery and let me handle the rest."

Relief slackened his father's face. He gave a slight nod and his eyes slowly closed. His heart rate decreased to a normal pace as he gave in to his body's demand for sleep.

B.J. strode into the room followed by one of the nurses. His brother motioned for Simon to step out of the room. Zoe followed him to the corridor where Liam sat in a chair beside the door.

He glanced up when they walked from the room. "How is he?"

"Disoriented. He was awake for a couple of minutes. Dad's more worried for Mom than he is for himself."

"Did he say what happened?"

"I didn't get a chance to ask him. Once he knew Bravo was protecting them, he went back to sleep. I'll try to get information when he wakes again, but I think our best bet is to find out what the police know. If they won't share the information voluntarily, I'll ask Zane for help."

"The crime scene techs have been on scene for several hours. They should have something by now."

"My sister, Tracey, can pressure the police for information." Simon's ring tone sounded. "Speaking of Tracey, that's her now." He pressed the phone to his ear. The longer he listened to his sister, the darker Simon's expression grew. He ended the call.

"Well?" Liam's eyebrow rose.

"My sister just got off the phone with the detective working Dad's shooting. The surgeon gave him the bullet. Dad was shot with a military-grade .308 round."

Zoe frowned. "What does that mean?"

"My father was shot by a sniper."

CHAPTER TWENTY-TWO

Simon's blood ran hot. Someone had tried to assassinate his father. Was Chris Hollister to blame? He intended to track down the trainee and confront him. Ethan's warning came to mind and Simon shoved the admonition aside. He'd protect his family, no matter the cost to himself. If Hollister had targeted Simon's father and Zoe, the trainee would pay.

"Have the cops located the sniper's hide?" Liam asked.

"Not so far."

"If I knew where your father was gunned down, I could pinpoint the location."

"It would give us an idea how good the shooter is and if Hollister might be our guy."

"We read the background data on him." Zoe edged closer to Simon. "He's a competitive shooter. You said he and Isaac were at the top of the class in marksmanship. Does that mean he's capable of shooting your father?"

"Competitive shooting isn't the same as hitting a live, moving target." Liam rose. "Call Tracey and have her smooth the way for me to look at the scene. The faster we find the hide, the sooner we'll have more information for law enforcement. We need to wrap this up soon, Simon. My family is in danger and we don't know who to look for."

"Agreed." He called his sister. "Do you know the detective working the scene?"

"Sure. Why?"

"Tell him to expect me and my teammate, Liam McCoy, at the crime scene."

"Look, I know you and your friends are super spies and play with guns and knives, but cops aren't well known for allowing civilians to meddle in their cases. I need to convince him that Liam has something to offer. Why should he let your friend on site?"

"Because he's a world-class sniper. You said the police haven't been able to pinpoint where the shooter set up. Liam will find the sniper's hide."

Tracey didn't say anything for a few seconds. "Your friend is a sniper."

"One of the best I've ever seen and worked with."

"What about you?"

His grip tightened around the phone. "I'm not in his class."

"But you can shoot long-range?"

"It's part of my job, Tracey." He'd be a terrible spotter for Liam if he couldn't shoot well.

"Sniper's kill people. You and your friend are like the man who tried to kill our father? How did I not know this? Been hiding things from us, bro?"

Simon's heart sank. "You've known about my job for five years."

"You told me you're in private security. Did you lie?"

"Of course not. Fortress does a lot of things, including train bodyguards. That's also part of my job."

"What about the other part of your job? Are you and your buddies trotting around the globe, killing people?"

"We deal with the worst of the worst, the people you don't want anywhere near your family. I won't apologize for doing my part to keep the world safe. Now, will you call the detective and tell him to expect us or should I do it myself?"

"You'll do this with or without my approval, won't you?"

"To protect Dad and Mom and the rest of you? Absolutely. We generally have good working relationships with law enforcement. If you're worried about your reputation taking a hit because one of your family members works in black ops, don't be. I won't embarrass you or come off as half-cocked and looking for trouble." He scowled. "Or worse, as a vet with a roaring case of PTSD with an itchy trigger finger. I'm not a danger to the public, just terrorists."

A soft gasp. "I didn't mean it like that, Simon."

"Yeah, you did." Simon wrestled down the disappointment and hurt. He never considered that his sister would view him as most of the public saw him. The public got a pass since they didn't know him. Tracey did. Or at least he'd thought she did. Guess he was wrong. "Will you give me the information or not, sis?"

Another short pause, then she rattled off the detective's name and phone number and the location of the shooting. "I'll call him and arrange everything. I'm sorry, bro."

Temper still spiking, he ended the call without replying. He slid his phone away. "Got the information. Dad was shot in our south pasture. I'll help you pinpoint the shooter's location." It would give him a chance to walk off some of the mad burning through him. He needed to do something physical and this would satisfy his need to assist in finding his father's shooter.

"I can work GPS," Liam said, his tone mild.

"I'm going." Waiting on the sidelines would drive him crazy. It's why he wouldn't have been happy as a military officer. After rising through the ranks too far, you rode a desk. Simon hadn't re-upped when he'd realized he was slowing down and his superiors were thinking of assigning him to push piles of paper across a desk or work behind a computer.

War was a young man's game, though, and Simon had seen more than his fair share of action over the years. He'd received an invitation to interview at Fortress a month after he returned stateside. He'd picked up the phone immediately and agreed to drive to Nashville to talk to Maddox. Accepting the job offer to work with a black ops team was a dream come true. Bravo was as much his family as his own flesh and blood.

His hand clenched. At least, his teammates understood the need to protect innocents. He and his team didn't glory in violence, but they used the skills the military taught them to continue protecting the vulnerable.

"What about Zoe?"

"I'll go with you," she said.

Simon hesitated. He didn't want her out in the open more than necessary. "It's a pasture. Wide open spaces with very little cover if trouble develops. You'll be vulnerable to attack."

"So will you whether I'm with you or not. Do you think the shooter is still in the same place, waiting to pick off the next family member who happens to wander by?"

He understood her need to do more than sit at his father's bedside. He refused to leave her at the hotel alone while he traipsed around the south pasture and up into the hills close by where he suspected the shooter had lain in wait. His teammates would be on guard around his father. "Probably not," he admitted, reluctant though he was to tell her the truth. Lying to her wasn't an option. He'd find a way to keep her safe. The alternative was unthinkable.

"I want to go with you. I'd love to see your family's ranch."

Simon glanced at Liam. His friend's eyes were lit with amusement. Yeah, he'd be laughing too if a confirmed bachelor with a reputation for being a hard nose had this much difficulty saying no to his woman. And she was his woman. Simon had claimed her and he wouldn't back out now, no matter the circumstances.

He blew out a breath. "All right. But you'll do everything I tell you to do without question, Zoe. If I tell you to drop, you hit the ground. Understood?"

Her lips edged upward as she saluted. "Yes, sir."

He tugged her into his arms and breathed in the familiar apple scent of her shampoo. "Brat." He reveled in his right to hold her in his arms. Too bad he didn't have the luxury of holding her for longer than a minute or two. He'd remedy that tonight. If nothing interfered, he'd set everything aside for a few minutes and indulge his driving need to hold her.

B.J. returned to the corridor. "Did Dad know who did this to him?"

"He was shot by a high-powered rifle. He won't know who pulled the trigger." But Simon would find out the shooter's identity if it was the last thing he did and he'd run this coward to ground. If the creep was lucky, he'd see the inside of a jail cell. The jury was still out on what Simon would do when that time came. "Is Dad all right?"

"He's resting peacefully for now. What stirred him up?"

"Hearing why he was in the hospital. He was more worried about Mom than himself."

"Typical." His brother's voice came out husky. "I know you need information to start your search, but give him a few hours to rest. His body has been through a serious trauma. We have to give him time to recover before you demand more answers."

Simon's cheeks burned. Did his other two siblings think the worst of him, too? "I didn't demand answers this time. I asked if he knew who shot him. He didn't."

"You can't badger him, Simon. Dad can't take it right now."

"I'm not an idiot. I have to leave for a while."

His brother scowled. "You're deploying now? Dad isn't out of the woods yet. What if something happens and we need you?"

Understanding punched through Simon's irritation. His brother was afraid and doing his best to hide it from Simon with a gruff attitude. "I'm taking Liam to the pasture where Dad was shot." Simon moved closer to his brother and dropped his voice to a murmur. "Liam is a sniper. If anyone can find the shooter's position, it's him."

"What good will that do?"

"The shooter will have left behind evidence of his presence. If we're lucky, the evidence will point to the shooter's identity." Doubtful, but every piece of evidence would help build a case against the culprit when he was caught.

"I see." B.J. turned and shook Liam's hand. "Thanks for helping Hanover's finest. We have a SWAT team. However, according to Simon, they aren't anywhere near the caliber of Bravo. They're just good old boys who are decent shots with rifles." He turned back to Simon. "I know you wouldn't leave without guards in place. Who's staying here with Mom and Dad?"

"Matt, our medic, Trent, and Cade. If anything happens, they'll protect Mom and Dad with their lives. You can trust them."

"Do what you have to do. I'll let you know if something comes up." He laid a hand on Simon's shoulder. "I'm sorry. I didn't intend to insult you. I overreacted because I'm worried about Dad."

"So am I." He shrugged his brother's hand off his shoulder and walked down the hall to call Trent and request Cade and Matt replace him and Liam on guard duty.

A minute later, he ended the call and held out his hand to Zoe. When she joined him, Simon glanced at Liam. "We'll meet you at the ER entrance." Ignoring his brother, he pressed his hand to Zoe's lower back and guided her to the elevator.

After the doors closed, enclosing them in the car, Zoe wrapped her arms around his waist. "Are you okay?"

"I will be."

"Your brother and sister hurt you."

"Yeah, they did. I didn't know my siblings thought I was a loose cannon about to explode or an unfeeling lout more interested in himself than his family."

She tightened her grip. "Now they know better."

True. Still, he couldn't help but feel they should have known the truth without him telling them. Did they think he enjoyed the ugly, dirty aspects of his job? He didn't, but someone had to step up and help those who couldn't help themselves escape dangerous situations out of their control. Simon had volunteered because he had the skills and the burning desire to protect. What he didn't have was an inclination to follow strict law enforcement rules which was the only other place he could use his military training.

He glanced down at her, dreading her answer to his next question. What if he'd miscalculated the strength of her feelings for him? He could lose her in the next minute. The possibility sent an arrow of pain straight to his heart. "Are you sure you want to be in a relationship with me, Zoe? This won't be the last time I'm viewed as a killer for hire."

"I'm not giving you up, buddy. I waited for months, hoping you would notice me and ask me out. Now that you have, I intend to enjoy every minute I'm privileged to be with you."

Thank goodness. Simon couldn't help himself. He bent his head and kissed her, hard and fast. A moment later, the car stopped at the first floor and the doors slid open. Automatically, Simon stepped in front of her until he was sure no danger lurked in the corridor or waiting area directly across from the elevator. He reached back and clasped her hand to lead her into the waiting area. He headed for Trent who stood near the corner of the room.

"Maddox called," Trent said. "Zane's picking up increased chatter on the Internet."

Simon's stomach knotted. "Why didn't Z call me?"

"You had just gone in to see your father. He didn't want to interrupt that time."

"What did he find out?"

"At least one contract killer is hunting for you and Liam."

CHAPTER TWENTY-THREE

Simon stiffened. A contract killer meant a professional, one who wouldn't hesitate to use anyone and anything to get to Simon. That included targeting the beautiful woman standing strong by his side. Then the words Trent had used registered. At least one contract killer. More than one shooter could be gunning for him and Liam.

He glanced down at Zoe's beloved face. Regret and guilt surged to the forefront. She was in the line of fire because of him. Simon should send her home to Otter Creek. Inside, he rebelled at handing her over to Shadow and Durango. Under ordinary circumstances, he wouldn't even consider the move. This information, though, proved his presence endangered Zoe rather than provided protection and safety. Being with him could get her killed. He couldn't lose her.

Zoe looked up at him, defiance in her eyes. "No."

He blinked, brows beetling. "No?"

"You're not sending me home. I'm exactly where I should be. At your side."

"I'm a target, Zoe. That puts you in more danger than I realized."

"Do you want to trust my safety to someone else?"

Everything in him rejected that option. "That would be the safest option."

"Not from my perspective. I'm staying. Besides, I can't open the bakery until the crime scene cleaners do their work and Mason does his. I figure I'll have to be closed for the rest of the week."

"Don't you want to go to Macy's funeral?" Trent asked.

"Her parents are transporting her body back to Illinois tomorrow. They don't want a service in Otter Creek. They told me not to come to her funeral. I think they blame me for her death."

Simon scowled. "Why? You didn't hurt her."

"If they talked to Chris before he disappeared, then they know Isaac blamed me. Maybe they believe Isaac had grounds for his statement."

"They're wrong." Trent's voice was flat.

Liam walked into the waiting room. His eyebrow raised as he approached the small group. "What's up?"

"Someone thinks we're worth killing." Simon coasted his hand up and down Zoe's back, offering her silent support and comfort.

A snort. "That's nothing new."

"This time, someone put money where his mouth is by offering a bounty for our deaths."

Liam stilled. "How much?"

"One million each." The corners of Trent's mouth lifted. "Apparently, you aren't worth much."

"Do Josh and Nico know?"

"Not yet. I just received word from Maddox five minutes ago about the contracts."

"I'll call them on the way to the Murray farm. They need to beef up security around Piper."

A nod from their team leader. "You better get going. Daylight will fade in the next two hours. You'll need every minute to find the shooter's location."

He faced Simon. "We'll take care of things here. Keep your head in the game. A mistake out there will have deadly consequences."

"Yes, sir."

Twenty minutes later, Simon parked near the knot of police cruisers and a crime scene van in the ranch's south pasture. Being out here was bittersweet. He loved the ranch and missed it like crazy while he was gone. Standing in this beloved place in the wake of his father's shooting muted his joy at being home. The violence he dealt with on missions shouldn't taint his sanctuary.

He motioned for Zoe to remain in the SUV while he and Liam scanned the area. Standing out in the open made them easy targets for a shooter. Simon didn't see any reason to enlighten his girl to the fact that he and Liam were using themselves as bait to draw out the shooter instead of waiting for him to take aim at her.

One of the policemen separated himself from a small group standing a short distance away and walked toward Simon and Liam. He held out his hand to Simon. "You have to be Don's son. You look just like him. I'm Ray Chisolm, the detective assigned to your father's case."

The detective, in his early forties, had a firm grip. "Simon Murray. This is Liam. The woman in the SUV is Zoe Lockhart. She's with me."

"I understand from the chief of police that one of you is a military-trained sniper."

"That would be me," Liam said. "I can help you pinpoint the shooter's position when he shot Mr. Murray."

"We could use the help," the detective admitted. "One of the department sharpshooters came out and gave me an estimate on the location. I can't find any indication the shooter was in that area," he said, frustration evident in his voice.

"Do you have the coordinates?"

Chisolm rattled them off. "I need a location before the rain hits at midnight."

"I'll do what I can to help." Liam eyed him. "I'll need to utilize my sniper rifle. I'd rather not be shot by your men."

"I'll inform the others." He activated his radio and passed along the information to the officers working the scene and searching the hillside for signs of the shooter. Once he'd received acknowledgments of his order to stand down and allow Liam to do his work, Chisolm turned back to Simon and Liam. "Okay?"

With a nod, Liam strode to the back of the SUV and lifted the hatchback. A moment later, Zoe joined the men.

Simon glanced down at her feet. He should have thought to get her a pair of boots. She wouldn't have a problem traversing the pasture in her running shoes. The hills around the farm would be more of a challenge. Tactical boots would have been handy.

"Ms. Lockhart can stay with me while you and your friend tromp through the hillside," Chisolm offered.

Flicking a glance at him, Simon shook his head. "She stays with me."

"You know the area around here is rugged."

"Zoe will be fine." He'd make sure she was. What he wouldn't do was let somcone he didn't trust implicitly protect the woman who was slowly stealing his heart.

The detective looked skeptical, but didn't argue further with him.

Liam returned with a pack on his back and rifle in his hand. He also carried Simon's pack. "What time was the shooting?" he asked Chisolm.

"Between 10:45 and 11:00 this morning."

"Simon, I need to know where the bullet hit your father for my calculations."

He sent a text to B.J. The reply came a moment later. Simon showed the text to his partner.

The operative nodded, pulled out his phone, and walked a short distance away.

"What's he doing?" Zoe asked.

"Checking the atmospheric conditions at the time of the shooting. We need to know the wind speed and direction to come up with an accurate guess."

"Does your friend have a kill book?" Chisolm asked.

Simon's eyes narrowed. "He keeps a record to improve the next shot he has to take to protect innocent lives. He might even be called on to save your life one day, Chisolm."

The detective held up his hand. "No offense intended. I'm curious. I've never met a sniper."

Relaxing, Simon said, "He's one of the best in the business. I've worked with two others in his class. Their skills are legendary in the military. There's no one I would rather have protecting my back than Liam, though."

"I understand you have friends who came to Hanover with you."

"My teammates," he clarified. "We work for Fortress Security."

Chisolm stilled. "The black ops group."

"You've heard of us."

"Who hasn't?" he muttered. Uneasiness filled his eyes as he glanced from Simon to Liam and back.

"Did you and your buddies decide if we're the good guys or the bad guys?"

"Opinions are evenly split. You're mercenaries."

"Operatives. We specialize in hostage retrieval and counterterrorism."

"What's your job?"

"I train bodyguards for PSI, the bodyguard training school for Fortress, and I'm assigned to a black ops unit where I serve as Liam's spotter." Among other tasks the good detective wouldn't approve of.

A muscle in Chisolm's jaw ticked. "You must be a good shot."

"Are you accusing me of shooting my father?" Although his tone was mild, Simon's emotions were volatile. "Let me set your mind at ease, Detective Chisolm. I was in Otter Creek, Tennessee at the time my father was shot. I have dozens of witnesses who will vouch for my whereabouts, one of whom is Zoe."

The detective shifted his attention to Zoe. "Ma'am?"

"He hasn't left my side in days, Detective." She wrapped her arm around Simon's waist and leaned into him, giving Simon much needed support. The detective took in their body language without comment, his expression blank.

Liam walked toward them. "Got it. Ready?" he asked Simon.

"Almost." Simon turned toward the detective. "Do you have a business card?"

The other man fished one from his pocket.

He glanced at the number and committed it to memory, then flipped it over and scribbled his own number on the back. "I don't know how long we'll be gone."

"There isn't much cell reception out there."

"I'm aware. I grew up out here, remember? We use sat phones. We won't have a problem. If you leave the area and assign other officers to maintain a perimeter, inform them of our presence. I'd prefer not to be shot in front of my girl."

"Like that, is it?"

Simon smiled for the first time in minutes. "I know a class act when I see one. I'm not about to let Zoe Lockhart get away."

Her head whipped his direction. Did she think he'd let her go now that he had a real chance with her? How many other women would have tolerated the danger she'd been subjected to at the beginning of a relationship without walking away? He knew now that Zoe Lockhart was strong enough to go the distance with him. They had a shot at a life together. But did she want that as much as he did?

His heart skipped a beat. A life together? Simon drew in a careful breath and faced the truth. He was in love with Zoe. The question was, what was he going to do about it? For her own sake, he should back away and let her go. He wasn't going to. Simon was too far gone over Zoe.

"Earth to Simon," a male voice said.

He glanced at his teammate, scowling. "What?"

"There you are. Nice to know you're paying attention to me and the lady."

"Sorry. What did you say?"

Liam rolled his eyes. "Come on. Let's get moving."

Cheeks hot, Simon clasped Zoe's hand and followed Liam to the edge of the pasture. Zoe didn't comment on his inattention. She was too busy studying the surrounding area, which he should be doing instead of studying her.

"This area is beautiful, Simon. You must miss it."

"I used to dream about the pasture and surrounding hills when I was in some of the worst cesspools in the world."

"You don't anymore?"

"Nope. Now I dream about you."

Her breath caught. "Simon."

He squeezed her hand. "It's the truth."

"We're a matched pair, then, because I dream about you at night, too."

"Perfect. Must mean I don't have any competition."

A choked laugh sounded up ahead. Although it wouldn't do any good, Simon glared at the back of his teammate's head, then focused his attention on the surrounding area. One of his favorite places on the ranch, he'd spent long hours out here. Simon couldn't count the number of times he and his brothers had camped out under the starry sky, told ghost stories, and made themselves sick on S'mores. He loved the rugged landscape where hidden pockets of beauty lurked if you knew where to look. He owed his father for teaching him to see beyond the obvious.

Ten minutes later, Liam stopped to check his phone. He turned toward Simon when he and Zoe caught up to him. "Based on the location of the wound, wind speed, and direction, the shooter set up somewhere in this area." He handed over his phone with a highlighted map of the hillside.

After sending a copy of the image to his own phone, Simon handed Liam's phone back to his partner. "Zoe and I will take the right side, you take the left. Watch your step out here. We have rattlers and rock slides."

"Fantastic," Liam muttered.

They separated and Simon guided Zoe toward the right side of the hill. At first, the hillside rose in a gentle climb. Within two hundred feet, the terrain grew steep.

He turned to Zoe. "The climb will be more difficult from here on out. Walk behind me and hold onto my pack strap. I'll help pull you up the hill."

"I can make it without help."

"You can," he agreed. "You'll make the climb with less slipping and sliding if you hold onto me. Next time we hike, I'm getting you a pair of tactical boots. You'll have better traction. Running shoes are great for running, not for hiking up a steep hillside."

"I'll take you up on the offer. Do they have pink camo boots?" she teased.

With a chuckle, Simon turned his back to her and felt a slight tug on his pack as she wrapped her hand around the strap. "Ready?"

"Let's go. I'm thinking about a steak and baked potato for dinner. The sooner we find the shooter's hide, the faster I get dinner. I'm counting that meal as our next date."

Although he was skeptical that Zoe would actually eat the steak, he appreciated her attempt at levity. As the light faded, Simon grabbed his small flashlight and continued up the hill.

Fifty feet ahead, he noted signs of recent passage. Disturbed earth, bent grass blades, broken bush limbs. He frowned. Whoever came this way hadn't tried to conceal his presence. The depth of the footprints and stride length told him he was looking for a male about six feet weighing in at 230 pounds or so.

Simon followed the trail into denser brush. Sweeping the small beam of his flashlight along the ground, he noticed black droplets leading further up the hill.

He knelt and touched one of the droplets. The substance was tacky. Simon sniffed and caught a whiff of iron. Blood.

Simon shifted the flashlight to his left hand and pulled his Sig from the holster at his thigh. "Stay behind me," he murmured to Zoe. He moved further up the brush-covered rise, keeping to the shadows as much as possible.

Ten minutes later, he stopped and listened, senses on alert. He'd heard something, but what? Simon waited, pleased that Zoe didn't ask questions. She remained motionless at his back, close enough that he could shove her to the ground to protect her if necessary and far enough away not to impede his movements.

A low moan drifted on the night breeze. Definitely not an animal. Simon turned off the flashlight, shifted his attention thirty feet to his left, and waited for his eyes to adjust to the starlight. "Don't move until I come back for you," he whispered as he nudged her under the branches of a tree and motioned for her to crouch at the base. She was concealed in shadows and would be overlooked unless someone looked directly at her or she moved and drew someone's attention.

"Be careful."

He cupped her cheek briefly before refocusing on his task. He slipped the small flashlight into a pocket of his cargo pants. With careful steps, Simon shifted into denser cover, breaths slow and steady. This was what he'd trained for. Hunting down the enemy was in his blood and, with Zoe only feet away, Simon had more incentive than ever to get to the bottom of what was going on.

A rustle of leaves to his left drew his attention. Simon paused at the edge of a small clearing. Another restless movement caught his eye and he spotted a prone figure wearing combat boots similar to Simon's. While he watched, the figure inched further up the slope, seeking higher ground.

Weapon raised and ready, Simon edged closer to his quarry. The man crawled into an area of the clearing illuminated by starlight. His jaw clenched and his hand tightened around the grip. "Don't move."

CHAPTER TWENTY-FOUR

The injured man on the ground froze. He turned his head slowly in Simon's direction. "Help me," he pleaded, his voice and breathing ragged. "I've been shot."

"I can see that. You armed, Hollister?"

The trainee shook his head. "They thought I was dead and took my weapons."

Simon's gaze raked over the younger man. "I'll need to confirm that for myself."

Hollister's mouth gaped. "You don't trust me?"

"About as far as I can throw you. Keep your hands exactly where they are or you'll have another bullet wound to add to the two you already have." Simon crossed the remaining ten feet between them and ascertained for himself that Hollister told the truth. Once he was sure the injured man wasn't a threat to Zoe, Simon went back for her and brought her to the clearing.

He slid off his pack and dug out his first aid kit. "What are you doing on my family's ranch, Hollister?"

"I came to help."

"Help who?" Simon handed his flashlight to Zoe and motioned for her to hold the light for him to see Hollister's injuries. He widened the rip in the thigh of the other man's left pant leg and winced at the still-bleeding gunshot wound. A through-and-through. Looked like the same situation in his side as well.

"The Barones."

Simon paused a moment, then dived back into his med kit for QuikClot and compression bandages. He called Liam. "I found Hollister. He's been shot in the side and leg. I could use a hand patching him up until the EMTs get him out of here." He rattled off the GPS coordinates.

"I'm not far from your position. Be there in five."

"Copy." He slid the phone back into his pocket.

Hollister groaned. "Why doesn't my phone work out here?"

"No cell reception. Fortress operatives use sat phones. We work in a lot of places with no cell reception." The trainee gave a hoarse chuckle as Simon examined the side wound and whistled. "You're lucky to be alive. A few more centimeters to the right and you wouldn't be."

"Yeah, lucky me."

"Tell me about the Barones." Simon ripped open a packet of the white powder and dumped it into the wound on Hollister's side. The trainee swore a blue streak until he caught Simon's scowl.

He glanced at Zoe. "Sorry, ma'am."

"The Barones?" Simon prompted as he applied the bandage.

Hollister hissed at the pain of the wound closing, then said, "They want you and McCoy dead."

"Why?"

"They said you made up information to get the old man convicted of stuff he didn't do."

"How do you know about our business with Matteo?"

"They told me and Isaac."

"And you believed them?" He rolled Hollister mostly onto his stomach and dumped another packet of QuikClot into the exit wound. This time, Hollister growled low and harsh, jaws clamped shut. After applying the bandage, Simon tugged down the trainee's shirt and positioned him on his back again. Treatment of the leg wound would have to wait until Liam arrived. Simon was out of QuikClot.

"I thought I could trust them. I went to school with them, sir."

A soft whistle sounded and Liam pushed through the brush into the clearing a few seconds later. He knelt beside the trainee. "You look the worse for wear, soldier."

"Yes, sir."

"I took care of the wound on his side. While you work on his leg, I'll call Chisolm and get some help up here."

"Go. Zoe and I have this."

Simon moved a short distance away and called the detective.

"Chisolm."

"It's Simon. We found a wounded man up here."

"The shooter?"

He glanced back at the man sprawled on the ground with Liam and Zoe working to render aide. "I haven't gotten the whole story out of him, but I don't think so based on his own wounds. His name is Chris Hollister. He's one of our trainees at PSI."

"What's he doing here? Are you sure he didn't shoot your father?"

"I don't know yet, but I'm hoping to find out before the EMTs whisk him off to the hospital. He needs a medevac. Hollister isn't mobile. He has a gunshot wound to the left side of his torso and his left leg. He's lost a lot of blood."

"Is there a place for the chopper to land?"

"Nope. The pilot will have to lower a basket." He gave the detective the coordinates. "Call me with an ETA on that bird."

"Copy that." He ended the call.

Simon knelt beside Zoe at Hollister's side. "Chopper will be here soon."

"We've done as much as we can," Liam said.

"Do you have water?" Hollister asked. "I haven't had anything to drink for hours."

He grabbed a bottle of water from his pack and elevated Hollister's head enough for him to take a few sips. "I'd give you more, but you'll probably be in surgery in the next hour or so. We shouldn't give you too much in case the anesthesia makes you sick. Did you shoot my father?"

"No, sir. I tried to hunt down the shooter and stop him before he took the shot." He grimaced. "I didn't know both of the Barones were here."

"Garrett and Blake?"

A small nod from the trainee. "Isaac and I tried to talk them out of their vendetta. They wouldn't listen."

"Why were the Barones funneling money into Wendy's second account?"

"How do you know about that?"

"Focus," Liam snapped. "You don't have much time before you're out of here and we need answers. My wife's life is at stake."

"We were being paid to find out any information we could about you and Murray."

"For what purpose?"

"We didn't know there was an agenda behind the request. Garrett asked us to keep tabs on you to make sure you and Murray didn't continue the smear campaign against the family. He said he needed information about your activities and the people you cared about to make sure you weren't given the chance to extend Matteo Barone's time in prison or try to set up another family member."

"You've trained with us for three months, Hollister. You've watched us in and out of the classroom, seen us with our families and friends. We don't operate outside of our missions based on personal agendas."

"With all due respect, sir, you and Murray aren't loose-lipped about your private lives. Isaac and I only knew that you were fiercely protective of your wife and Murray was nuts about Ms. Lockhart. We also knew when you were out on missions, but not where you were deployed."

Simon glared at Hollister. "No one knows where we operate except for two people at Fortress. Most of our missions are out of the country. Several are government-sanctioned which means they're classified. In our business, loose lips endanger people's lives. Our families don't know the details of our missions. There's no chance we'd talk to trainees about our missions."

"You tried to find the shooter," Liam said. "What happened when you did?"

Hollister winced. "They spotted me before I saw them. They ambushed me, stripped my weapons, and took off."

Liam snorted. "They didn't check to see if you were dead?"

He shook his head.

"Sloppy."

"Did you know they were targeting my father?" Simon asked.

"I tried to talk them out of it. They threatened to kill Wendy, sir. I had to protect her so I pretended to see reason and promised to keep quiet."

"They would have killed you. You're a loose end."

"They tried hard enough." Disgust rang out in Hollister's raspy voice.

"You should have come to me and Liam. We would have helped you." And maybe a sweet woman and Hollister's friend wouldn't have been murdered, and Zoe and Piper wouldn't have been injured.

Simon's forehead furrowed. If the Barone cousins were behind the attacks on Piper and Zoe, why didn't they kidnap or kill the women? Something must have spooked the killer before he carried out his agenda.

Either that, or this was an elaborate scheme to set up Simon and Liam so they would end up behind bars like Matteo Barone. That would explain the clumsy attempts to frame Simon. If the efforts had been successful, the frame job would have shifted to Liam.

Simon's phone rang. As soon as he answered, Chisolm said, "Ten minutes. You need to give the pilot some kind of signal so he knows exactly where to hover and lower the paramedic with the basket."

"Copy that." He looked at Liam. "Ten minutes. We'll have to signal the pilot."

With a nod, the sniper turned his attention to Hollister. "You and Lyons were to feed the Barones information. Did they kill Lyons and Macy?"

A slight nod. "We met them for dinner a few weeks ago and they tried to recruit us to kill you. We pretended to think about it, then turned them down. We hoped that would be the end of it and the Barones would move on to another plan."

"You tried to handle it yourselves." Simon dragged a hand down his face. Good grief.

"Why didn't you come to us?" Liam asked. "We would have helped you. Macy and Lyons would still be alive if you had talked to us."

"We took bribes to spy on you. You would have kicked us out of the program."

"Kicking you out was one option. Instead of learning the punishment and taking it like a man, you skulked around in the shadows and tried to sneak up on a viper that whipped around and bit you."

Another hard swallow. "Yes, sir."

"Lyons' attitude since nearly the beginning of his training was prompted by the false information, wasn't it?" Simon asked.

A slight nod. "The Barones contacted us two weeks after we arrived at PSI. We believed what they told us. You don't understand, sir. They're practically royalty where we live."

"Matteo tried to kill us and Piper several times, all to continue lining his pockets with money on gun sales. Garrett and Blake lied to you and Lyons."

"I see that now." The trainee glanced at Zoe. "I didn't know they planned to hurt you. And I sure didn't know they would kill Macy." His voice broke on that last word. "Isaac was crazy about her. He lost it when he found out about her death."

"Why did he blame me?"

"The Barones said they were going to scare you, rough you up a little, and set up your boyfriend to take the blame. But Macy was working that morning. She wasn't supposed to be there and the Barones had never seen a picture of either one of you."

"They killed the wrong woman." Simon's gut clenched.

"I didn't know they planned to kill Zoe. I swear. I would have come to you if I'd known."

"But you thought it was okay for them to hurt her to frame Simon?" Liam scowled at Hollister. "Our mission is to protect the innocent. You seem to have forgotten that part of the training."

Abruptly, Zoe stood and moved to the other side of the clearing, her back to the trio of men.

Simon and Liam looked at each other. The sniper gave a slight nod and Simon followed her.

"Sweetheart?" he murmured.

"It's my fault," she whispered.

"None of this is on you."

"I asked Macy to give me a hand because I wanted to spend a few minutes with you before the shop opened. If I hadn't, she would still be alive."

"And you would be in the morgue." Simon turned her to face him. His heart clenched at the sight of her tear-stained cheeks. "I'm sorry that she's dead, but lay the blame for her death at the feet of the ones responsible. The Barone cousins. One or both of them killed your friend. They had a choice to walk away and come at me and Liam directly instead of using the people we love in some sick act of revenge."

Her gaze lifted to his face, eyes wide. "The people you love?"

Rotten timing and the wrong place, but he'd own it. "Didn't you know? I'm falling in love with you, Zoe Lockhart."

CHAPTER TWENTY-FIVE

Zoe stared in wonder at Simon. "What did you say?"

His lips curved. "You heard me. I don't want my feelings to scare you off. If you don't love me, I'll find a way to deal. However, I'm warning you up front that I'll use every skill in my arsenal to change your mind."

Her laughter was soft and husky. She wouldn't expect any less of a man who fought against the odds and won on a regular basis.

"We'll get back to that later. What I'm trying to say is that Macy's death isn't on you." Simon cupped her face between his palms. "Don't let the Barones convince you otherwise. One or both of those clowns killed her to get back at me for my role in the downfall of Matteo Barone."

"That's what the scrawled words on my bedroom wall meant. They killed the wrong woman." How could people she'd never met decide the best way to reach their goal was to kill her?

"So it seems." Simon wrapped his arms around Zoe and held her tight. "We'll track them down and stop them."

"Promise?"

"Count on it. We won't rest until it's done. No one is going to take you from me, and my teammates and I will fight to the death to protect Piper and the baby."

Zoe rose to her tiptoes and brushed her lips over his in a gentle kiss.

"Simon."

He glanced over his shoulder at his teammate.

"Chopper's close."

Simon brushed the moisture from Zoe's cheeks and led her across the clearing. He reached into his pack for a larger, more powerful flashlight.

He flicked on the light and aimed the beam upward. Liam did the same with his flashlight. Two minutes later, the chopper hovered over the clearing. A figure lowered a basket to the ground and followed it down.

"What have we got?" he asked, voice raised to be heard over the helicopter's rotors.

"GSW to the left torso and leg. He's lost a lot of blood."

A quick nod. "Let's get him into the Stokes basket. You friends of his?"

"That's right."

"We're taking him to Hanover Medical Center. You can catch up with him there."

Following the paramedic's directions, they loaded Chris into the basket and another EMT in the helicopter hauled the wounded man into the belly of the machine. When the rope was extended to the ground again, the paramedic hooked his safety belt to the line and was pulled up. A moment later, the helicopter flew away.

"Call Trent." Liam gathered the trash from their medical triage on Chris. "He should be on hand in case the Barone boys find out Hollister survived and decide to snip off another loose end."

Simon grabbed his phone. When he finished the call, he said, "Trent's on his way to meet the chopper. He wasn't happy with Hollister."

"Will Chris be kicked out of PSI?" Zoe asked.

"I don't know. At the very least, he'll be rolled back to the next class. He can't train until his injuries heal and any physical therapy prescribed is completed."

"Maddox could go either way on that decision," Liam said as he stood, the last of the medical trash in his hand. He shoved the garbage into a bright red bag and stashed it in his pack.

"Did you find the sniper's hide?"

"Yeah, right when you called."

Simon glanced at Zoe. "You up for a short hike?"

She didn't want to be left behind or for Simon to be away from the hospital longer than necessary. "Of course. Can we use a flashlight now?"

"No problem." He removed the small flashlight from his cargo pocket and flicked the switch.

Zoe breathed a sigh of relief when the darkness receded far enough to see where to put her feet. To require a second run by the EMTs to get her off the mountain if she sprained an ankle or broke a bone would be embarrassing.

She considered Simon's broad shoulders and muscular arms. Then again, if the injuries weren't too bad, Simon would carry her out himself. While she wouldn't mind a lift if it was necessary, Zoe didn't want to further delay their return to civilization. She looked forward to a hot meal and perhaps a cup of hot tea. It might be summer in Texas, but she was downright chilly at the moment.

Simon wrapped his hand around her free one and followed Liam. Within ten minutes, they stood in front of an outcropping of rocks.

Liam inclined his head toward the stones. "The sniper took position up there. View's good with a clear line of sight. I'm not sure if your father moved at the last second or if the shooter isn't that good. Either way, your father is lucky to be alive."

"What did he leave behind?"

"He didn't police his brass and left behind a couple of cigarette butts as well."

"Probably didn't think the cops would find this place."

"His mistake. Fingerprints and DNA will nail the shooter's hide to the wall."

Satisfaction swept through Zoe. If the police arrested the right man, the physical evidence left behind would help convict him. Maybe Simon would be satisfied to allow the law to exact justice for his father's injury. She and Simon might not have been an official couple for long, but she knew him well enough as a friend to understand he would balance the scales of justice himself if law enforcement couldn't do it themselves.

Simon looked at the rocks and blew out a breath. "I want to see for myself. May I borrow your rifle?"

Without a word, Liam slid the weapon from his shoulder and handed it to Simon.

He clambered up the rocks and lifted the scope to his eye. Within a couple minutes, he climbed down and handed the rifle to his partner. "I'll notify Chisolm."

Simon glanced at Zoe as he pulled out his phone. "We may be up here a while if he wants us to wait until he arrives with the crime scene investigators."

"No problem. Is it safe to sit on one of the nearby rocks?"

"Let me check it out first."

She eyed the fat boulder glowing in the starlight. Right. In this wild, untamed part of the ranch, snakes and who knew what else might lurk in the darkness surrounding the rock. Zoe shuddered and stood where she was while Simon called the detective.

After he slid the phone away, Simon inspected the area around the rock Zoe had indicated. Finally, he said, "It's clear."

Thank goodness. Zoe perched on the rock and settled in to wait for the police to arrive. She listened to Simon and Liam as they reported in to Trent first, and then Maddox. By the time they finished, the lights from the police flashlights were cresting the hill.

Chisolm picked his way along the uneven terrain to stand beside Simon. "Where?" His gaze scoured the rocks.

Using the beam of his flashlight, Simon showed him the place where the sniper had hidden among the rocks and propped his weapon.

The detective motioned for the crime scene techs to see what they could find. He turned back to the two operatives. "The man you found arrived at the medical center a few minutes ago. The doctor is examining him now. Who is this guy?"

"Name's Chris Hollister. He's one of our PSI trainees."

"What's he doing out here?"

"He's AWOL."

His eyes narrowed. "Is he your father's shooter?"

"No."

"You sure this isn't a case of partners in crime turning on each other?"

Zoe's respect for the police detective rose a notch.

"He says not."

Chisolm eyed him for a moment. "Do you believe him?"

"I do."

"Why?"

Simon glanced at Liam. "Your call."

"No choice."

Simon explained about the Barones and his and Liam's roles in the downfall of the Barone empire. After he finished summarizing the events in Otter Creek and repeating the information Chris had given them a few minutes earlier, Chisolm dragged a hand down his face.

"I've heard of the Barone organization. People in law enforcement circles speculated about the group who had brought down Matteo Barone. We all figured it was an interagency taskforce of some kind. Should have known a taskforce wouldn't be able to get the job done. Barone probably had people tucked away in key positions in law enforcement to give him a heads-up about action headed his way. I doubt a taskforce would have been weasel free. How many Fortress people got the job done?"

"Two full teams. About ten operatives."

The detective's mouth gaped. "How many people did you go up against?"

"About forty." Liam's lips curled. "We didn't have time to take a count."

A soft whistle. "Holy cow. And the local cops didn't have anything to say about it? We usually don't cotton to outsiders taking over our operations and snagging credit for a big bust."

"They were persuaded to stay out of it by the feds. The feds were on cleanup and claimed the credit. Operatives who work in the glare of media spotlights don't stay alive long." Simon wrapped his arm around Zoe's shoulders. "I have an excellent reason to stay alive."

"Incredible work, then. I'm amazed no one dropped the Fortress name in all the media interviews." He glanced at his cell phone. "Look, I know you'll want to go back to the hospital to check on your father, Simon. I'll need a statement from all of you about Hollister. I'd like to take care of that when I leave here. I'll swing by the hospital and we'll take care of it tonight. The sooner I get everything down, the better. I need every detail I can get. I'll run the Barones through the system, see what pops. My guess is, though, that they cleared out of the area. These guys seem like the type to hit and run."

Zoe didn't think that was the case and Simon's expression indicated that he disagreed with the detective as well. The Barones had wanted to draw out Simon and Liam to kill them. Why would they leave before the job was done, especially since their targets were in the same place and unable to leave until Mr. Murray was stable?

"You know where to find us," Simon said as he threaded his fingers through Zoe's. "You'll keep us in the loop?"

"What I can tell you, I will."

Which meant he would tell them nothing. Zoe couldn't say she was surprised. The Otter Creek police were closed-mouthed about their cases, too. At home, though, the grapevine was alive and well and more accurate than the police wanted. She'd heard of more than one dressing down by Ethan Blackhawk when an officer let information slip. From what she'd seen over the past year, the police chief was excellent at his job and he demanded the same from his people.

Simon squeezed her hand. "We'd better get moving. We have a long walk ahead of us to the SUV and it will take longer in the dark."

More like it would take Liam and Simon longer with her along. Zoe suspected most of their operations were conducted at night under cover of darkness. The operatives were used to working under these conditions. She would slow them down.

The men flanked her as the trio made their way down the hillside and navigated around brush, rocks, and crevices. She imagined the area was beautiful in the daylight. At night with deep shadows cast by objects in the natural environment, the going was treacherous. Zoe lost count of the number of times Simon and Liam steadied her when her feet slid or she stumbled over an exposed tree root hidden in the darkness.

"The first thing we're doing when we return home is buying those hiking boots," she muttered.

Simon grinned. "Right. Pink camouflage."

Liam gave a huff of laughter. "This I've got to see."

Soon, Simon slid behind the steering wheel of the SUV and drove them toward town. "While we were talking about strategic options on the jet, you researched the Barones. What did you learn?" he asked Zoe.

"Not a lot. We already know both of the men attended UAB with Chris and Isaac, and then enlisted in the Army."

"Both of them served in the Army?"

"Yes."

"What kind of information did you find on their military service?"

She twisted to look at him. "How do you know I found anything?"

"You used the Fortress search tools. We're able to access more information than a casual searcher would find with a traditional search engine."

"This time, your search tool let me down."

"Why do you say that?" Liam asked.

"I didn't find anything about their service record except that the years they served. I couldn't even find out what job they did in the military or the units they were assigned to."

Simon's head whipped her direction. "You found nothing?"

"That's right."

He glanced in the rearview mirror at his partner, his expression grim.

Liam growled.

Alarmed, Zoe looked at the sniper. Raw fury hardened his features. "What is it? What did I miss?"

"There's only one reason you couldn't find anything out about their military service," Simon said. "The Barones were in Special Forces."

CHAPTER TWENTY-SIX

Simon parked near the ER entrance and kept Zoe close as he escorted her inside the medical center, his gaze scouring the darkness, alert for a threat. A sniper possibly having Zoe in his crosshairs at that moment infuriated him. The only thing he could do to protect her and his family was find the clowns threatening them. If the Barone cousins were Special Forces, the level of danger had just risen one thousand percent.

He glanced at his teammate and saw the same mixed feelings brewing in Liam. Dealing with this kind of danger was bad enough on missions and an accepted risk. Their loved ones weren't supposed to be in the line of fire. The Barones had changed that by betraying the ideals instilled during military training. The cousins used their training to harm innocents instead of protect them. If they wanted to come at him and Liam, let them come. Their loved ones should be off the table. But they weren't.

His hands fisted. The Barones had no honor and were the antithesis of everything Special Forces soldiers stood for.

Simon felt sick at heart. He expected to defend himself and his teammates against terrorists, not fellow soldiers, men he would have bled and died to protect on the battlefield. The cousins had betrayed him and other Special Forces soldier with their choices.

He glanced at Zoe. Would she trust him now that she knew who and what he was or paint him with the same brush she did the Barones? Seeing disappointment in him in her eyes or, worse, fear, would destroy him.

Zoe looked at him, an unspoken question in her eyes.

Simon shook his head. This wasn't the time or place. They'd talk at the hotel. First, he wanted to check on his parents. After that, he'd take Zoe to dinner or order room service if she was too tired to eat in a restaurant.

They exited the elevator on the sixth floor where Cade was on watch at the door to Don Murray's room. The EOD man met them a short distance from the room.

"Did you find the traitors?"

The bad-tempered question brought a slight smile to Simon's lips because that was the perfect description for the Barone cousins. "No, but Liam located the sniper's nest. The crime scene team is processing the area now."

"We'll find them, Simon."

Would they find the men before they hurt someone else he loved? As much as he worried about Zoe's safety, he couldn't forget his brothers, sisters, their spouses, and his nieces and nephews were vulnerable. While Zoe had the best protection detail available, his brothers and their families didn't. His sisters had police protective details. His brothers had refused police protection.

Simon walked into his father's room where Matt and his mother sat. Liam remained in the hall with Cade. "How is he?" he asked his teammate.

"Drifting in and out, but resting comfortably. His wakeful periods are coming more frequently and lasting longer, a good sign."

"Has the doctor been by?"

A nod. "Your father's surgery progressed like he anticipated, and Don came through it like a champ."

Simon wrapped his arms around his mother and held her tight. She trembled in his grip. This had to be agonizing for her. She and his father were soul mates. He spoke past the lump in his throat. "What are his chances of a full recovery, Matt?"

"Excellent. Your brother, B.J., confirmed my assessment and that of Don's doctor."

Thank God. He drew his first free breath since he'd received the call from his mother. Simon kissed her cheek. "I need to speak to Matt. We'll be in the hall if you need us."

She stepped out of his hold. "I'll be fine, honey. Do what you need to do."

"Is there anything you need, Mrs. Murray?" Zoe asked.

"It's Lisa, and I'd love a soft drink. Anything is fine."

"I'll be back soon." She followed Simon and Matt. "The vending machine is down the hall to the right. Do any of you want a cold drink?"

"Something with caffeine, please," Cade said.

Matt nodded. "Same for me."

"And me," Liam chimed in.

"Simon?"

"Same. Do you need help?"

She shook her head. "I've got it."

Simon watched her until the corridor curved and he lost sight of her, making him twitchy. If she didn't return soon, he'd track her down.

He angled his body to talk to his teammates and monitor the hallway for Zoe's return. Between him and Liam, they updated their teammates about Hollister and the Barone cousins.

Matt scowled. "We need to track these guys down before they cause more trouble for your family or Zoe."

Cade looked around. "Speaking of Zoe, where is she? I thought she'd be back by now."

Liam frowned. "Maybe the vending machine isn't working and she had to find another one."

Simon's stomach knotted. "I'm going to look for her." He left his teammates to guard his parents and moved swiftly along the corridor Zoe had taken. Before he reached the alcove filled with vending machines, Simon heard her voice.

"You're sure he's all right?" Zoe asked the person on the phone. "Well, that's something at least." Silence, then, "I don't know, Nick. Not for a few days at least. Simon's dad is doing well, though. Yes, I'll tell him. Thanks for calling." She slid her phone into her pocket and gathered the soft drinks in her hands and turned.

Zoe gasped. "Oh, wow. You scared me, Simon. I didn't hear you walk up. You guys should wear bells. You don't make any noise."

His lips curved. "Moving without making noise is necessary for our work. Anything wrong?"

"Nick Santana called to tell me the crime scene cleaners finished the bakery bathroom. He also mentioned someone broke into Mason Kincaid's home."

Simon took the soft drink from her hands. The break-in artist couldn't be the Barones unless they'd split up. Hollister said both the cousins were here in Hanover. Had they shot his father and returned to Otter Creek? If not, who was responsible for the invasion of Mason's place? "Did he take anything?"

"Nothing. Like Macy's place, the drawers were open and the dressers in the master bedroom and guest room had been moved slightly."

"No wholesale destruction?"

"Apparently, that honor is reserved for me."

"Hey." He stopped and turned to face her. "We're working as fast as we can to smoke the Barone cousins out.

As soon as we do and I'm sure Dad's stable, we'll return home and reclaim your life, including opening your bakery." Simon leaned down and brushed her mouth with his. "We'll get to the bottom of this."

"I know." She sighed. "I'm sorry. I don't mean to complain, but we're hitting walls at every turn."

"We're frustrated, too, but making progress. We know the names of the men targeting me and Liam. When we find them, we'll confirm who's funding the bounty."

"Confirm?" she repeated. "Do you know who it is?"

"I have a couple of ideas."

"Care to share?"

"Not yet. I'm still thinking through some things and need to do more digging." He got them moving again. "We'll get past this and things will go back to normal." As normal as life could be for her when dating an operative. "You were amazing out there tonight, Zoe."

She looked skeptical. "At what? I was along for the ride. The best thing about that adventure was spending time with you and watching you work in the field."

He stopped again. "Are you kidding? You walked in the darkness through rough terrain, hunting for a sniper's hide, not knowing whether the shooter was still there or had set a trap for us. We were out there for four hours and you didn't utter one complaint." Simon inched closer and lowered his voice. "You went with me so I wouldn't be distracted or worried about you even though you aren't a fan of the great outdoors."

Her lips curved. "The great outdoors and I have a terrific relationship as long as I stay inside. Did I slow you down too much? I tried not to hold you back."

"What do you think?"

"I held my own pretty well for a couch potato."

Simon chuckled. "You did, at that."

"I'm grumpy because I'm tired, hungry, and need a kitchen. Baking is in my blood and I'm restless when I don't have a chance to mix batter, dough, or icing."

"If the kitchen withdrawals grow too bad, let me know. We'll go to the ranch and bake cookies or something. Mom always keeps the kitchen stocked with ingredients for cookies, cupcakes, and pies for the kids."

Zoe brightened. "I'd love that. Come on. We should deliver the soft drinks while they're still cold."

Matt and Cade turned at their approach, relief filling their eyes. "Thought you might have gotten lost, Zoe," Matt teased.

"Nick Santana called me." She explained about the break-in at Mason's home. "He wanted an update on Simon's dad and a possible timeline for our return to Otter Creek."

"Mason's okay?" Cade asked.

"He wasn't home and nothing was taken. Only the dressers were moved and the drawers pulled out."

"Like Macy's home." Matt frowned. "That doesn't make sense. Why would he search furniture?"

Simon rubbed his jaw, frowning. "Doesn't Mason live in Rio's old house?"

"That's right. Why?"

"Rio must have tight security installed. Maybe the cameras caught something."

"Call him and ask." Cade leaned one shoulder against the wall. "He'll find the similarities between Macy's break-in and Mason's interesting."

"It can't be a coincidence."

"Think the Barones are behind this latest incident?" Matt asked.

"I don't see how unless they chartered a plane and flew out right after they shot Dad and tried to kill Hollister. I think Zoe is right. This feels like two different groups."

"Ethan will be ticked off at the crime spree."

No doubt about that. The police chief took crime personally.

Simon's mother came to the doorway. "Simon, your father's awake and asking for you."

He hurried into the room with Zoe trailing a step behind him. "Dad."

His father's hazel eyes locked onto his. "Simon?"

Despite the barely audible whisper, joy exploded inside Simon at the sound of his father's voice. "I'm here. You're going to be fine, Dad."

"Shooter?"

"They're still at large."

Don Murray's eyes widened.

Simon covered his father's hand with his own and squeezed. "We believe there are two men involved in your shooting. You were shot at long range by a trained sniper. We're aiding the police in their investigation." Bravo would also be tracking down information the police wouldn't have access to through legal channels. A few people owed Simon favors. If necessary, he'd cash in a few to find the Barones.

"Check my computer." Stare intense, Don continued. "Threat."

Simon scowled. "Target?"

"Zoe."

CHAPTER TWENTY-SEVEN

Zoe's heart jolted into a frantic rhythm as Simon's face hardened into a fierce expression. Why would someone send Don Murray a message threatening her? Wouldn't the threat have been more effective emailed to Simon?

Perhaps the sender couldn't find Simon's email address. The operatives didn't share their personal information and if the threat had been sent to Fortress, Zane would have tracked the IP address unless the sender masked his trail. She didn't think the shooter and his buddy were that tech savvy.

She frowned. The Barone organization should have access to computer professionals. Could one of them track down Simon's email? Why have a bounty placed on Liam's and Simon's heads if someone from the Barone family was to kill the operatives? Perhaps the Barone cousins weren't supposed to go after Liam and Simon in the first place. If they had, the job would have been a debt of honor rather than for money. Something to think on and share with Simon.

"Go to Otter Creek. Protect her," Don insisted.

A smile curved Simon's mouth. "Dad, she flew to Hanover with me." He caught Zoe's hand and tugged her gently forward. "This is Zoe Lockhart. Zoe, Don Murray, my father."

Incredible hazel eyes shifted to her, eyes so like Simon's. Relief flooded his features. "You're safe."

"Yes, sir. Simon is an amazing bodyguard."

He was silent a moment, studying her face. "Is that all he is to you?"

Don Murray might be on pain medicine, but he was sharp and saw more than she was comfortable with. Now she knew where Simon inherited part of his intuitiveness. Simon's mother had asked several pointed questions in the few minutes they'd been together without him. "No, sir. He matters a great deal to me." Zoe was crazy about the operative standing beside her.

With a slight nod, he turned his head toward Simon. "Do you know who shot me?"

"We know their names and motivation. We'll find them soon, and you and the rest of the family will be safe again."

"Zoe?"

"No one will hurt her again on my watch."

A frown. "Again?"

"We think the same men attacked Zoe in her bakery after stabbing her friend. Macy didn't survive."

By the time Simon finished a summary of the events in Otter Creek, Don's eyes had grown heavy. "Rest now, Dad."

Don roused enough to focus on Simon again. "You look tired."

"I'm used to little sleep."

"Zoe isn't. Take care of her."

She noted Simon's flinch at his father's words and laid her hand on his arm. "He's taking great care of me, Mr. Murray."

"Don. Mr. Murray is my father." He settled deeper into the pillow with a pained grimace. "I need a minute with Simon."

"Dad."

"No, Simon. It's all right. I'll wait in the hall with the others." After squeezing Simon's hand in support, Zoe went to talk to Matt and Cade while Lisa slipped back into the room with her husband and son.

Simon joined Zoe a short time later. He trailed his hand up and down her back. "Do you want to go to the hotel with Matt? He'll stay with you in the suite until I get there."

Zoe leaned against his side. "I'll go when you do. You might need me."

"Are you sure? I won't be able to leave until 2:00 tomorrow morning."

She shrugged. "I'll be fine. I can research recipes for next month's specials at the bakery and bring food or more drinks for you and the others." She glanced around and frowned. "Where's Liam?"

"With Trent, providing security for Hollister," Cade said. "When the Barones find out he survived their bullets, they'll want to finish the job. If he's alive, he's a threat to them."

Simon dragged a hand down his face. "We need help covering shifts. We can't stay on duty 24 hours a day."

"Trent's on the fourth floor, east wing." Matt sipped his drink. "Talk to Trent about the security arrangements. We have your father covered."

"Do you want to wait here or go with me?" Simon asked Zoe.

"I'll go, too. If we find a steak and baked potato on the way down, I'm ordering a meal to go. Maybe dessert, too."

The operatives chuckled.

"We'll see if the cafeteria has something acceptable for dinner." Simon glanced at her. "I owe you a steak dinner with all the trimmings."

"That's a deal. I can wait knowing I have that to look forward to."

"Be back in a few minutes with food," Simon said to his teammates, and guided Zoe to the elevator.

As soon as the doors close, she asked, "Is your father all right?"

"I think so." Simon wrapped his arms around her and pulled her close. He rested his chin on the top of her head. "He wanted to know my intentions toward you." He sounded amused.

Surprised, she looked up at him. "Did that make you angry?"

He laughed. "No, that's what I expect from my father. All I've done for months is tell my folks how crazy I am about you. He wanted to make sure I wasn't stringing you along, that I was being upfront and honest with you about everything."

Zoe scowled. "Did he ever consider I might have been the one without honor, out to sponge meals and have you cater to my every whim without any intention of being in a serious relationship with you?"

"Um, no. I didn't have the best rep in high school. I was an All-State football player and used that to my advantage with the ladies. You wouldn't have liked me when I was younger." His smile faded. "This relationship won't be easy. You still have time to back out if you want although I'm praying you don't. I think I'm too far gone to back away now."

"I'm in this as deep as you are, Simon. Being with you is worth every challenge."

Simon's expression softened and he pressed a gentle kiss to her mouth as the elevator slid to a stop. When the doors opened, he escorted her into the hall and turned left.

Zoe's eyebrows winged upward. Did he have a map in his head? "How did you know where to turn?"

"Matt said Trent was in the east wing. It's this way."

"I need landmarks to find my way around," she muttered. "Maps remind me of a child's scribbles. Colorful, illegible, and full of information I can't figure out how to use. I rock at using GPS, though."

Simon blinked. "Good to know."

"Don't laugh."

"No, ma'am. I'm smarter than that."

She smiled. Smart aleck. Liam and Trent stood in the hallway, keeping watch outside the entrance to the surgical suite.

"Sit rep," Trent said.

Simon updated his team leader, ending his report with, "Is the Texas team available?"

"Let's find out." Trent grabbed his phone and called their boss. "It's Trent. We have another complication in Hanover." He explained about Hollister and the threat looming over both the trainee and Simon's parents. "We need another team to help cover security shifts."

Bravo's leader listened a moment, then said, "Yes, sir. Bravo could use four hours at least to function at peak capacity. If another team is assigned, Bravo will turn its attention to hunting down the shooters."

After another short conversation, Trent ended the call. "The Texas team will be here in two hours. As soon as we talk to Brody, we'll go to the hotel for the night."

"We'll stay on Hollister until Texas relieves us," Liam said.

"Do you need food or drinks?" Zoe asked.

"I'd love coffee and a sandwich. Trent?"

"Same. I'm not picky. Whatever looks good."

"I'll take care of it."

"We'll take care of it," Simon corrected. "I'm not comfortable with you wandering around the hospital on your own."

She had to pick her battles. This one wasn't worth causing Simon more stress. "Probably wise. I'll have a difficult time carting food and drinks from the cafeteria for your team. You make a great tote goat."

He gave her a smart salute. "At your service, ma'am." Simon turned back to Trent. "Any estimate on how long Hollister's operation will take?"

"Two hours, maybe more. Depends on the extent of the damage."

"Did you talk to him?"

"For a minute. He apologized for not coming to us when the Barones approached him and Lyons. Hollister and his buddy didn't know what they were up against."

"Maybe. I'm still angry that they thought so little of me and Liam that they assumed the Barones told the truth despite a lack of evidence to back up their claims."

"Water under the bridge." Liam leaned against the wall. "Focus on the fallout."

"After you deliver the food and drinks, take Zoe to the hotel," Trent said. "We can't do anything more tonight. We'll put together a plan after sleeping for a few hours."

A nod from Simon. "I'll have breakfast delivered to the suite for the team. Once we make our plans, we'll coordinate with Texas."

When Trent's phone signaled an incoming call, Simon and Zoe headed for the cafeteria. They loaded up on sandwiches, chips, and drinks, and delivered the bounty to the members of Bravo.

That done, she and Simon returned to the sixth floor to check on his parents and eat their meals with Simon's mother and the other two operatives. The chicken sandwich wasn't bad, Zoe decided. She couldn't wait to return to a kitchen again, though. She longed to inhale the scent of chocolate chip cookies or cinnamon rolls baking in the oven.

After speaking to his father for a moment, Simon hugged his mother, explained about the second team soon to arrive, and promised to return in a few hours. "Get some rest, Mom. If you need me for any reason, call me. We're staying at the Westgate."

Lisa rubbed his back. "I'll be fine. If your father's condition changes, I'll call. Go rest and take Zoe with you. She looks like she could sleep standing up."

An accurate description of how she felt. "Do you need anything before we leave?"

Simon's mother hugged her. "No, dear. The sandwich and green tea you brought me were perfect. If I need something else, I'll get it myself."

"Ask one of the bodyguards to go with you. The danger to you and Dad isn't over," Simon said.

"There are security guards everywhere," Lisa protested.

"The men we're after are dangerous, Mom. You need one of us."

She kissed his cheek. "All right. Go rest so I won't worry about you."

Simon escorted Zoe from the room and looked at Matt.

The medic nodded. "I'll keep an eye on them."

Simon and Zoe walked to the elevator. "Do you need anything before we go to the hotel?"

"Like what?"

"Tea, coffee, ice cream?"

They stepped inside the car. As soon as the doors slid closed, Zoe turned into his arms and hugged him. "I'm fine, Simon. Please don't worry about me."

"You're important to me."

"Makes things nice and balanced because you're important to me, too."

His arms tightened around her. Twenty minutes later, Simon opened the door to the suite and set their bags against the wall. After turning on the light, he held his finger to his lips in a bid for silence.

Zoe watched in fascination as Simon toured the room with a small black gadget in his hand. The chaser lights remained green as he walked around the suite.

When he returned, he said, "It's safe to talk."

"What were you checking for?"

"Electronic signatures of cameras and listening devices."

"Is it likely the Barones would break into the suite to spy on us?"

"Zane reserved the suite in my name. A resourceful person could pass along a few twenties to find out which room we'd been assigned. If the roles were reversed and we needed information on our targets, I'd offer a bribe. Which bedroom do you want?"

"If it doesn't matter to the security arrangements, I'll take the room on the right."

He carried her bag into the room she chose. Simon turned and drew her into his embrace. "You must be exhausted. Are you too tired to sit with me a few minutes? We could watch an episode of something fun or part of a movie."

"Don't you need to sleep?"

"I need you more."

Zoe's heart squeezed. Simon needed comfort and a distraction to get his mind off the circumstances for a few minutes. She understood that. Simon had been her respite for the past week. She was thrilled to provide the same comfort for him.

She led him back to the living area. "What are you in the mood for?"

"Something relaxing. Maybe an action movie."

Right. That wouldn't have been Zoe's first choice. However, Simon probably thought those types of movies were fun. "I'm disappointed. I thought you'd choose a romantic comedy. Too bad we don't have popcorn to make the movie choice tolerable."

He grinned. "I can buy soft drinks and candy bars from vending machines."

Contemplating either of those options this late at night made her stomach churn. "Pass. I'd prefer kisses during commercials instead of soft drinks and candy any day."

His eyes heated a little. "Great plan." They sat on the couch and Zoe handed Simon the remote.

"You can choose. I'll watch anything as long as I can hold you for a while."

She shook her head. "You need to control something right now."

Simon rested his forehead against hers. "You're right. Everything is out of my control and I hate that."

"Everything is out of control for the moment. We start again tomorrow morning after a good night's sleep. The Barones are as good as smoked out of hiding."

"I like the way you think." He cradled her against him for a minute, then eased back, his expression serious.

Uh oh. She knew that look. "You want to talk before we watch television."

"The Barones will keep coming after you and my family unless we stop them, and they have the skills to do the job, courtesy of Uncle Sam. We should hide you in one of the Fortress safe houses."

Stunned, Zoe stared at him. "You're willing to trust my safety to another operative?"

Simon scowled. "No. I'll ask Maddox to send us to one house, my parents to another, and Liam and Piper to a third. That will give us time to regroup and track down the cousins through their electronic footprints."

"Fortress has that many safe houses?"

"We have them all over the world. Some we rent for short term assignments. Others belong to a holding company to hide the Fortress name."

"Wow. Impressive. I won't outright refuse, but I think your parents will. We don't know how soon your father will be released from the hospital and when he is, he'll need to be close to good medical care in case of a problem. He'll have follow-up appointments, too."

"Fortress has a doctor on staff in Bayside, a few hours from here. Dr. Sorenson is one of the best trauma surgeons in the country. Dad couldn't be in better hands."

"You still have to convince your parents. You said yourself that your father will want to recuperate at home where he can direct the ranch hands and organize their duties."

"I want them safe. It's impossible to monitor and control access to 500 acres."

"I understand, but I know you can keep them safe on the ranch. Your father will heal faster at home, Simon."

"I'm still going to talk to them about it when the doctor gives us a release date. Will you consider the safe house?"

"I can't be stashed away for long. I have a business to run and now I don't have an assistant to keep the place going while I hide. If I'm closed for too long, I won't have money to pay bills."

Zoe kissed him with a gentleness that she hoped showed him her heart. "Liam won't want to run with his pregnant wife. Like you, he'll want to hunt for the men who are threatening Piper. Neither of you will allow danger to stalk those you care about."

"How did you get to know me and my teammates so well?"

She laughed softly. "What else would I do for those long months while I waited for you to ask me on a date? I watched and listened to you and the others talk in general terms about your missions and deduced the rest." Her face burned. "I also dogged Del, Josh's wife, for books about the military, military units, and deployments. The stack she gave me included several books about Special Forces soldiers. I put the information together and figured out you and the others weren't ordinary front-line grunts. All of you are alpha to the max. You won't wait for the Barones to find you. You'll go after them."

CHAPTER TWENTY-EIGHT

Simon woke the instant the key card slid into the lock. Sig in hand and aimed, he was on his feet before the door opened to admit Liam. Simon returned his weapon to his holster.

"Your parents are safe. Matt said your father is stable and resting comfortably. The Texas unit's medic took the watch for him. Jesse Phelps won't let anyone past him."

Jesse was a big man and as fierce as they came. His parents were in good hands. "Thanks."

"How's Zoe?"

"Finally sleeping. Took her a long time to unwind."

"How much have you slept?"

"Enough. I'll take the watch. Go sleep."

"Wake me at five if I'm not up. Trent wants to meet at six."

His partner closed himself inside the second bedroom, fatigue evident. He had a feeling Liam hadn't slept much after Piper's injury and learning she carried their child.

Simon prepped the coffee maker and waited impatiently for the brew cycle to finish. When the pot was full, he poured the steaming liquid into his mug and walked to the balcony doors where he could survey the front of the hotel and watch the door in case the Barones attempted to infiltrate the suite, hoping to catch him off guard.

When he was satisfied all was as it should be, Simon returned to the couch and grabbed his laptop. This was a good time to look into the Barone cousins' background.

His frown deepened the further he read through the information Fortress had amassed on the cousins in the past few hours. Both men had been Army Rangers. Simon's jaw clenched. So had he, but he didn't remember hearing about them. With men like the Barones, their reputation usually made the rounds of the Special Forces units.

While Zoe hadn't been able to access their military records, Zane had. The more Simon read, the lower his opinion became of the Barones. They might have been Rangers, but they didn't have the honor or code of conduct of elite soldiers.

He wondered if Ethan knew Blake and Garrett Barone. A glance at the corner of his screen told Simon it was too early to call the Otter Creek police chief. A text would elicit results in a few hours.

He slid his phone from his pocket and sent Ethan a text message. That done, he turned back to the computer only to have his attention diverted by a call.

Simon checked the screen and sighed. "Sorry to wake you," he said, careful to keep his voice pitched low enough that he wouldn't disturb Zoe.

"I was up anyway," Ethan said. In the background, a child wailed. "Lucas has an ear infection."

"Ouch. Poor kid. I'm sorry."

"Yeah, me, too. There's nothing worse than knowing your child is in pain and you can't do much to stop it. Hold a second." Ethan's voice became muffled as he spoke to Serena, his wife, and gradually, the cries faded. "Tell me what's going on, Simon."

"We found Chris Hollister in the foothills of my family's ranch. He'd been shot twice, once in the thigh, once in the side. Both were through-and-though."

"Is he alive?"

"Yes, sir. I received a text from Trent an hour ago confirming that."

"He's not responsible for shooting your father."

A statement, not a question. "No, sir. Hollister knows who did."

"He recognized the shooter?"

Simon told him about the deal between the trainees and the Barone cousins, the solicitation to murder, and the bounty on him and Liam.

"What else?"

"Blake is skilled at knife work and has a reputation for enjoying it."

"Garrett's the sniper, then. What do you need from me?"

"I've lost touch with my unit, but you're still connected to the Special Forces network while not being in the circle. Have you heard anything about these two men?" Simon had his own suspicions about them.

"I've heard rumors. Nothing confirmed."

"Come on, Ethan. My life is on the line and so is Liam's. Zoe is in danger as well as my family, and all of Bravo's families."

Silence greeted his outburst. Finally, Ethan said, "If Serena was in the line of fire, I'd feel the same. I don't have proof of what I'm going to tell you, but I know the CO of their unit. He's a friend. We served together for two tours. Rothchild mentioned a couple incidents that occurred while the Barones were under his command, incidents that led him to demote them and recommend they be sent back to a regular unit."

His eyebrows rose. "Go on."

"Blake and Garrett were sent on a scouting mission in Afghanistan to collect intelligence and return to the base camp. They returned two hours late. Rothchild caught Blake washing blood from his hands. The CO questioned him and Blake claimed he defended himself against a wild animal and his cousin backed him up. Three days later, Rothchild learned that a woman had been raped and knifed to death in a village in the area where the Barones were sent to scout. When my friend confronted the pair, the Barones denied any knowledge or involvement. No one in the village saw or heard anything since the woman was attacked and killed outside the village. The CO believed Blake was guilty, but he didn't have proof."

Disgust swamped Simon. No man worthy of the name would ever treat a woman like that. "What about the second incident?"

"Another village where the Barones were operating was decimated. Most of the men were away fighting the Taliban. Only the old and sick plus the women and children were living in the village." Raw fury filled Ethan's voice. "The CO believes they killed everyone in that village, including the kids. But once again, there was no proof so he couldn't charge the Barones. The best he could do was write them up every time they screwed up and send them back to a regular unit with demotions. Both were skilled, but had no respect for authority or the chain of command. They mustered out and returned home. Rothchild lost track of them once they were stateside."

And these were the men targeting Zoe? Resolve hardened in Simon. These clowns were not going to get their hands on his woman again.

"I'll be two hours from Hanover later this morning."

He blinked. "Why?"

"Lost child in the national park. The little girl wandered away from her family's campsite while everyone was sleeping. The local cops haven't had much luck tracking her down. Neither have the S & R teams. I'll be flying in to track her. If I have a chance, I'd like to stop by to see your father."

"Dad would love to see you again."

"Good. Simon, I don't have to tell you how dangerous the Barones cousins are if what I know about them is true. They're good at killing and like it. You and Liam need to watch your backs."

"Believe me, we are."

"I assume you have a watch on Hollister."

"Yes, sir."

"Keep someone on him. Your trainee is a loose end. You're still a target along with those you love. The cousins won't think twice about using any one of your family members or Zoe to draw you out. Don't give them an opening."

"I won't."

"I'll be in touch soon." Ethan ended the call.

Simon returned to his research, sending an email to Zane with a few questions five minutes before Zoe's door opened and she stepped into the living room.

He set the computer aside and met her halfway. Simon gathered Zoe into his arms and held her for a moment. He was still amazed that she melted against him instead of pushing him away. After what he'd told her of his skills, he was grateful every time she allowed him to touch her. Maybe in fifty years, that expectation of rejection would leave. "Hi."

"Hi, yourself," she said, her voice still husky from sleep. "Any news from the hospital?"

"Dad's fine. Hollister, too."

"Good." She eased back to meet his gaze. "Sorry I conked out on you last night. You should have woken me and told me to go to bed instead of carrying me there."

"I enjoyed doing it. Don't rob me of the pleasure of carrying my girl against my heart."

Her breath caught. "Simon."

"I speak the truth." He brushed a gentle kiss over her mouth. "Did you sleep okay?"

Zoe gave a short nod. "What about the rest of Bravo?"

"They'll be here in a few minutes. We need to order breakfast."

Once they perused the menu, Simon called in the order. "Would you like hot tea? I brought tea packets with me from home for you."

Her lips curved. "I'd love a cup."

Simon nuked a mug of water with a tea bag. When the heating cycle ended, he led Zoe to an outdoor couch on the balcony. At this hour of the morning, he didn't believe she was in danger. The town hadn't begun to wake and no other buildings close by were tall enough for a sniper to get a good bead on Zoe.

She looked surprised as he sat beside her on the couch. "Is it safe to be out here?"

"It's fine as long as we're seated. I thought you'd enjoy the fresh air and quiet atmosphere before the day cranks up."

"No, this is perfect. You knew I was feeling hemmed in, didn't you?"

Instead of answering, he kissed her temple and draped his arm around her shoulders.

She settled deeper against his side and sipped her tea. As they enjoyed the silence and peace, Hanover began to stir and the stars faded as the sun rose to reveal a cloudless sky, hinting at the day's warmth.

Simon thought of the little girl, lost somewhere in the national forest to the north of his hometown and prayed Ethan found her trail quickly. So many dangers lurked in the area for someone young and inexperienced in survival. This little one was defenseless against the natural predators in the area, not to mention the challenges of navigating the terrain.

"What are you thinking about?" Zoe asked, voice soft.

"I talked to Ethan an hour ago. He's flying to a town two hours from Hanover."

"Why?"

"A missing child."

"Why is Ethan coming for that?"

"He's one of the best trackers in the country. Law enforcement agencies call him when they need help with a search for missing children."

"He's that good?"

"I wouldn't want him on my trail if I needed to stay hidden."

"I'll be sure to stay off his radar if I'm on the run."

Bravo joined them in the suite for breakfast thirty minutes later. While they ate, Simon and his teammates exchanged information and bounced ideas off each other on ways to protect his father when he returned to the ranch. His father would insist on returning home as soon as possible, more than likely before the doctor wanted to release him. Bravo needed a plan before that happened.

With the breakfast cart consigned to the hall, Simon and Zoe headed to the hospital to check on his father. The rest of his team would arrive within the hour to take over the watch from the Texas unit.

Because of the early hour, Simon easily found a parking space. Circling the SUV, he opened Zoe's door. Before she could slide to the pavement, Simon cupped her chin and captured her lips with his own. He was dying for a taste of her.

A moment later, he eased back, pleased with the dazed look in her eyes. "Thank you."

"For a kiss?"

He chuckled. "That and for coming with me instead of overseeing the remodeling at your shop."

"Being with you isn't a hardship."

Simon dropped a light kiss on her lips and stepped back, hand extended to help her to the asphalt. As they walked toward the hospital, two men dressed as orderlies raced from the entrance.

Senses prickling, Simon moved in front of Zoe, his hand edging toward his holstered Sig. At that moment, the two men spotted them. One of them smiled and aimed a weapon at Simon.

He pivoted, grabbed Zoe, and took them both to the ground behind a car just as the gunman fired the first shot. Adrenaline pouring into his veins, Simon lifted her into a crouch and motioned for her to follow him. He led her toward the corner of the lot where bushes were thick with foliage and large trees spread branches laden with leaves, creating a pocket of gloom.

Choosing a large SUV with a good size wheel well, Simon positioned Zoe in the deepest shadows against the wheel. He shifted in front of her. "Watch behind us," he whispered. He didn't think there was a third thug in the vicinity, but he never assumed anything.

When she nodded, he grabbed his Sig and scanned the area. One of the gunmen ran toward the far side of the parking lot while the second man searched for their location.

Simon volleyed his glances between the approaching man and his retreating buddy. Everything in him urged him to turn the tables on the two men and stalk them. If he left Zoe's side, however, she'd be vulnerable to attack.

He glanced back at her, grateful she chose to wear black today. She'd be hard to spot.

"Go get him," she whispered. "I'll be fine."

Torn, he checked the position of the men again. When he heard an engine crank at the far end of the lot, he nudged Zoe toward the bushes. "Hide in there. Don't move until I tell you it's safe to come out."

Zoe moved silently between two of the nearest bushes and disappeared behind the dense foliage. Excellent. If Simon couldn't see her, the thugs wouldn't either.

He focused his attention on the thug heading his direction. The man moved like he was trained. No sound. Economy of motion. Every move practiced and eyes continually scanning. When sirens sounded, the man scowled and cursed.

When his partner drove toward the corner where Simon and Zoe were located, the closest gunman shifted position. He stilled a moment, then aimed toward the bushes where Zoe hid.

Simon pulled the trigger, hitting the gunman center mass. The thug looked down at his chest, stunned shock on his face. His knees gave out and he dropped to the asphalt.

The car with the second thug raced toward Simon. At the last moment, he swerved around his fallen partner and sped through the parking lot toward the street. The car skidded onto the main street, turned away from the approaching sirens, and disappeared from view.

Weapon trained on the fallen gunman, Simon kicked away his weapon and checked for a pulse. Nothing. After a final glance around to be sure there was no other threat to him and Zoe, he holstered his weapon. "Zoe, you can come out now."

She appeared seconds later and threw herself into Simon's arms. "Are you hurt?"

"That was going to be my question to you."

"A scratch from the bush. You?"

Thank God. "Uninjured." Keeping his body between Zoe and the dead man, he called Trent. He'd need help protecting Zoe in two minutes or less.

"St. Claire."

"It's Simon. I need you at the hospital."

"What happened?"

"Two gunmen shot at me and Zoe."

"Are they dead?"

"One of them. The other got away."

"Injuries?"

"None for me. A scratch on Zoe. I'll need help covering her while the cops sort everything out."

"Copy that."

Simon slid his phone away and wrapped both arms around Zoe. He breathed in the familiar apple scent of her shampoo. He could have lost her in a heartbeat if the gunman had fired before Simon pulled the trigger. The idea made him break into a cold sweat. "Are you sure you're all right, baby?"

She nodded.

"Here's what's going to happen. The cops will be here soon. My teammates will be right behind them. I'll be handcuffed. It's standard procedure when the police realize I'm armed with a man dead on the ground. Things will work themselves out. But it may take a while for the evidence to bear out our story."

Zoe's head lifted, her eyes wide. "He's dead?"

"He aimed his weapon at the bush you hid behind and was ready to pull the trigger. I didn't have a choice."

She cupped his face. "I know you wouldn't kill without a reason, Simon. I know."

Simon rested his forehead against hers and waited for the police. Thankfully, Bravo arrived before the police. Trent volunteered to stay with Zoe and sent the rest of the team to check on Simon's parents and the Texas unit.

Within less than a minute of law enforcement's arrival, Simon was in handcuffs and stuffed in the back of a patrol car, sans his weapons. He breathed easier when Detective Chisolm arrived thirty minutes later. A patrolman spoke to the detective and gestured toward the car where Simon sat.

Chisolm dragged a hand down his face and made his way to the car. He opened the door and helped Simon out. "Why am I not surprised?"

He scowled. "I didn't go looking for trouble."

"No, but it sure found you, didn't it? Who's the dead man?"

"Garrett Barone."

The detective narrowed his eyes. "The sniper who shot your father?"

"Although I don't have proof, he's probably the trigger man."

"Tell me what happened and don't omit anything, Murray, because this doesn't look good."

Simon relayed the incident from the time he and Zoe arrived at the hospital to the moment he made the decision to pull the trigger to protect Zoe.

"How many shots did you fire?"

"One."

Chisolm stared at him. "What about the shooter? How many times did he fire?"

"Seven."

"Did he hit anything?"

"Not us, which is all I care about. The owners of cars with busted windows and bullet holes in the doors will think otherwise."

"How can a trained sniper miss two targets?"

"Hitting a moving target is harder than it looks."

"You didn't miss."

"I have more training than he did and I'm on the gun range more often. We train bodyguards. Can't have green recruits shooting better than we do. We train for missions of our own and I'm partners with our team's sniper. I've learned a lot from him."

"Sounds like our sharpshooters could use lessons with McCoy."

"He's a great trainer. Hanover PD wouldn't be the first police department to bring Liam in to conduct training sessions."

A wry smile curved the detective's mouth. "I'll pass the word along the chain of command."

"Good. Now, what about removing these cuffs? I can't protect Zoe as well like this."

"Looks like your friend has her covered."

"She's mine to protect."

"I'll unlock the cuffs, but you stay put until I finish Zoe's interview."

Simon turned his back to the detective and a moment later, his wrists were free. He signaled Trent to stay with Zoe.

As she talked to the detective, Simon watched Zoe's face and body language. When she rubbed her arms despite the heat of the day, he straightened. She needed a blanket or sweater and a drink with sugar in it. Maybe the hospital cafeteria sold hot tea. He'd give Chisolm five more minutes before he insisted Zoe go inside the hospital. The detective could finish the interview later.

At the five-minute mark, Chisolm motioned to Simon. He jogged to her side and drew her against him to share his body heat. "Am I free to take Zoe inside? I need to check on my parents."

"I'll go with you. The ME's at the scene of a fatal accident on the other side of town and will be another thirty minutes."

Simon led the way to the hospital with Zoe tucked against his side and Trent at his back. Once they were inside, Simon's urgency to reach his parents escalated. Yeah, his teammates were on watch and would have notified him if the gunmen had reached his father's room. Simon worried about the repercussions of fear and stress on his father.

CHAPTER TWENTY-NINE

Simon strode into his father's room with Zoe and Trent on his heels. Since Hollister's room had also been a target according to the Texas unit's leader, Detective Chisolm opted to begin his interview with the trainee.

Simon's mother launched herself at him. Arms closing around her, Simon hugged her. "Are you okay?"

She shuddered. "I'm still shaking, but we're fine. Thank God for your friends."

He looked at his father over her shoulder. "Dad?"

His eyes gleamed with a mixture of fury and concern. "I want out of this room. I'm a trapped rat in here. There isn't another exit and I'm weak as a newborn colt."

"As soon as the doctor says you're ready, we'll get you out."

"Make it happen, Simon. Those men could have hurt Lisa. It's one thing for them to come after me. I have to protect my wife."

"I'll talk to B.J. Maybe he can convince your doctor to release you early. If it's not safe for you, you'll have to deal. I won't put your life at risk by taking you away from medical care you need."

"Find a way," his father snapped.

Don Murray might be injured, but he still had a steel spine and a stubborn streak a mile wide. "I'll do my best."

A commotion sounded outside the room. Simon released his mother and moved in front of her and Zoe. He and Trent prepared to defend his loved ones from a new threat until he heard his sister Tracey's angry voice in the hallway.

Terrific. She sounded like she was on the warpath. "I'll be back in a minute." Optimistic thinking, that. He glanced at his team leader who gave a short nod.

He entered the hall to see Tracey trying to bulldoze her way past Matt and Jesse.

"Get out of my way before I have you arrested," his sister hissed, her face flushed, eyes glittering.

"Tracey."

She shifted her ire to Simon. "I should have known you'd be here. Are these goons with you? Tell them to step aside."

Wow. She was in fine form this morning. "Chill, Tracey. This is Trent, Matt, and Jesse. Guys, my sister Tracey Bolliver, mayor of Hanover."

Bravo's leader nodded in acknowledgment. "Ma'am."

"Now that we're best friends and all, step aside, boys." Tracey's words practically dripped with sarcasm.

Trent glanced at the nurse who watched them with a frown on her face. When she gave a curt nod, the operative stepped aside.

Tracey marched past the men into their father's room, trailed by her bodyguard.

"Sorry about that," Simon murmured to Trent. "Tracey's driven and intense."

His friend stared. "I worked with SEALs who weren't that intense. Your sister is in another category."

"She's like a category 5 hurricane. Dad claimed she'd rule the world when she grew up."

Matt glanced at him. "I would have let her go in the room, but the nurse insisted the room had too many people inside. Tracey argued with her and tried to throw her weight around. That's the only reason I stepped in."

"Dad, you can't do that!" Tracey's voice raised in agitation. "I won't allow it."

This time, Simon looked at the nurse, his eyebrow raised.

She rolled her eyes and waved him on.

"I'll wait with Trent and the others," Zoe said.

"Go," his team leader said. "I've got her."

Simon retraced his steps and grasped Tracey's arm. "Come with me." When the bodyguard made a move to intervene, Simon stopped him with a pointed stare. The guard didn't like it, but he backed down.

"Let go of me," she snapped. "I'm not finished."

"Yeah, you are, Sis. Let's go. Dad, Mom, I'll return in a few minutes."

He propelled Tracey to the empty family waiting room. As soon as he released her arm, Tracey rounded on him, eyes lit with fury.

"You don't drag me from our father's bedside, Simon. I'm not some terrorist you need to subdue."

"Based on the way you're acting, that's debatable. You were upsetting Dad."

"Do you know what he asked me?"

"I can guess. He wants to leave the hospital. I don't blame him."

"He just had surgery. Dad can't check himself out of the place and go home to recuperate without a doctor's care."

Oh, man. He should have figured his father would find a way to get what he wanted if Simon didn't move fast enough. "B.J. will talk to him."

"You said the men guarding Dad were the best. How did a killer come so close to him?"

"If they weren't the best, the killer would have breached the room and finished the job he started yesterday morning."

She snorted. "I'm not convinced, bro. We need to have a family meeting."

"Agreed. Dinner at the ranch tonight?"

A scowl. "Why the delay?"

"It's a long story, one I'd prefer to tell you at home." Nothing like having to tell his family that he'd killed a man to protect his girlfriend and confirm their worst suspicions. "We need to give the overnight bodyguards time to talk to the police and rest a few hours before my team is free to leave the hospital."

Tracey's eyes narrowed. "No one said anything about inviting your team to this meeting. What part of family don't you understand?"

His temper spiked. "You're asking me to trust our entire family's safety plus Zoe's life to a dozen ranch hands. That's not going to happen."

"Your girlfriend?" She stared. "You mean the pretty woman with you?"

He nodded. "That's Zoe Lockhart."

Delight chased the anger from his sister's face. "You're dating the Otter Creek baker? It's about time, buddy. Congratulations."

He stared at his sister, unable to fathom the quick turnaround in attitude. Usually she was like a bulldog. Once she sank her teeth into something, she didn't let go. "Thanks."

"How serious is this relationship?"

"I want to marry her. She doesn't know yet so I'd appreciate you not mentioning it until I broach the subject with her. We're still in the early days of dating."

Her jaw dropped. "But you already know you want to marry her? You don't believe in wasting time, do you?"

Not in his line of work. Every mission could be his last and he wanted every single minute he could get with Zoe. "I'm in love with her. There is no other woman for me and never will be."

"Do Mom and Dad know?"

"Yes, and they approve." He'd been floored when his parents gave him their blessing yesterday. He thought they'd demand he slow down. Instead, they'd greeted his announcement with enthusiasm.

"How does Zoe feel about the sudden shift in your relationship?"

"She says she's in this as deep as I am."

"Have you told her you love her?"

"Why is that your business?"

Tracey grinned. "You might want to clue her in since you're already planning on buying matching wedding rings."

"Yeah, yeah. The right time hasn't popped up yet. I need to convince her that we're perfect for each other and I'll do everything in my power to make her happy."

She threw her arms around him and hugged him tight. "I'm happy for you, Simon. You better not screw this up."

A wry laugh escaped. "Thanks for the vote of confidence."

Tracey eased back. "Dinner. Are we ordering pizza or something else?"

"I vote for pizza. I've been craving Antonio's pizza for months."

She pointed a finger at him. "If you had bothered to come home last month like we planned, you wouldn't be suffering from withdrawals. We ate a ton of pizza at the last family dinner."

He scowled. "Don't rub it in." Simon had been deployed with Bravo at the time. "You want to arrange for delivery?"

"I'll pick up the pizzas myself. How many people from your group are coming?"

"Counting me, six." He'd leave the Texas unit on guard at the hospital.

"Dessert?"

Simon started to tell her to pick up dessert pizzas, too, but thought of Zoe's longing to be in a kitchen. "I'll take care of it. Zoe might want to bake something. If not, I'll grab something from the local bakery."

The smile slid from Tracey's face. "Back to Dad's crazy idea. Find a way to derail his plan or Dad and Mom will be joining us for this family dinner."

"You're the oldest and the mayor."

"Doesn't mean I have any power. Will the kids be safe tonight?"

"My team will be on full alert and we'll bring some of the hands closer to the house to help secure the perimeter. As long as the kids stay within the safe zone, they'll be fine." Especially since the sniper was lying dead in the parking lot at the moment. Blake preferred to work in close quarters.

His sister glanced at her security guard. "Have the car brought around." After he left, Tracey turned back to Simon. "I'm sorry for coming on so strong. I'm just worried about Dad."

"We're all concerned. Dad's not as young as he used to be and he won't bounce back from this as fast."

She hugged him. "I love you, Simon."

He held her a moment. "Even though I rank a little above a terrorist?" he teased.

Tracey gave a wry laugh. "Not my finest moment, I'll admit."

"It's okay, Sis." She wouldn't be the last person to lay that label on him. Simon released her. "Go on. You have a world to conquer."

With a grin, she smacked his shoulder and joined her bodyguard in the hallway. They left together.

Simon returned to his father's room. His mother rose, her brow furrowed. "Where's Tracey?"

"Gone back to work." He winked at her. "She has world domination to plot."

Lisa exchanged glances with her husband, then turned back to Simon. "What's wrong?"

He sighed, his forced smile fading. "I could never pull anything over on you."

"Your eyes give you away every time."

"Remind me to wear sunglasses next time," he muttered.

"Son, despite appearances to the contrary, I can handle bad news," his father said. "What I can't handle is a secret that concerns me or your mother. Talk to me."

Simon felt a small, warm hand on his back, offering silent support. He twisted slightly and wrapped his arm around Zoe's shoulders. "The men who tried to breach your room ran from the hospital as Zoe and I were walking toward the entrance. They fired on us. We evaded. They kept coming."

He didn't want to tell his parents that he'd killed a man, even in defense of his own life and Zoe's. They knew what he did for a living. Didn't mean they wanted to be confronted with the reality.

"Bottom line, Simon."

"I killed one of the men as he was about to pull the trigger. The other escaped."

Lisa gasped, one hand pressed to her throat. "You and Zoe aren't hurt?"

"We're fine."

Don's hand fisted. "Could have turned out otherwise. I want to take Lisa somewhere safe, a place that's defensible and I want my handgun."

The corners of Simon's mouth tipped up. Guess he'd gotten the protective streak from his father. "I know, Dad. I'm working on it."

"Simon, the detective's here to talk to Lisa and Don," Trent said.

He turned to his parents. "I'm taking Zoe to the cafeteria to get her some hot tea. Do you want anything?"

When they both refused, he escorted Zoe from the room. At Chisolm's scowl, Simon held up one hand. "We're going to the cafeteria. We won't leave the building."

"Good. Once I'm finished here, I'll need you both to come down to the station to make a formal statement."

In other words, Simon was in for a long interview session with the good detective. He might need one of his teammates along to provide protection for Zoe until Chisolm was satisfied that all his questions had been answered and Simon wouldn't be changing his story. "Whenever you're ready for us, we'll be available." As long as he took care of Zoe first.

After purchasing a steaming to-go cup of tea for Zoe and coffee for himself, they returned to his father's room to wait for the detective to finish taking statements from his parents. Ten minutes later, Chisolm emerged.

"Let's go," he said curtly. "I have questions for both of you."

"Will I need an attorney?" Simon asked.

"You have that right."

The question was, should he avail himself of that privilege? He'd hold off for now. If things looked like they were turning against him, he'd invoke his right to counsel and call Fortress. "We'll follow you."

A narrow-eyed glance from the detective. "I know where you live."

"I'm not running, Chisolm." He motioned for the other man to lead the way.

"Bravo is taking over the watch," Trent said. "Texas unit will be going to the hotel to sleep. If you need help, call me. The Fortress lawyer is already on standby."

Ten minutes later, Simon walked into the police station with Zoe. Since the cops had confiscated his weapons earlier, he didn't have to worry about losing them now. He'd restock his weapons when he returned to his SUV. He always carried multiples of every weapon.

"This way." Chisolm led into the interior section of the police station. He stopped halfway down a corridor and motioned to a room on the right side. "Murray, you'll be in here. Ms. Lockhart, you'll be in the room across the hall."

"She needs an officer you trust implicitly stationed outside the room until you finish with me."

"You're not in charge here."

"Zoe's safety is my priority. Either you get an officer to stand watch outside her interrogation room or I put in a call to an attorney and bog down your case."

"And if there isn't an officer available?"

"Then we wait until one of my teammates arrives. I'd rather trust her life to one of them."

With a scowl, Chisolm said, "Wait here. I'll see who I can find to babysit."

Simon held Zoe against his chest.

"I don't have to have anyone with me," she murmured.

"For my peace of mind, you do."

Two minutes later, the detective returned with a linebacker-sized man dressed in a suit. The shield on his belt told Simon the man was a detective.

"This is Detective Moran, a ten-year veteran with the force. He also did eight years in the Marines. No one gets past Moran unless he wants them to. We'll also keep the door cracked to this room so you can hear what's happening in the hallway, Murray. Does that work for you?"

He nodded. "Thanks."

A snort. "Not like you gave me much choice. I don't want to spend the whole day waiting for your attorney to arrive when I could be hunting down the second thug from the hospital. Detective Moran, escort Ms. Lockhart into the interrogation room across the hall and I'll start with Murray."

"Would you like me to interview her? Save you some time."

Chisolm looked at Zoe. "Is that acceptable to you?"

"It's fine."

"Murray?"

"As long as he stays with Zoe until we're finished." He pinned the second detective with his gaze. "I don't want her left alone, Moran. She's a target of a killer."

"Understood. If another detective needs the interrogation room, Ms. Lockhart will be at my desk in the bullpen."

Simon shook his head. "Too much exposure in a large, open room. Is there somewhere else to take her that's close to this room?"

Moran was silent a moment. "We have an empty office off the bullpen. I can close the blinds. No one will be able to see her in there."

The knot in his stomach smoothed away. "That's perfect." He brushed a gentle kiss over Zoe's mouth. "You're okay with this arrangement?"

"I want this over with as soon as possible. I don't want to forget anything."

"This way, Ms. Lockhart." Moran indicated she should precede him from the room. He closed the door most of the way. A moment later, the door to the other interrogation room closed.

Chisolm indicated for Simon to take a seat on one side of the table. He sat on the opposite side and opened his notebook and grabbed a remote. "I'm going to record this to be sure I don't miss anything. Now, take me through the events of this morning again, Murray."

CHAPTER THIRTY

Zoe paced the empty office as she waited for Detective Chisolm to finish questioning Simon. She glanced at the utilitarian clock on the beige wall and scowled. The detective had been hammering at Simon for six hours. What could be taking so long?

Detective Moran tapped on the door to the office and stepped inside. "Need anything else?"

She shook her head. The detective had already brought her lunch and a drink as well as two bottles of water. He'd even escorted her to the restroom and stood guard outside the door until he walked her back to the safety of the office. "I'm fine, thanks."

"Shouldn't be long now."

"That's what you said two hours ago." Should she ask Liam to notify the Fortress attorney? Would Chisolm arrest Simon for murder?

He'd killed Barone to protect her. The shooter would have kept firing unless Simon had stopped him. If Barone pulled the trigger that last time, he would have hit her.

"I've been walking by the room every half hour. Chisolm is wrapping up this round of interviews."

"This round?" Her jaw dropped. "How many rounds should we expect?"

"As many rounds as it takes to catch the second man. Each time we question witnesses and suspects, we learn something new. Every piece of information will help us find the shooter's partner." He glanced over his shoulder. "Here's your boyfriend now."

Within seconds, Simon entered the office followed by Chisolm.

Zoe jumped up and threw her arms around Simon, relief melting the ball of ice in her stomach.

He hugged her close. "Ready to leave?"

"More than. No offense, Detective Moran, but I'm sick of these four walls."

His grin made him seem younger than she suspected he was. "I understand. I feel the same after most shifts."

"Thank you for watching over me. What do I owe you for lunch?"

Moran waved her inquiry aside. "It's on the house. Consider lunch a reward for doing your civic duty."

Simon slid his arm around her waist. "If you have more questions, Detectives, contact the Fortress number I gave Chisolm."

"Do I have to tell you not to leave town without notifying me?" Chisolm asked.

"I'll be available as long as my team isn't deployed. If it is, I'll have to go but I will tell you." Simon escorted Zoe through the bullpen and into the late afternoon sunlight.

"Where are we going now?" Zoe asked. She didn't really care as long as she was in a space larger than the office she'd paced for the past four hours.

"Depends."

"On?"

"If you want to bake dessert for our dinner at the ranch tonight."

She smiled. "I'd love to. Do we need to stop by the grocery store for ingredients?"

"I don't think so. Mom has all kinds of ingredients in the ranch kitchen. She loves to spoil Dad, the hands, and her grandchildren." Simon unlocked his SUV and lifted her into the passenger seat.

When he drove from the lot, she asked, "Do the kids like chocolate chip cookies? They're quick and make the house smell amazing."

He chuckled. "You'll be everyone's favorite person tonight. The kids beg Mom to bake those cookies."

"What about you? Do you like chocolate chip cookies?"

"Who doesn't?"

"Handy for me that you're a great kitchen assistant."

After a call to his parents to check on them, Simon headed toward his family's ranch. Now that she studied the terrain in daylight, the landscape amazed her with its beauty. The night before, the only thing that registered was the open land in the pastures and near the house. "This is gorgeous."

He kissed the back of her hand. "We think so, too." Soon, he turned into the long drive that led to the front of the two-story house. After parking, Simon circled the vehicle and opened her door.

As soon as Zoe's feet touched the pavement, a Blue Heeler trotted toward them, tail wagging.

Simon gave the dog a good body rub, then scratched behind his ears. "This is Bow. His brother, Arrow, is probably out in the pasture with the cattle."

"Will he let me pet him?"

"Oh, yeah. Bow loves to be petted and loved on. He'll get his attention fix, then go find his brother. Arrow loves the same treatment, but he's not as insistent."

"Will I meet Arrow later?"

He gave her a pointed look. "This won't be the last time we visit my parents."

Afraid to guess the meaning behind that statement, Zoe showered Bow with attention for a few minutes. When he trotted off toward the pasture, Simon guided her to the back of the house and unlocked the door. He turned off the alarm and relocked the door.

Zoe glanced around the enormous kitchen with commercial-grade steel appliances and gleaming granite countertops. "This is a dream kitchen. I would love to have one like this in my home someday." Maybe after her bakery was on solid footing.

"Mom loves it. Dad had the kitchen remodeled for their fortieth wedding anniversary."

"Did he win points for that?"

"Major points. Dad said it was a win-win for him. She's happy and he gets the benefits of eating food prepared in a gourmet kitchen with a content chef."

She smiled. Simon's parents reminded Zoe of her own. "Same with mine. Mom owns a bakery and invested her money in a to-die-for kitchen at her shop. The one at home was old fashioned and cramped with very little counter space. Dad worked as much overtime as he could for a year to pay for the remodel of her home kitchen. According to him, the smile on Mom's face every time she walks in there was worth every penny he paid for it."

"Do you think you can work in here?"

"Let me wash my hands and I'll show you."

They gathered the ingredients she needed for the cookies, preheated the oven, and mixed ingredients. Soon, the scent of freshly-baked chocolate chip cookies filled the kitchen. Because Simon's family was so large and his teammates also loved the sweet treats, she tripled the recipe. If they didn't eat all the cookies tonight, she would take some to Don and Lisa tomorrow.

By the time the last batch of cookies cooled on the wire rack and the cookie sheets were washed and dried, Bravo had arrived and laughter filled the dining room and kitchen. Soon, chaos reigned in the house when Simon's siblings arrived with their families.

The women found paper plates and napkins, set out cold drinks, and opened pizza boxes. They let the kids eat in the den with a movie playing since the adults didn't want their conversation to upset the young ones more than they already were.

Following dinner while Simon, Cassie, Tracey, James, and B.J. plus Cassie's and Tracey's husbands sat in the dining room and talked about the risk of Don leaving the hospital too early, Zoe and Simon's sisters-in-law straightened the kitchen and stored the leftover pizza. As they cleaned, the kids wandered in and out of the kitchen, grabbing cookies and drinks, and taking them outside to eat and play while it was still daylight.

Since the Murray siblings were still enmeshed in the debate and on alternatives if Don's doctor released him from the hospital early, Zoe, Andrea, and Emily went to the patio to talk and keep an eye on the children.

Fifteen minutes later, one of Andrea's daughters fell and skinned her knee. She and Emily insisted the rest of the children come inside.

"I don't mind watching them," Zoe said.

"The sun's down anyway." Andrea glanced around, frowning. "Where's Naomi?" she asked an older boy.

"She went around the side of the house to get her ball. She said she'd be right back."

Zoe rose. "I'll find her."

"Thanks, Zoe."

When Zoe rounded the corner of the house, she slowed, surprised at the lack of light on this side of the Murray home. Maybe the security light had burned out.

She frowned. Would Naomi search for her ball in the dark? "Naomi?" A quiet sob reached Zoe's ears. "It's Zoe. Are you hurt?"

Nothing.

"Naomi?"

"If you want her to stay alive, keep walking," a deep male voice said.

She froze. "Who are you?" Her gaze scoured the darkness.

"Your worst nightmare, lady. Do what I told you or I'll hurt this pretty little thing."

Another quiet sob.

"Don't hurt her." Zoe moved in the direction of the man's voice. Was this Blake Barone or one of the ranch hands the Barones had turned against Simon and his family?

Five feet, ten, twenty.

"That's far enough." A dark-haired man moved forward. Naomi, B.J.'s daughter, struggled to free herself to no avail. "Come with us, nice and quiet. If you don't, I'll kill you both. It's only fair since your boyfriend killed my cousin."

Blake Barone. Ice water coursed through Zoe's veins. "Leave Naomi here. If you want Simon, I'm your best leverage. You don't need a defenseless child. Leave Naomi here and take me."

Blake tilted his head. "You'll go with me willingly?"

"If you promise to release Naomi unhurt, I'll go with you." Where were the ranch hands or one of Bravo? Simon's teammates were supposed to be stationed close to the house.

"You don't have any bargaining power, Zoe." An ugly smiled curved his mouth. "If you don't do what I say, I'll hurt you and enjoy every minute of it."

"If you harm Naomi, I won't cooperate and I won't go down easy. I'll raise such a ruckus, the hands will come running. You won't be able to escape. These cowboys don't appreciate a coward who hides behind women and children."

Blake's eyes narrowed. "She comes with us until we're out of sight. Walk to the trees to your right. No more negotiating. I don't want to hurt a kid but I will."

The man had no honor, but refusing wasn't an option. She couldn't take the chance that he would carry out his threat to harm B.J.'s daughter.

"Move," Blake hissed as he gestured at Zoe with the gun clenched in his hand. "Last warning."

She walked where he indicated. Fifteen feet from the house, she stumbled over an object on the ground. She sucked in a breath. Cade. Oh, no. "Is he...?"

"Stun gun. He's fine as long as you cooperate."

When Blake shifted the weapon toward the fallen operative, Zoe moved forward, forcing the thug's attention back to her. In the heavy tree shadow, Zoe almost fell over another body, a man she didn't recognize. Must be one of the ranch hands.

Just inside the tree line, Zoe stopped. "I'm not going one more step unless you release Naomi."

Blake pointed the gun at her. "You'll do what I say unless you want a bullet in the gut."

"You won't shoot me. The gunshot will bring Simon, his friends, his brothers, and the ranch hands. You can't escape that many angry men."

He was silent for a beat. "Fine. I'll let her go after you strip every bit of jewelry from your body."

CHAPTER THIRTY-ONE

Simon glanced up as the back door flew open and slammed into the wall. Naomi ran into the house, tears streaming down her cheeks.

"Daddy!"

B.J. shoved back from the table. He hurried to his daughter and knelt in front of her, scanning her small body for evidence of injury. "What's wrong? Did you fall?"

She shook her head as she wrapped her arms around her father's neck. "You have to help her. The bad man took her."

Adrenaline poured into Simon's veins, dread coiling in his gut. "Help who, Sprite?"

"Zoe."

Blood drained from his face. "Who took Zoe?"

"The bad man. He grabbed me and Zoe came. She made him take her and let me go. You have to get her back, Uncle Simon. You have to."

He grabbed his phone and logged into his email to pull up the picture of Blake Barone that Zane had sent him. How had Barone made it to the house without one of the ranch hands or a member of Bravo seeing him? The "bad man" had to be Barone or one of his cronies. Who else would kidnap Zoe? "Do you know where he took her?"

"To the trees. That's where Zoe made him let me go."

No way would that clown stay there. He had to suspect that Naomi would head straight for the house and tell him and her father what had happened. Simon turned his phone around and showed his niece a picture of Blake Barone. "Is this the man who took Zoe?"

She looked at the screen and nodded. "You have to get her back."

"I will. I promise." He kissed her forehead. "Are you sure the bad man didn't hurt you?"

Naomi shook her head. "He's scary." Her lip quivered.

"Yeah, sweetheart, he is." And he had Zoe. Simon ruthlessly controlled his anger at Barone and fear for Zoe's safety.

"You said you and your friends had security covered. Find this guy and take him down," James snapped. Accusation and fury shown in his brother's eyes.

"That's the plan. Stay in the house and keep everyone else in here." He rose and headed toward the back door, activating his comm system. "We have a security breach. Barone has Zoe."

"Bravo, check in," Trent ordered. Everyone but Cade responded.

"I'm headed to his post now." His post was on the way toward the tree line. Simon stepped outside, weapon in hand, and headed to the right side of the house. He noticed the security light was off and scowled. If Cade was down, no doubt he'd noticed the same thing and been ambushed while checking it out.

Simon searched that side of the yard and found Cade's prone body in a pocket of deep shadow. Oh, man. He closed the gap between them in a few strides and crouched beside his teammate, checking for a pulse. He breathed a sigh of relief when he found a steady beat. Thank God.

Simon activated his comm system again. "Cade's unconscious twenty feet from the house on the west side."

"On the move," Matt said. "Injuries?"

"Unknown. The security light's out."

"Copy."

"My niece said Barone took Zoe toward the tree line. I'm also calling Zane to have him activate her trackers." Thank goodness he'd arranged for her to have the jewelry.

He called the Fortress tech guru.

"What do you need, Simon?"

"Activate Zoe's trackers. She's been kidnapped by Blake Barone."

"Hold." A moment later, Zane said, "Done. Coordinates have been sent to your phone, but you should be able to see her. The trackers are showing that she's one hundred feet to the north of your position. Her phone's been turned off."

Simon's head snapped up. Zoe was still in the trees? Fear gnawed at his gut like a deranged rat. Had Barone hurt her, possibly kill her? Breath strangled in his lungs. No. He couldn't go there. He wouldn't be able to function for the blind rage and driving need for revenge. "Copy that," he murmured and ended the call.

Activating his comm system, he reported in to Trent as he brought up the GPS coordinates on his phone.

"Copy. Wait for me. Two minutes."

Staying put took every ounce of discipline he had. His gaze remained locked on the tree line at the back of the house. True to his word, Trent arrived in two minutes.

Together they approached the tree line and discovered another man on the ground. A glance told Simon the man was one of the ranch hands. Again, this man was unconscious. Trent notified Matt who promised to check on him once he moved Cade inside the house.

After Simon gave Trent the GPS coordinates, the two operatives split up and infiltrated the woods twenty feet apart. Simon chose his footing carefully to mask the sound of his approach. Still no movement from Zoe.

He and Trent moved in on the coordinates from opposite sides. In the middle of a small clearing sat a large flat gray stone that Simon and his siblings had enjoyed playing on when they were young. Zoe and Barone were nowhere in sight.

As he and Bravo's leader zeroed in on that rock, the clouds cleared and a shaft of moonlight lit bits of metal on the rock's surface. "No." Simon's voice came out choked. He shoved a hand through his hair. Barone had forced Zoe to remove her jewelry. Simon had no electronic way to track her location.

When they were certain that Barone and Zoe weren't in the vicinity, the operatives grabbed their penlights to hunt for tracks. Aside from a few tracks in the dirt near the rock, they couldn't find signs of their passage.

Simon crouched near the last tracks and carefully studied the area. He could understand Barone being able to conceal his tracks, but not Zoe. She wasn't trained. She should have left some sign. The knowledge that she hadn't stoked his fear for her safety.

"We can't track her in the dark, Simon," Trent said softly. "We might destroy the very signs we're hunting for and not know it."

Simon stood, grim determination filling him. "I'm not leaving her in his hands for one minute longer than I have to."

"We'll go after her at first light."

"Not good enough. We can't track her in the dark, but I know someone who can." He looked at Trent. "Ethan."

"By the time we fly him out here, it will be daylight."

"He's in Texas on a search for a five-year-old girl."

"And if he hasn't found the child?"

"It won't hurt to ask. If he isn't available, maybe he knows someone close who can do what he does." Except no one was as good as Ethan Blackhawk.

Simon also knew it was probable that Barone had a vehicle stashed nearby and any tracks would lead to a dead end. He prayed that wouldn't be the end result. He wanted the upper hand in the negotiation sure to come. Zoe's life might depend on it. "What about one of the satellites?" He needed a contingency plan in case Ethan was unavailable.

Trent shook his head. "I checked. They're not in the right position."

Grabbing his phone, Simon called the one man who might be able to give him an edge. He placed the call on speaker for Trent to hear the conversation.

"Yeah, Blackhawk."

"It's Simon. You're on speaker with Trent."

"How can I help?"

"Barone kidnapped Zoe."

"I'm on my way."

"Ethan, what about the little girl?"

"She's currently on her way to the hospital to be checked out, but aside from a few cuts and bruises, she looked good to me. I'm already heading your direction. I'll be in Hanover in an hour. Where do you want me to meet you?"

Simon gave Ethan the address of the ranch. "Barone probably had a vehicle stashed somewhere close."

"Maybe. We'll find out. In the meantime, gather supplies and gear up. We may be in for a long night."

He slid the phone into his pocket. An hour would seem like an eternity.

Trent clapped Simon on the shoulder. "Come on. You heard the man. Let's find out what supplies your parents have that we can use. We need to create a Go bag for Ethan."

The corners of Simon's mouth edged upward. "Ethan just completed a hunt. He might need to replenish his supplies, but he has his own gear with him."

The two men retraced their steps to the ranch house. All conversation ceased when they entered through the back door.

Naomi's lips quivered and tears pooled in her eyes. "Where is Zoe? You said you would bring her back."

"I will," Simon vowed, no matter what it took. "It's going to take me longer than I'd planned."

Liam scowled. "What happened?"

"Barone forced Zoe to remove her jewelry."

"What's the big deal about that?" Cassie asked.

"The jewelry had GPS chips embedded in the pieces. We found the jewelry, but not Zoe."

Matt frowned. "You didn't find tracks?"

"We found some that ended a few feet from the jewelry. After that, nothing."

Matt, Liam, and Cade exchanged grim glances.

"How did Barone get the drop on you?" Trent asked Cade.

"When I checked out the blown security light, he hit me with a stun gun. Never mind about me. How are we going to find Zoe?"

"We called the best tracker in the business."

A blink. "Ethan will take hours to get here."

"He should arrive in 45 minutes," Simon said. "He was in the area on a search-and-rescue mission. He found the child and was on his way to Hanover to see Dad."

"Who is Ethan?" Tracey demanded. "Another of your workmates?"

"He's the Otter Creek chief of police and one of the best trackers in the world. If anybody can find Zoe, it's Ethan." Although not being able to do the job himself galled Simon, he'd take any help he could get. He just wanted Zoe back in his arms.

Trent looked at Cade. "You up to the task?"

"By the time Ethan arrives, I will be."

With a nod, he turned to Matt. "How's the ranch hand?"

"Same as Cade. A little shakier than Superman here."

"Good enough. Simon, we need the rest of the hands to set up a perimeter close to the house and station two inside with your family."

"We don't need them inside," Tracey said.

Trent frowned. "Ma'am, I need Simon focused. He's already distracted because Zoe's been taken. Having you and the rest of the family inside this house without protection isn't an option."

"Listen, Trent, I appreciate your concern for the helpless women and children in the family, but let me clue you in. My father taught me and Cassie to shoot as well as my brothers. I know Simon has more training than we do, but we can hold our own. We have guns and we're not afraid to use them."

"The man we're after has Special Forces training. He's far beyond a gun-toting cowboy. I'm not questioning your ability to shoot. Two ranch hands will be inside this house because you'll need every bit of firepower you can get if he slips past the rest of the hands and breaches the house."

Silence fell on the Murray siblings and spouses.

"This guy is that dangerous, Simon?" Cassie asked.

"Do you want to chance it?" he countered.

"Is he as good as you and your friends?"

"No, but he's dangerous enough to be a serious threat to your safety. He doesn't have a conscience, Cass. Barone will do whatever he has to do to achieve his objective."

"Which is?"

"He wants me dead."

She scowled. "Why?"

"I killed his cousin earlier today at the hospital's parking lot. He was going to shoot Zoe."

"I don't understand. He was just some random shooter?"

Simon shook his head.

"How did you become involved with this guy?"

"The head of the Barone family tried to kill my wife," Liam said. "Simon and I helped put him in prison."

"We all had a part in it," Matt reminded him. "By your logic, Blake Barone will come after the rest of us eventually."

"That's why we'll stop him here." Trent eyed his team. "We have families to protect. We can't allow Barone anywhere near Otter Creek again. I won't leave my wife vulnerable to attack while we're deployed."

Tracey, Cassie, James, and B.J. exchanged glances in a silent communication. "Think about the kids," B.J. said to Tracey. "We'll have our hands full keeping them calm and protecting them if trouble comes to us. What will it hurt to have a couple of hands inside the house to help us protect our families?"

Tracey's husband looked her direction. "Tracey." Nothing more in his quiet voice, just her name.

She sighed. "All right. Two ranch hands inside the house. How can we help you and your men prepare, Trent?"

"Make sure all windows and doors are locked. We also need water and protein bars if you have them. We don't know how long we'll be out there. Might be an hour or two days, depending on whether Barone hid a car close by or set up camp on the property."

"We'll take care of the windows and doors. Simon, show your teammates where Mom and Dad keep the supplies." She glanced at her other siblings and their spouses. Andrea and Emily were with the rest of the children to be sure they didn't go outside.

Simon led his teammates into the storage room where his father kept the equipment they needed. As he stocked his pack with supplies for himself and Zoe, he prayed she was of more value to Barone alive than dead. After all, what better way to ensure that Simon would do anything Barone wanted than by threatening to kill Zoe in front of him?

Although he and the others made plans for every contingency, Simon's skin was crawling with the need to go after his woman by the time a black SUV slid into view. He'd been hoping for contact from Barone with a demand to meet. No such luck. What was the creep waiting on?

The Otter Creek police chief exited the vehicle and grabbed a pack. He met Simon at the porch steps. "Any word?"

"Nothing."

A nod. "Didn't expect you would. Barone is messing with your head. Don't let him."

"Hard not to."

"I know. Do it anyway. Nick called a few minutes ago. He made an arrest that you'll be interested in."

Simon frowned. "Who did he nab?"

"A man breaking and entering houses and searching dressers."

He froze. "He broke into Zoe's house?"

"That's right. The perp was looking for a packet of loose diamonds hidden in a dresser that was sold at the flea market. Zoe happened to be one of the customers who bought a dresser from the right vendor. The man also searched Mason's place as well as Macy's."

"Who would hide loose diamonds in a dresser?"

"An old man who didn't trust banks and didn't want his thieving relatives to steal the diamonds. Unfortunately, the relatives were too eager to clean out the house and get rid of the old furniture before they realized they'd gotten rid of the old man's stash of wealth."

"Huh. Is he the man who hurt Piper?"

"He says he's not responsible for that. He didn't hurt anyone, just searched the dressers."

"One of the Barone cousins must have hurt Piper."

"That's my guess."

Time to refocus. "We have water and protein bars for you as well as MREs that we always carry. Didn't know how much of your own stash you'd used during your search."

Simon led him inside the house and introduced him to the family. By the time he finished the introductions, Naomi had edged closer to Ethan, her dark brown eyes showing her wariness and worry.

Ethan crouched beside her. "My name is Ethan. What's yours?"

"Naomi."

"That's a pretty name."

"Thank you."

"Did you want to ask me something, Naomi?"

She nodded. "Will you find Zoe?"

"I'll do my best. She's a friend of mine."

"She made the bad man let me go."

His face softened. "That sounds like something she'd do."

"But he might hurt Zoe. Uncle Simon said so. I heard him even though I wasn't supposed to listen. I should have stayed quiet. If I didn't cry, the bad man wouldn't have her."

Simon's eyes burned. He should have realized what she was feeling. He'd been too focused on his own anguish and fear for the woman he loved.

"You did exactly what you should have," Ethan said. "You kept yourself safe by not making the bad man angry and you listened to what Zoe told you to do. She wanted you to be with your Mom and Dad."

"But I don't want him to hurt her anymore."

Fists clenched, Simon closed his eyes for a moment as the realization sank in. That jerk had hurt Zoe. Barone was a dead man. He just didn't know it yet.

"Listen to me, sweetheart." Ethan laid his hand on her shoulder. "Zoe is one smart lady. She'll do everything she can to keep herself safe. Because you're here, she doesn't have to worry about your safety as well as her own. We'll find her and free her."

"I want to help, too."

Simon swallowed past the lump in his throat. His niece was killing him. So brave with a big heart.

Ethan gave a nod. "We can use it. Help the adults keep the other kids calm and inside the house. We can't let them outside. You could find a movie to watch or play a game that involves everyone. If they want a snack, you can bring them snacks and drinks. That will encourage them to stay together in one room. Will you do that?"

She squared her shoulders and nodded. "Okay."

"Good girl. Thanks for the help, Naomi." Ethan rose, shoved the supplies set aside for him into his pack, and looked at Simon. "Show me."

After handing Ethan a spare comm system and shrugging on his pack, Simon led Ethan and the rest of Bravo to the woods where he'd seen the last signs of Zoe. The surface of the stone was empty now, Zoe's jewelry safely tucked into Simon's pocket. He'd give them back to her when he found her.

He and his teammates stayed at the edge of the clearing, letting Ethan search. Ethan crouched at the last place Simon found signs of Zoe's foot tread in the dirt. After a moment, he glanced over his shoulder at Simon. "Got it. Let's go."

CHAPTER THIRTY-TWO

Simon and his teammates trailed Ethan as the police chief tracked Barone and Zoe through the wooded section of the Murray ranch. The further they walked, the more confident Simon grew that Barone had set up a base camp somewhere close. Although he couldn't see a trail, Ethan led them away from a place where a vehicle could easily travel.

He thought about the direction they were heading. That whole area was a dead zone as far as cell coverage went. Perhaps that was the explanation for why Barone hadn't made contact with Simon. If the thug had called and demanded Simon trade himself for Zoe, Simon would have done it in a heartbeat. He could handle whatever Barone dished out. The same couldn't be said for Zoe.

Ten feet ahead, Ethan raised his hand and made a fist. Bravo stopped and waited.

Simon's heart skipped a beat when the chief crouched and appeared to study the ground for an extraordinary length of time. Had he lost the trail? Unable to stand the suspense any longer, he glanced at Trent for permission, then moved closer to the police chief. "What is it? What do you see?"

"Barone brought friends to the party." He looked over his shoulder. "At least five other men joined them here, maybe more. The prints are overlapping so much I can't tell an exact number. One of them dropped a small bit of C-4. My guess is they set up a few surprises in case you came after them."

"No way I wouldn't."

"Of course not. They hoped you would come while it was still dark. Much easier to miss the signs of a bomb in the darkness." He stood. "Is Cade up to the task?"

"Let's find out." Simon motioned for his teammate to join them. When he did, Simon said, "Barone and his buddies may have set booby traps. Ethan found C-4. Are you operational?" Cade was the best around in handling explosives. Doing that job when you were still woozy from being zapped by a stun gun was foolhardy.

"I'm fine now. Let me look around before Ethan moves ahead."

The police chief moved back.

Cade grabbed his flashlight and began to search the area. About 25 feet ahead, he crouched, playing the light across the ground in slow motion. He shifted to the left a few feet, stopped, examined the dirt, then slid his pack from his back.

Simon joined him. "Need help?"

"Hold the flashlight." He showed Simon where to aim the beam. "You sure you want to offer assistance? I'm not as steady as I usually am."

Oh, man. "You said you were operational."

"I am, but I'm not operating at the normal level."

Small comfort. What choice did they have, though? Trent had some EOD training. He could be Cade's hands if necessary. "Trent can handle the delicate work if you need him. What do we have?"

"IED with a pressure plate. Would have been obvious in daylight. It's practically invisible at night." Within a few minutes, Cade had safely disassembled the bomb. He got to his feet. "This could be a long night if those clowns left many of these."

He prayed that wasn't the case. Simon needed to find Zoe. "You want to stay with Ethan? He can follow the trail while you keep an eye out for more IEDs."

His friend nodded.

Simon returned to the rest of Bravo. "Watch where you step. Barone brought friends and one of them left an IED behind."

"Terrific." Trent scowled. "Spread out and be alert."

Trotting back to his original position, he signaled for Ethan to proceed. Three more times, the police chief held up a fist and Cade had to dismantle more bombs. The volume made Simon worry that there might be more they didn't see. The cattle, ranch hands, or one of the kids might stumble upon one accidentally. He vowed to have a bomb-sniffing dog search the area before he allowed anyone in this part of the spread.

Three miles from the main house, Ethan came to a sudden stop and signaled the team behind him to scatter before taking shelter himself.

From behind the shelter of a large rock formation, Simon watched as a man dressed in black camouflage walked into view carrying an M5. When his path took him into a patch of moonlight, Simon spotted his sidearm and a Ka-Bar strapped to his thigh. One of Barone's men.

Five feet from Simon's position, the thug stopped and scanned the area, a frown forming. Had he seen movement from Bravo or Ethan? No way. If Simon didn't know where his teammates and Ethan had taken shelter, he wouldn't be able to spot them.

A moment later, the silence of the night was broken by the crackle of a radio. Though the volume was low, sounds carried long distances at night.

"Ashton, report," snapped a disembodied voice.

A scowl from the thug. "Nothing yet," he growled.

"You sure?"

"Yeah."

"I don't like it. The woman's boyfriend is out there somewhere. I've seen them together. Murray is gone over her. He won't wait until daylight. Stay alert."

"Yeah, copy that." Ashton shoved the radio back into his pants pocket, cursing.

Simon glanced at Trent who was in his line of sight and received a nod of agreement.

The thug glanced around the area one more time, then pivoted to return the way he'd come.

Keeping to the shadows, Simon circled around to the right to another stand of trees and waited for Ashton to pass his position. When he did, Simon slipped behind him and tackled him.

The man fought like a cornered wildcat. Simon had been trained in the same hand-to-hand combat techniques in the military, then added more training with Fortress. His teammates had taught him several skills learned from their various military backgrounds. Within two minutes, Ashton was moaning on the ground, restrained and stripped of weapons and his radio.

Simon and Liam frog-marched him to a tree stump a few feet away and shoved him down. "Let's talk, Ashton," Simon said, arms folded.

The thug sneered. "Got nothing to say except you need to let me go if you want your woman to survive the hour."

Trent snorted. "It's not smart to remind Simon that you and your buddies have his girlfriend. He holds grudges and enjoys dishing out punishment."

"You don't scare me."

The gaze shifting from one member of Bravo to the other said he was lying. Simon took out his own Ka-Bar and pretended to examine the blade. "You should rethink that."

Ashton swallowed hard, his gaze locked on the knife. "What do you want?"

"Zoe. Where is she?"

The man remained mute.

Liam, who stood behind the thug, glanced at Trent, eyebrow raised.

Bravo's team leader turned to Ethan and Cade. "Keep going. Make sure we don't have any more surprises waiting for us while we take care of Ashton."

After the two men left, Trent nodded at Liam. The sniper clamped a hand over Ashton's mouth and pressed hard on a pressure point on the thug's shoulder. Immediately, the man gave a muffled scream, sweat beading on his brow as he fought against the zip ties securing his wrists behind his back and struggling to free himself from Liam's hold. He failed. At Trent's signal, Liam eased off although he retained his controlling hold on the man.

"Where is Zoe?" Simon snapped. "My friend can keep this up all night. I'll warn you, though, the pain will only continue to get worse if you refuse to answer my questions."

"You don't understand. He'll kill me."

"Then you better pray we get to him first."

Trent tilted his head. "I don't think he believes us." He flicked a glance at Liam who covered Ashton's mouth and shifted to another pressure point. The response was immediate. More violent thrashing and louder screaming. By the time Trent signaled Liam to ease off, tears were streaming down Ashton's face.

"Where is my woman?" Simon growled. "And don't bother to lie to me. I'll know."

"Cabin," the man said, shuddering with relief.

"Which one? There are three in this area." He had a good idea which one, but he didn't want to waste time going to the wrong cabin. Every minute counted. The more time they had to form a plan, the better. He had to see for himself if Zoe was all right. Not knowing was driving him crazy.

"East of here about two clicks. It's a big one."

Old man Walters' cabin. That place was empty except when the large Walters clan came to visit. Simon turned to Trent. "Tell the others to hold position."

With a nod, Bravo's leader activated his comm system.

"How many people does Barone have, Ashton?"

"Twelve," he muttered. "Too many to take on a small unit of wannabe mercenaries. We could have handled it without the others."

"My feelings are hurt," Liam said.

Matt rolled his eyes. "Wannabe mercenaries? If we're not the real deal, how did we capture you?"

Ashton scowled.

"Are Barone's people mercenaries, military, what?" Simon asked.

"Half are former military. The other half are civilians. Family members."

"Civvies mess up everything."

"You got that right." Disgust filled the thug's voice. "Barone's family doesn't know how to take orders. They argue with him all the time. I was glad to go out on patrol just to get away from the bickering."

"What are they fighting over?" Trent asked.

"Who gets the girl when Murray is dead, who collects the bounty, and who takes power and restarts the family business."

"How will Barone play this?"

A head shake. "I don't know."

Liam adjusted his hold.

Ashton jumped. "I don't know," he insisted. "Barone won't tell anybody his plan. He's a paranoid jerk who doesn't trust anyone."

"What else do you know?"

"After you're dead, he'll kill your girl, then go after the rest of the men involved in that business in Alabama."

Exactly what he'd thought. Bravo couldn't afford to let Barone slip away. If they did, the rest of Bravo and their families were the next targets.

CHAPTER THIRTY-THREE

Zoe rubbed the zip ties restraining her wrists against the metal bracket of the bed frame. She didn't know if she was making much headway, but she felt more play in the restraints.

As she worked, Zoe listened to the argument raging in the living room on the first floor. Although she was on the second level of the log cabin, almost every word drifted up the stairs.

She grimaced at the creative ways the jerks were coming up with to make her pay for associating with Simon. According to the Barone clan, she was tainted goods now. That left the other men who acted like they were military. They didn't mind getting their hands dirty with her.

The thought of one or more of them touching her made Zoe want to barf. It also spurred her to work faster to free her wrists. At this rate, she'd be lucky if she made progress with the plastic before one of the men returned to stare and taunt her again.

A short time later, Zoe heard heavy male footsteps on the stairs. Great. Which one was coming this time? The man with curly black hair or the straw-colored blond with the crooked nose? She shuddered. Either one made her uncomfortable. Something in their eyes caused her pulse to race and her stomach to churn.

Curly and Blondie were the embodiment of evil. They liked to hurt people. Given what she knew of the Barone cousins, Zoe wasn't surprised that they had gathered people like these two men to go after Bravo.

She kept sawing at the plastic around her wrists until a shadow appeared on the corridor wall. Blondie strode into the room farther than the earlier times he'd checked on her.

"Miss me?" he murmured, gaze drifting over her body.

Zoe fought a shudder. She didn't want to give him the satisfaction of knowing how much he affected her. "Like a bad rash."

His eyes narrowed. "You don't want to make me angry."

"Barone won't like it if his leverage is mishandled." At least she prayed that was true. She needed to stay alive because Simon was coming. Zoe felt that truth to her bones. He wouldn't give up until she was back in his arms.

Blondie crouched beside her. "Barone won't always be around. Sometime soon, he won't need you anymore. Then you'll be mine. Maybe you won't mind as much as you pretend. Your boyfriend isn't much of a man. The coward hasn't even bothered to track you down yet." He smiled. "You don't have to worry about that with me. I'll always find you and bring you back. You won't like the punishment, but I will."

Zoe glared at him. "Simon is more man than you'll ever be. He has honor and integrity. You're nothing but a two-bit thug with a bad attitude, a gun, and a pea-sized brain."

Before she could draw in a breath, Blondie slapped her. Zoe's head whipped to the left as something crashed to the floor and broke. Pain radiated from her cheekbone in waves. Despite Blondie using his open hand to hit her, Zoe saw stars and wondered if she was going to pass out again. From the feel of her jaw, Barone had slugged her to knock her out for transport to this place, then hauled her away from the Murray home.

"Hey," Barone yelled up the stairs. "Everything okay up there?"

Blondie's eyes glittered. "Yeah, she's fine." He leaned close enough to whisper, "But not for long." He stroked the top button of her shirt. "You're going to pay." He stalked from the room, slamming the door behind him.

Zoe blinked away the tears in her eyes. She could cry later when she had an ice pack pressed to her face and Simon's arms around her. Man, she missed him so much she could barely draw in a breath.

She sat up to resume the work on the zip ties when her foot slid on something. She glanced down. A shard of ceramic. Her eyes widened. Would the broken piece have enough of a sharp edge to cut through the plastic?

Only one way to find out. Zoe used the edge of her shoe to maneuver the shard toward her hands. She twisted and turned, pushing the ceramic close enough to grasp.

Zoe's breath puffed out as though she'd run a marathon. Nice. Who knew twisting yourself into a pretzel winded you? After a moment, she positioned the piece so a sharp edge lay against the plastic and began to saw.

"Come on," she muttered after a while. "Give way already." Minutes later, the restraint broke and Zoe's hands were free.

She scrambled to her feet and hurried to the closest window. Back pressed against the wall, she moved the curtain enough to see that this was the side of the cabin with a straight drop to the ground. Wonder Woman could do it. Unfortunately, Zoe wasn't a superhero.

Ducking under the window frame so she wouldn't be visible to someone on the ground, she crossed the room to the other window and wanted to scream in frustration. That window faced the front of the house where two men stood.

Zoe eyed the door. She didn't remember Blondie locking the door and realized the lock was on her side of the doorknob. She could get out, but big deal? From the sounds of the continuing argument downstairs, this time over the best ways to handle Simon, there were several men on the first floor. She would never escape by using the main stairwell.

Did this place have stairs at the back of the house? With her luck, they led into the kitchen, a place where one or more of the guards could be drinking coffee or eating a snack. No, if back stairs existed, they would be her last resort.

If her prison was at the front of the house, there must be other rooms on the other side of the hallway. Those rooms might give her a better option for escaping from Barone and his cronies. If she put enough distance between her and the creeps, there were plenty of places to hide and wait for daylight or for Simon.

Knowing she didn't have much time before either Curly or Blondie returned, Zoe twisted the knob. She eased the door open an inch and waited to see if someone noticed that she was free.

After a moment, she concluded that she was safe. Opening the door wider, Zoe peered down the hall toward the stairs. No guards on this level. She saw a closed door across the hall and decided it wasn't safe to open. What if one of Barone's men was asleep in there? Another room to the left had an open door. She would try that one.

Zoe slipped into the hall and hurried into the darkened room. She didn't see or hear anyone. Although she hated to close the door and alert one of the men to a change, she hated even more to leave herself vulnerable. Maybe she could find a weapon to protect herself even if an escape route wasn't available.

Decision made, Zoe closed and locked the door, then went to the window. No escape. Straight down. She glanced to the right and spotted French doors. A balcony?

Heart beating faster, she unlocked the French door and opened it a fraction. Cool night air rushed into the room and made her doubly glad she'd shut the door to the hall. Definitely a balcony or a deck. She opened the door wider and checked for guards standing on the wooden surface. The balcony was empty.

Zoe stepped out and closed the door behind her. She glanced around. Although the guards weren't in evidence on the ground, she knew that wouldn't last long. The men were thorough and seemed to know what they were doing.

No stairs. The balcony was enclosed. However, a large tree was close enough for Zoe to grab one of the branches. She'd never been a tree climber. Guess she was going to learn. Anything to escape Curly and Blondie and their pals.

Zoe heard a noise from below and lay flat on the wooden surface of the balcony, hoping she wouldn't be seen. The lighting was dim on this side of the house, something she knew Simon wouldn't have allowed if this were his place.

Soon, the guard disappeared around the side of the house. Zoe popped up, reached for the tree limb, and hauled herself onto the rough surface. Inch by inch, she felt her way to the trunk of the tree, then reached for the next lower branch with the toe of her tennis shoe. She was so getting hiking boots before the week was out.

Zoe made her way carefully to the ground. Now what? She glanced around. Not seeing or hearing a guard, she mimicked what she'd observed of Simon's movements during their mission the night before. She hugged the shadows, careful not to step on something that would break or crack and give away her position.

Urgency drove her to move faster. Curly or Blondie would check on her soon. Once they knew she was gone, they'd sound the alarm and she would have a bunch of thugs on her trail.

Zoe reached the safety of the woods when a shout came from the house. She glanced over her shoulder. Her heart sank. Time was up.

CHAPTER THIRTY-FOUR

Simon activated his comm system. "In position," he murmured, gaze locked on the 6,000-square-foot cabin where his woman was being held against her will. Someone would pay for taking Zoe. Barone would pay more for hurting her. Before he left the house, Naomi had informed Simon that Barone punched Zoe in the face.

"Hold," Trent whispered.

Simon scanned the area, skin prickling. Where were the guards? Barone should have posted guards to alert him to unwanted visitors. Only a fool would assume that Simon and his teammates wouldn't track Zoe. Were the guards good enough that Bravo and Ethan missed them or were they gone?

Grabbing his NVGs, Simon studied the cabin. Two people moved about freely on the first floor. A ball of ice formed in his gut. Neither one appeared to be Zoe.

He scanned the top floor again. No heat signatures. Had Barone moved Zoe when Ashton didn't check in?

Jaw clenched, Simon vowed to capture one of the men left behind and force him to divulge where Barone took

Zoe. He didn't care what kind of force was necessary to learn the truth.

Ethan's voice sounded over the comm system. "I located several sets of footprints leading away from the cabin. One set belongs to Zoe."

Simon froze. "Trent?" His voice came out rough, gut screaming that Zoe was in trouble. He had to find her.

"Ethan, location?"

"Back of the cabin, west corner at the tree line."

"Simon, go."

He skirted the perimeter of the structure, hugging the shadows to avoid alerting the two clowns in the cabin that Bravo had located their hideout. They must have a way to communicate with Barone.

When he located Ethan, the police chief pointed at the prints in the dirt. "Zoe has several men after her." He turned to Simon, expression grim. "She won't be able to elude them for long."

And when they found her, they would be furious. Remembering the sheer brutality highlighted in Blake Barone's background, Simon activated his comm system. "Looks like Zoe escaped. The rest of the men must be combing the area for her."

"Copy. Five minutes. We need to secure the guards before we go after Zoe. Do not proceed until the cabin is secured."

Simon's hands fisted. "Copy."

While they waited, Ethan studied the footprints while Simon scouted the area for more indications of the direction Zoe went. How ironic that one woman ignited an all-out search when Barone or one of his men could have handled the search with a second person for backup.

"Eight or nine men are on her trail," Ethan murmured. "They'll split up and run her to ground."

"You're not helping."

"You can handle the truth better than a pretty lie." Dark eyes glanced his way. "Zoe is smart. She'll do her best to protect herself and she has an excellent motive to survive. You."

Simon hoped that would be enough, but going up against a Special Forces unit without protection or experience was a recipe for failure.

At the five-minute mark, the rest of Bravo joined them. Trent glanced at Simon. "You and Ethan take point. Stay on Zoe's trail. The rest of us will peel off to track the rest of them. Zoe is your only priority."

"Yes, sir." He set off with Ethan, following the smaller footprints in the dirt. Simon's tracking skills weren't in the same class as Ethan's, but he recognized the place where Zoe realized the thugs were on her trail. Her tread patterns became more distinctive with a kickout in the heel digging deeper when his girl began to run.

Simon fought the need to sprint after her, forcing himself to consider what he was seeing with cool logic. She was using as much hard surface as she could find to lose her pursuers. Unfortunately, she left enough prints behind to gain a few minutes before the men caught her trail again. About three hundred yards further, Barone and his merry band of thugs split up to cut off Zoe's escape routes.

Simon glanced over his shoulder as Trent divided the rest of his team. Although they were outnumbered, Bravo thrived in games of cat-and-mouse. Still, tracking down more than one opponent would slow their progress. Simon didn't want to contemplate the possibility that Barone's men seeded this area with IEDs. The men didn't seem to be avoiding one particular direction. If he was smart, Barone left himself and his men an escape route. If there was a safe zone, Simon prayed Zoe stayed inside the boundaries.

When he and Ethan broke from the trees, Simon oriented himself and sucked in a breath, dread coiling in his gut. Ethan glanced back at him, eyebrows raised. "There's a gorge half a mile from here with a steep drop to the river. In the darkness, Zoe might not see it until it was too late." Or she wouldn't have a choice. Barone might force her over the edge to rid himself of a problem.

He activated his comm system and informed the others about the gorge, receiving four clicks in silent acknowledgment. The information would be enough for his teammates. They could take care of themselves. Zoe needed help derailing the goons on her trail.

Simon was surprised that she'd eluded her pursuers this long. Was Barone toying with Zoe, heightening her fear before pouncing? Based on his profile, Barone wasn't above using psychological torture to get what he wanted.

"Ethan, how many men are tracking her?"

"Three."

"One of them has to be Barone. He wouldn't leave her recapture to an underling. That leaves six who are circling to cut her off."

They continued in silence. Although Simon wanted Ethan to push the pace, they risked missing a sign of her passage through the area and having to retrace their steps to pick up her trail again if they were wrong. Zoe couldn't afford for them to make a mistake.

The closer they moved to the gorge, the more Simon's fear grew until the urgency to find Zoe before Barone or his cronies did consumed him.

When they were close to the edge of the gorge, a woman screamed. Zoe! Simon surged ahead of Ethan and raced toward the sound of male laughter.

CHAPTER THIRTY-FIVE

Zoe glared at Barone, fighting against Blondie's hold. Seconds later, his hold shifted and Blondie brandished a knife in front of her face.

"I like my women to fight," he growled. "Makes it more enjoyable."

"For who?" she muttered.

"Me."

Her attention swung to Barone. "Let me go," she demanded.

"Sorry, pretty lady," he said, not sounding sorry in the least. "You're too valuable to release."

"What do you want?" Despite knowing the answer to her question, Simon needed time to find her. In other words, she had to stall Blake Barone.

"Your boyfriend," he said in answer to her question. "You're the bait."

Blondie dragged Zoe tighter against his chest. "You promised to give her to me. I don't want to wait until later."

His boss looked thoughtful a moment, then shook his head. "Too dangerous to have you distracted."

A snort from the man holding her caged against his body. "You don't have anything to worry about. Whoever told you Murray and his team were an elite unit didn't know squat. Murray should have been here long before now even with the surprises we left behind to slow him down." Blondie nuzzled Zoe's temple. "You'll find out what a real man is like soon, sweet cheeks."

Eww! She turned her face away, disgusted and terrified that he would do what he wanted as soon as Barone's back was turned. Simon was coming. The question was if he would arrive in time to spare her from this thug's intentions.

Unfortunately, Curly stood on her left side, a grin on his swarthy face, black eyes glittering. "She don't want you, man. She prefers a real man like me."

Curly was right. She did prefer a real man--Simon. Zoe caught movement in the trees. She dropped her gaze and fought in earnest.

The shadowy figure didn't move like an animal. Providing a distraction was the only thing she could do to help. Was the mysterious figure Simon? She couldn't be sure.

The terrible threesome laughed again at her futile struggles. "You're wasting your strength," Barone said, a smirk on his face. "You'll need your strength later because Jenks is all about obedience and pain."

That she could believe.

A noise to her right had the three men pivoting that direction. Jenks kept her squarely in front of his body, the jerk. Barone and Curly had weapons in their hands, aimed that direction.

Zoe waited for another noise or for movement on her left where she'd seen the shadow figure. Unfortunately, Zoe's new position prevented her from seeing the progress of the operative closing in.

Another noise came from the right in the trees. Barone frowned and glanced at Curly. "Check it out."

The thug took off for the trees and melted into the darkness. A moment later, a muffled thump sounded. Barone stiffened. "Hatcher?" he called.

Nothing broke the silence aside from the night breeze. A scowl. "Hatcher."

Tension filled Jenks' body. "Something's wrong."

Barone sent the man a derisive look. "You think?" He waited another moment and called out again. When he received no response, Barone glanced at Jenks. "Give her to me and find Hatcher. Be alert."

"I'm not planning on napping in the dirt," he growled as he shoved Zoe into Barone's arms. "Remember who she belongs to, Barone. I want her in good shape. I've got plans for sweet Zoe."

"Move," Barone snapped.

Jenks slid his knife away, palmed his gun, and headed for the trees where his cohort had disappeared.

Barone dragged Zoe farther from the trees. She twisted to free herself from his hold. Barone countered every movement until she was pinned so tight against him that she couldn't move. Great. How could she help herself and the operatives now?

Zoe's attention shifted to the left. Though the area was shrouded in darkness, she had the impression of a vast open space. A ravine? If she could free herself, a ravine offered ample places to hide until Simon or one of his friends found her.

But the space felt bigger than a ditch. The lack of light frustrated her. Distraction. She needed to distract Barone from his intense focus. Physically fighting this Special Forces soldier wasn't an option. His hold was unbreakable. That left breaking his concentration. "If you want to survive this night, let me go."

Barone gave a rough laugh. "Trying to scare me is a waste of your time. I don't scare, sweetheart, and I'm

303

certainly not afraid of your boyfriend. He's all talk and no action."

"You're an idiot."

"I couldn't have said it better myself." Simon stepped out from the stand of trees, although he was still in the shadows. "Let her go, Barone. You want me, not her."

"Look who finally showed up to the party late. Simon Murray, the coward responsible for sending my uncle to prison."

"Matteo sent himself to prison by breaking the law."

"He was taking care of his family." The muscles in Barone's body hardened.

"By selling weapons illegally. How many innocent families were torn apart by your uncle's business? Too many to count, Barone."

"Stop talking about Uncle Matteo." He pressed a gun to Zoe's temple. "Get over here, Murray, or I'll kill your woman in front of you."

"And lose your only leverage? I don't think so. If you shoot her, I will kill you before you take another breath."

Barone stilled. "She'll still be dead and you'll have to live with the knowledge that you're to blame."

Simon moved closer. "You want me? Come get me." He gave a "come on" gesture.

The man holding Zoe captive growled and threw her to the left.

Zoe screamed as she fell into the darkness.

CHAPTER THIRTY-SIX

Horror filled Simon as Zoe disappeared over the edge of the gorge, a scream ripping from her throat. "Zoe!" He tore his gaze away from his greatest nightmare and refocused on the man bearing down on him like a freight train. The sooner he dispensed with Barone, the faster he could find Zoe and provide medical assistance. He refused to even consider that she was beyond help.

Simon shifted his weight at the last second, twisted, and used the thug's momentum to slam Barone to the ground on his back. He rammed his fist into Barone's face twice, splitting his lip and breaking his nose, blocked a roundhouse punch to the jaw, and landed more blows to the man's face.

A moment later, he sailed over Barone's head when the soldier tossed him off. Simon hit the ground on a roll that ended in a fighting stance. He blocked kicks and punches when Barone came at him again, landing blows between each of his opponent's failed attempts.

Barone's attacks slowed, more attempts to hit Simon missing his target than hitting. Enough. He'd wasted too much time on this clown. Simon swept the other man's feet out from under him and followed him to the ground. After another two punches and an elbow strike to the temple, Barone was out.

Breathing hard, Simon grabbed his Sig and aimed at the man coming from the trees. He lowered the weapon when Ethan strode into view.

"Go," the police chief said. "I've got Barone."

Simon leaped up and ran to the edge of the gorge. "Zoe!"

"Simon, help me. My hands are getting tired."

Her voice helped him pinpoint her location. She clung to a slender tree growing into the side of the gorge. If she lost her grip, Zoe would fall at least twenty feet before she hit a ledge. "Don't let go, baby. I'll come get you in a minute."

Simon ran to the tree where he'd left his bag. Digging out his rope as he returned, he caught more movement to his right and Bravo emerged from the tree cover. "Zoe fell over the side of the gorge."

Matt slid his Go bag from his shoulder and grabbed his flashlight. He hurried to the edge and aimed the light into the gorge. After a moment he glanced over his shoulder. "I'm going down there. We don't know what kind of injuries she's sustained. It's not safe to move her until we know for sure."

"Leaving her hanging there isn't an option. She won't be able to hold on much longer." Simon stepped into his harness and secured it to the rope, then attached a second one from Trent to his harness. Cade took the other end of the rope and secured it to a nearby tree. Trent did the same for Matt's rope. When his teammates indicated that all was ready, he and Matt turned their backs to the gorge and began a careful ten-foot descent to Zoe.

When Simon drew even with her, he slid the extra harness around Zoe's waist and secured it. He glanced up to be sure his teammates were ready and received a hand signal to proceed. Simon wrapped his arms around her. "Let go, sweetheart. Your harness is attached to mine."

"I'll be too heavy and pull you down with me."

"Trust me," he murmured into her ear. "Lean against me and let me take your weight. I won't let you fall." A moment later, she let go of the tree.

Matt came to a stop on Zoe's other side. "Where are you hurt?"

"Everything hurts. My right ankle is the worst."

"I'll check that when we're up top. Will you let me check your ribs?"

She nodded. Her breath hitched when Matt pressed against the middle of her ribcage.

"Tender?"

"Very."

"I don't think the ribs are broken, Simon, but I want to be safe anyway until I'm sure."

With a nod, Simon glanced at Trent and Liam. "Haul us up, nice and easy," he called. As his teammates pulled them up, Simon leaned back and "walked" the side of the gorge with Zoe cradled against him.

When they crested the top of the gorge, Trent and Liam lifted them to solid ground while Cade and Ethan held the rope steady.

A moment later, Matt hauled himself over the edge and got to his feet. "Get the harness off her, then I'll check Zoe's ribs before I work on that ankle."

Once their harnesses were removed, Simon eased Zoe to the ground while Matt retrieved his mike bag. As the medic checked her, Simon sat with his chest to Zoe's back for her to rest against and cradled her hand in his. "Did Barone or his cronies hurt you?"

When she didn't say anything, Matt glanced at him, flicked his gaze to her face, then returned his attention to her ribs.

Stomach knotting, Simon leaned to the side to see her face. When she turned her face away, he gently cupped her chin with the palm of his hand and turned her face toward him.

He gritted his teeth when he saw the injuries to her beautiful face. "I should have killed Barone."

"I'm all right, Simon. I'll heal." She smiled. "I'm proud of myself. I escaped from a Special Forces team and almost made it to safety by myself."

Simon's teammates and Ethan chuckled at that. He didn't. The terror of almost losing her still rode him hard. Simon pressed a gentle kiss to her bruised mouth.

"Barone took my phone. Lyons told him about the jewelry. He heard one of the other wives talking about it and figured you gave me a set as well. Barone made me take them off."

"I found the jewelry. They gave us a starting point to track you."

Matt straightened. "Ribs are bruised, but I don't feel any broken bones, Zoe. I'll check your extremities, then focus on your ankle."

Simon remained quiet while Zoe answered Matt's questions, reveling in the pleasure of having her with him again. When the medic reached Zoe's ankle, he handed Trent a flashlight to illuminate the injury. Simon whistled softly. Zoe's ankle was swollen to twice it's normal size.

"Bet that hurts," Liam said.

"You are the master of understatement," Zoe said, voice tight.

"I'll use a vacuum splint on your ankle until you reach the hospital." Matt grabbed his equipment from the mike bag, positioned the splint, and pumped air into it. He turned to Simon. "She needs to have an x-ray as soon as possible."

"Is it safe for me to carry her?"

"I think so." Matt turned to Zoe. "If the way Simon holds you hurts, you have to tell me. We have other ways to transport you. Promise?"

She nodded.

"Let's get her out of here."

Liam and Simon lifted Zoe from the ground. Once she was steady, Simon slid one arm behind Zoe's back and one behind her knees and settled her against his chest. "Is this okay?" he asked Zoe.

She wrapped her arms around his neck and nodded. "Don't forget my phone."

Simon looked at Liam.

His best friend jogged to the moaning man and searched until he found the phone. Liam slid it into a compartment of Simon's vest.

"I'll stay with Barone and drive to the hospital when the local cops arrive on the scene."

"Thanks, Ethan," Simon said.

The police chief nodded. "Get your girl to a doctor. I'll see you in a few hours."

Simon set off with Zoe in his arms, his teammates surrounding them for protection. When they arrived at the cabin, Simon set Zoe on the wicker couch on the porch and elevated her injured foot. He called for an ambulance since the SUVs were still at the ranch. Although he could have carried Zoe longer, he wanted her examined by a doctor as soon as possible.

Within minutes, an ambulance parked in the driveway, followed by the local police. Trent motioned for Simon to accompany Zoe to the hospital while he and the others provided explanations to law enforcement, including the locations of Barone and his cronies. They had noted the GPS coordinates where they left each thug.

When one of the EMTs insisted that Simon ride in front with the driver, he glared at the man. "I'm not leaving her."

The other man sighed. "All right. Just stay out of the way."

Ignoring him, Simon climbed into the rig and sat near her head. The ambulance doors closed and they sped down the driveway with lights flashing and siren blaring.

When they arrived at the medical center, Simon contacted Texas unit's leader to provide backup.

Brody Weaver arrived two minutes later. "Sit rep."

Simon reported what had taken place in the hours since he and Zoe had left the hospital. While he talked to the other team leader, Simon kept an eye on the door to the examination room. When he finished his report, he turned back to Brody. "I think the danger to Dad is over but I'm not positive."

"We'll stay on duty for now." Brody lifted one shoulder. "We want you focused on Zoe."

He couldn't deny the relief that swept through him at the other operative's words. "How are my parents?"

"No incidents while you were gone. Have you had anything to eat or drink for a while?"

"No, sir."

"You burned a lot of fuel. I'll be back in a few minutes with a snack."

The next two hours passed in a blur as the doctor examined Zoe and sent her for x-rays on the ankle. He was by her side when the doctor returned with the news that Zoe had a severe sprain that required a walking boot or crutches.

Zoe made a face. "Boot, please. I'll be a hazard to everyone around me if I'm using crutches."

When the doctor released her clad in a walking boot, she had a prescription for pain medicine in her hand. As she hobbled down the corridor toward the elevator, Simon stayed close to her side, steadying her when she staggered.

"This is ridiculous," she grouched. "I feel like a toddler just learning how to walk."

"While the boot provides stability for your abused joint, the weight throws you off balance,"

She sent him a suspicious look. "I'm aware. You've worn one of these contraptions?"

"More than once. I'm not a fan of crutches, either."

They arrived at his father's room to see Ethan in a conversation with him.

Lisa Murray leaped to her feet, worry filling her gaze. "Zoe! What happened to you?"

"It's a long story that I'll let Simon tell you. Do you mind if I sit down?"

"No, of course not."

While his mother fussed over Zoe, Simon helped her settle into a chair. He glanced at Ethan, his eyebrow raised. Had the police chief told his parents anything of the night's events?

Ethan gave a slight head shake in answer to Simon's unspoken question.

"Simon, what's going on?" Don frowned. "You look like you've been in a fight."

He glanced at his mother. "You'll want to sit down for this."

"That bad, huh?"

"A long, involved explanation." He spent the next hour relaying the events of the night and answering his parents' questions.

Lisa rubbed Zoe's shoulder. "Are you sure you're all right, Zoe? Those awful men had you in their hands for several hours."

Simon watched closely for Zoe's reaction. He hadn't had the privacy to ask Zoe for details of her time in the hands of Barone and his buddies. Would she have told him if the thugs hurt her in ways he couldn't see?

"I'll heal."

A ball of ice formed in his stomach. What if Barone or his buddies had raped her? Simon doubted Zoe would blurt out the truth to his mother. He vowed to get the truth from her as soon as they were alone.

"Simon, do you have a recommendation for a good hotel close by?" Ethan asked. "I need to sleep a few hours before I make arrangements to return to Otter Creek."

He told Ethan the name of their hotel. "I'll tell the front desk to add your room to my tab."

"That's not necessary, my friend." Ethan clapped him on the shoulder. "I'm glad I was in the area and able to help." A few minutes later, the police chief took his leave after promising to stop in before he left town.

Simon's father looked at him. "Is the danger over, son?"

"I'll know more in another 48 hours." He had already contacted Maddox with an idea to end the threat to Bravo and their families from the Barone organization. If the plan worked, they'd know by that time. If not, he and the rest of Bravo would shift to more drastic measures. No one threatened their loved ones without serious repercussions.

"Go rest, son. You and Zoe look exhausted."

"Only because we are." Zoe smiled. "Do you want us to sneak anything in for you when we return?"

"I'd love a real cup of coffee."

"We'll take care of you, Dad." Simon hugged his parents, then helped Zoe to her feet. "See you later," he said over his shoulder as they left the room.

He stopped a moment to check on Jesse and Max. "You two okay to stay on duty?"

"Won't be the last time we go 24 hours without sleep," Jesse said. "I understand the docs are planning to release Hollister sometime today."

"I'll touch base with him before we leave." When he and Zoe were in the elevator, Simon wrapped his arms around her, grateful he could. "Do you mind one more stop before we leave? We won't take long."

She shook her head. "As long as I'm with you."

He longed to tell her he was in love with her and wanted her by his side permanently. This wasn't the time or place for such a declaration and he'd prefer to have Zoe all to himself when he did. Perhaps tomorrow. His father was right. They were both exhausted.

They exited on Hollister's floor and walked to his room. Sawyer greeted him, his curious gaze shifting to Zoe. "Sweetheart, this is Sawyer Chapman. Sawyer, Zoe Lockhart, my girlfriend."

The operative smiled. "Great to finally meet you, Ms. Lockhart. Simon talks about you every time we work with Bravo." Sawyer turned back to Simon. "Logan's inside with Hollister. Got a plan for when he's released?"

"Working on it. He has a lot to answer for back in Otter Creek." Simon tapped on the door. "It's Simon. I'm coming in soft." He eased the door open and moved into the room ahead of Zoe.

Hollister gave him a wary glance and shifted his attention to Zoe. His eyes widened. "Zoe! What happened?"

"Barone kidnapped her." Simon folded his arms across his chest. "Lyons told him about the GPS jewelry our women wear. Barone made her strip it off. Took me hours to track her down. Barone and his buddies hurt her before I found her."

The trainee winced. "I'm sorry, Zoe. I didn't know Isaac told them. Are you all right?"

"I will be."

He looked at Simon. "What happens when I'm released, sir?"

"You'll return to Otter Creek eventually."

"To PSI?"

"You'll talk to Josh Cahill and the members of Durango. What happens after that depends on your answers to their questions."

Blood drained from his cheeks. "Yes, sir."

"Until you're deemed fit to travel, you will stay at our hotel. Your only job for now is to rest, recuperate, and answer questions truthfully from us or the cops."

"I understand."

With a nod, Simon turned to Logan. "Can you and Sawyer stay on duty? I want to take Zoe to the hotel. She needs to ice her ankle."

"We're fine. Take care of your woman."

"I owe you."

A slow grin curved Sawyer's mouth. "Shouldn't spread your favors around, my friend. I'm liable to take you up on it one of these days."

When Simon ushered Zoe into the suite, he said, "I won't be surprised if the police knock on our door soon."

Zoe frowned. "Do you think they'll come talk to us about what happened tonight?" She lowered herself to the couch.

"They might. I'm more concerned with the dirty looks I received from the night clerk when she saw your face. She might call the cops to report that I abused you."

She settled deeper into the couch cushions. "Don't worry. I'll defend your honor."

Simon chuckled. "Good to know. What do you need?"

"You. I just need you."

He positioned the ottoman in front of the couch and lifted her feet to rest on the surface. "I'll make an ice pack for you in a few minutes. Right now, I need to hold you something fierce."

Simon sat by Zoe and wrapped his arm around her. She relaxed against him with a sigh.

"I was so afraid," she whispered.

"I know. I'm sorry."

"It's not your fault, Simon. You did everything possible to protect me. You didn't know Isaac told Barone about the jewelry."

He kissed her temple. "Rest for a bit, then I'll get the ice."

With a nod, she closed her eyes. Within a couple minutes, Zoe was asleep.

Simon shifted to settle her more fully against his chest. He needed to talk to her soon about how he felt. Hiding it would be impossible after the scare they'd survived this night.

Sometime later, his phone signaled an incoming message. He checked the screen. His teammates were on the way to the hotel. Good. He'd feel better with backup close at hand.

Zoe sighed and snuggled closer. "Everything okay?" she murmured, eyes still closed.

"The team is returning to the hotel. I need to ice your ankle or Matt will have my hide."

After brushing a light kiss over her mouth, Simon levered himself up, and found a plastic bag for the ice. After making an ice pack, he removed Zoe's walking boot and draped the bag over her swollen ankle.

He returned to his previous position and wrapped his arm around her shoulders.

Minutes later, Simon aimed his weapon at the door when a key card slid into the lock. He relaxed when Liam walked in followed by the rest of Bravo. They looked tired but uninjured. They also carried multiple bags of food from the best hamburger joint in town, one that happened to be open 24 hours a day.

"Didn't know if you were hungry, but we bought extra food for you and Zoe," Trent said.

"Great. I'm starving. What about you, Zoe?"

"The idea of eating a hamburger this early in the morning isn't appealing."

Matt smiled. "Good thing I insisted we stop for a blueberry bagel. Comfort food should settle easily on your stomach. How is your ankle?"

"It hurts," she admitted. "The pain has been steadily increasing for the past thirty minutes."

"Did the hospital give you a prescription?"

"We filled it before we left the medical center," Simon said. "She hasn't taken a pill yet."

Matt looked at Zoe. "Take the meds to get ahead of the pain."

"The doctor said the medicine will probably knock me out. I was saving it for when I really needed it."

The medic glanced at Cade, who found a bottle of water and handed it to Zoe. "Take the meds."

"What if the police show up to question me?"

"They can talk to me," Simon said. "I'll take you to the station tomorrow to answer questions. You have to take care of yourself. After all, you have to be mobile to reopen your bakery."

That last bit of logic seemed to do the trick because Zoe stopped protesting and swallowed a pain tablet. Matt badgered her into eating half the bagel before she waved him off with a promise to finish the rest later.

When she fell asleep in his arms a few minutes later, Simon looked at his teammates. "We have some loose ends to tie up."

Liam's hands fisted. "The bounty."

"You have a plan?" Trent asked.

"I have a few ideas."

CHAPTER THIRTY-SEVEN

When Zoe woke hours later, the suite was quiet, lit only by the early afternoon sun peeking through the cracks in the curtains, and no one else in evidence except Simon who held her securely in his arms. She could get used to this. Waking in Simon's arms was a pleasure like none she'd ever known and addictive to boot.

"Feel better?" Simon murmured.

"How long did I sleep?"

"Ten hours."

Good grief! "Please tell me you slept, too."

He tightened his hold around her shoulders. "I've never slept better in my life. You didn't answer my question. How do you feel?"

"Sore," she admitted. "My ankle is achy. Other than that, I'm grateful to be alive and in your arms."

He pressed a tender kiss to her forehead.

"Where is everyone?"

"The rest of the team relieved the Texas unit. Brody is sleeping in the other bedroom so we'll have backup close at hand if we need it."

"Aren't Barone and his buddies in jail?"

"They are. We still haven't resolved the problem with the bounties."

She twisted to face him. "What will you do?"

"We have a plan. If it works, I won't have to do anything."

"And if it doesn't?"

"I'll do anything necessary to protect you, my family, and my teammates."

That's what she thought he'd say. "Will you tell me the plan?"

"Zane and I are gathering information on the major players in the Barone organization."

"Information?"

"The incriminating kind."

"Of course."

"We'll email an ultimatum to the head of the family organization tonight at midnight. Either the bounties are withdrawn or the first packet of information including pictures and documentation of crimes committed by a major player will be delivered to the FBI within 24 hours. For every 24 hours that passes with the bounties still active, another packet will be sent to the FBI. If they delay too long, their top lieutenants and family members will be arrested for various crimes. If we have to, we'll send every last one of them to prison and drain the bounty account ourselves. How this plays out is ultimately up to the Barones."

"Do you think the plan will work?"

"From what Zane and I unearthed in the past few hours, the head of the family doesn't know Blake and Garrett were after the bounty for themselves. The information ties attempted murder charges back to the family name and the person who funded the account."

"Do you know who funded it?"

"Matteo's wife. If she doesn't drain the account, she'll either end up in prison or a coffin. I don't care which option she chooses as long as the danger to the people I care about ends now."

She studied him for a moment. "Would you kill her?"

"Do you need me to answer that?" he asked, voice soft.

"No, I don't. You will kill her without a second of regret if she continues to threaten those you love."

He stilled, intense gaze locked on her. "That's right, Zoe. That includes you."

Her breath caught. Did he mean what he said? "Simon?"

"I know it's too soon to say this, but after almost losing you to Barone and his cronies, I can't keep the truth to myself any longer. I'm in love with you, Zoe Lockhart."

Joy exploding inside, she smiled as wide as her sore mouth would allow. "I love you, too, Simon Murray."

"Enough to make me the happiest man alive by becoming my wife?"

"That much and more." Zoe wrapped her arms around his neck and dived into a long, heated kiss. She would never forget this moment, she realized. Finally, she was free to share the depth of her feelings without fear that the handsome operative would reject her. Building a life with this man would be the greatest privilege imaginable.

They ended the kiss when both were desperate for air. Simon hugged her tight. "Don't make me wait long to place a wedding band on your finger. A long engagement might kill me."

Zoe laughed. "We need to give your father time to heal and you have yet to meet my parents."

"Fine. Can you plan a wedding in two weeks?"

More laughter. "Let's aim for three months." When Simon protested, she kissed him gently. "Three months," she repeated when she eased back. "I need to find the perfect dress and line up a baker to cover for me when we're on our honeymoon. That takes time."

"Not one day longer," he insisted. "Or I'll kidnap you and whisk you off to Las Vegas for a quickie wedding."

"Deal. How long will our honeymoon last?"

"A lifetime."

Those two words melted Zoe's heart. "I need to know how many days to arrange for substitute bakers, Simon."

"Four weeks. I want to spend every minute of my month off mission rotation with you."

Wow. Four weeks alone with Simon? She couldn't think of anything she wanted more. "When you give me a definite start date, I'll make the calls." A few of her baker friends owed her favors. Maybe the best thing to do would be to arrange for several bakers to pick up a couple of days so covering for her wouldn't be a hardship on anyone.

"Perfect." Simon dropped a quick kiss on her mouth and helped Zoe stand. "Come on. You'll need extra time to get ready and we have to stop by the police station once we eat. Detective Chisolm wants to interview you as soon as possible. He's waiting for us. After that, I want to check on Dad." He smiled, eyes alight. "I can't wait to tell my parents we're getting married."

The rest of the afternoon and evening passed in a whirlwind of activities, including a lengthy interview with the detective. At the hospital, Simon led her into his father's room with a grin on his face.

His parents looked at each other, then back at their son. "Spill it," Don demanded. "You're about to burst with a secret."

Simon threaded his fingers through Zoe's. "Zoe and I are getting married."

Lisa enfolded Simon in a hug, then turned to embrace Zoe. "Congratulations. We're thrilled for both of you."

"Good work, Simon. I'm proud of you and happy you wised up. When is the wedding?" Don asked.

"Too far off," Simon complained.

Zoe smiled. "We don't have an exact date yet, but around three months from now. We have to find out when Simon will be off mission rotation and I need to line up bakers to cover my shop for me."

"Do you know where the wedding will be held?" Lisa asked.

"Otter Creek. We have many friends who will want to attend." Zoe knew without asking Simon that most of his friends wouldn't be able to leave Otter Creek. After all, Durango and the other members of the staff and instructors at PSI had to keep the classes going on schedule.

Throughout the rest of the evening, Simon touched base with his siblings and gave them the good news. He accepted all the razzing with a tolerant smile and assured his brothers and sisters that he would take good care of his bride-to-be.

Finally, they returned to the hotel. After nailing down details and gathering the last of the data for the first volley with the head of the Barone family, the email prepared by Zane and Simon appeared in Mrs. Barone's email at midnight.

Simon wrapped his arm around Zoe. "Now, we wait and hope for the best." Twelve hours later, they had their answer. He turned his computer around for Zoe to read the response.

"The account's been drained. How do we know if she'll live up to her bargain?"

"We'll wait a few more days before we relax our guard, but Zane will monitor the Barone family's communications and accounts from now on. He'll also periodically send reminders of the consequences of breaking the bargain. However, based on what I'm seeing, I don't think we have anything more to worry about from the Barones."

When his father was released from the hospital four days later, Simon and Zoe accompanied his parents to the ranch. Once his father was settled, Don looked at Simon and said, "It's time for you to return to work."

"Dad, I can take a leave of absence to help out around here."

He shook his head. "I'll be fine now. You've been invaluable and I've treasured every minute with you, but you're restless and itching to be back on duty. My healing process will be long and slow. I don't need you here for that."

"What if you need me?"

"I'll grab my phone and call. Go home, Simon. You and Zoe have a life to plan and jobs to return to."

Lisa hugged Simon, then Zoe. "I'll update you on his progress. Be at ease, Simon. You've done all you can. It's time for us to release you back to your work. We love you."

Simon chuckled and wrapped his arm around Zoe's shoulders. "I know a town that will be thrilled to have your bakery open for business."

"Working will be interesting with this boot on my foot."

After Simon notified Trent that they were ready to go home, they returned to the hotel and packed their bags. The team loaded their gear into the SUVs and helped Hollister into Trent's vehicle.

Within minutes, they boarded one of the Fortress jets that had been waiting on the tarmac to fly the rest of Bravo to Knoxville. Once the bird leveled off, the operatives and Hollister settled down to sleep for the return trip.

"Are you glad to be going home?" Simon murmured.

"I've missed being in the bakery. What about you?"

"My day is not complete without a five-mile run or a chance to grouse at my trainees."

Zoe laughed softly. "You know what I'm looking forward to the most?"

"What?"

"Planning our wedding and building a life with you. I love you, Simon."

He kissed her, slow and sweet. "I love you, too, baby. I'll work hard every day to be worthy of your love. I'll do anything I can to make you happy."

"That will be easy. All I need to be happy is you."

He groaned. "This is going to be the longest twelve weeks of my life."

"The wait will be worth it." The two of them had a lifetime to celebrate their life together and their love. A few weeks was nothing compared to a lifetime of bliss with the man of her dreams.

DON'T LET GO

ABOUT THE AUTHOR

Rebecca Deel is a preacher's kid with a black belt in karate. She teaches business classes at a private four-year college outside Nashville, Tennessee. She plays the piano at church, writes freelance articles, and runs interference for the family dogs. She's been married to her amazing husband for more than 25 years and is the proud mom of two grown sons. She delivers occasional devotions to the women's group at her church and conducts seminars on personal safety, money management, and writing. Her articles have been published in *ONE Magazine*, *Contact*, and *Co-Laborer*, and she was profiled in the June 2010 Williamson edition of *Nashville Christian Family* magazine. Rebecca completed her Doctor of Arts degree in Economics and wears her favorite Dallas Cowboys sweatshirt when life turns ugly.

For more information on Rebecca...

Signup for Rebecca's newsletter: http://eepurl.com/_B6w9

Visit Rebecca's website: www.rebeccadeelbooks.com

Printed in Great Britain
by Amazon